Sherlock Holmes

Consulting Detective

Volume Fifteen

AIRSHIP 27 PRODUCTIONS

TM

Sherlock Holmes Consulting Detective, Volume 15

Editor: Ron Fortier
Associate Editor: Gordon Dymowski
Production and design by Rob Davis
Promotion and marketing by Michael Vance

Published by
Airship 27 Productions
www.airship27.com
www.airship27hangar.com

ISBN: 978-1-946183-80-4

Printed in the United States of America

10 9 8 7 6 5 4 3 2 1

Sherlock Holmes
Consulting Detective
Volume XV
TABLE OF CONTENTS

Sherlock Holmes

in

"The Impossible Coin"

By
I.A. Watson

"How are you getting on with Sherlock Holmes?" young Stamford asked me as we met again at the Criterion Bar. "You have survived almost three months with the fellow. That must be a record."

"We're rubbing along quite well, actually," I admitted to my old Bart's dresser.[1] "We take it in turns to be sullen and uncommunicative, to mess up our living area, to get up and go out at all odd hours. He smokes a strong shag mix tobacco and I have my Ship's, so we choke each other. And we have a superior landlady."

I had taken shared rooms with Sherlock Holmes after the New Year. On the 4th of March, he confessed to me his occupation, the unique role of 'consulting detective' whereby he offered advice and support when other investigators were baffled. Over three days he had laid open his world to me as he investigated the death of Enoch J. Drebber, an affair which Holmes then called "the finest study I ever came across", and which was so extraordinary that I made notes so that I could render an account of events for myself.[2]

Stamford's lips quirked. "I wondered what you might make of him. He is an odd character with some eccentric capacities."

"His ability to read people's professions and habits by simply looking at them? He has a remarkable acuity for that, borne of intense and detailed study of the signs."

"You know he has published monographs on his studies?"

"I am aware of some of them. The privately-printed volumes are on our bookshelf: *Upon Tattoo Marks*, *Upon the Tracing of Footsteps*, *Upon the Distinction Between the Ashes of the Various Tobaccos*, and so on. He invited me to cast a medical eye over his recent paper on tests other than the guaiacum method for blood on cloth; I could not fault his research."[3]

---

1 That is a surgical houseman at St Bartholomew's Hospital, London, what is nowadays called a Pre-registration House Officer, a newly qualified doctor working a six-month supervised probationary period prior to being fully registered with the General Medical Council.

2 "I have all the facts in my journal, and the public shall know them," Watson promised Holmes in response to inaccurate press reportage of their first case together. These notes, formatted by literary agent Arthur Conan Doyle, would eventually inform Dr Watson's first published record of Sherlock Holmes in *A Study In Scarlet* (1888).

3 Application of a tincture of guaiacum from the West Indies lignum vitae tree, along with drops of hydrogen peroxide in ether was a standard test for bloodstains; if haemoglobin

"But his habit of reading one's mind?" Stamford was clearly disturbed by my fellow lodger's abilities.

"I find it fascinating. What appears at first to be supernatural omni-science is in fact informed by observation, deduction, and the application of research. He has elevated the procedure to an art form."

Stamford snorted. "I can see you two are well suited, then. But how are you doing otherwise? Recovering from your wound?"

He referred to the rifle-shot I had taken from a marauding Afghan last summer at Maiwand Pass, the injury which had shattered my health and kept me in a camp hospital for four months before my medical discharge back to England. "It pains me sometimes," I admitted, "but for the main part I am slowly improving."

"Will you return to medicine, then?"

I was unsure. "I have never run a general practice," I pointed out. "I progressed from the University of London Medical School to my residency at Bart's to my training as a military surgeon at Netley, and almost immed-iately I was dispatched to the 5th Northumberland Fusiliers and shipped off to India. I have no idea how to run a domestic surgery, no funds to purchase one if I did, and my health is too variable to sustain a regular routine."

"Perhaps some locum work?" Stamford suggested.

"Perhaps later. I will give it some thought."

In honesty, I did not intend to consider any such work. In April of 1881 I was a man adrift, without any plan or hope for the future. But Sherlock Holmes thought differently.

�

In my bad dreams I was always by the dry ravine, half in cover behind the twenty-foot raise from the valley floor. The big guns were thundering continuously, Ayub Khan's artillery formed in a semi-circle at the west end of the gulley, thrashing us to pieces. After three hours' exchange our own field weapons had fallen silent. The 2nd and 4th companies of Jacob's

---

is present the mixture turns bright blue. The process is detailed in the 1880 edition of the *Encyclopaedia Britannica*.

Holmes was working on "an infallible test for blood stains… a re-agent which is precipitated by haemoglobin, and by nothing else" to replace the guaiacum test or microscopic examination for blood corpuscles at the time of his first meeting with Watson in a laboratory at St Bart's Hospital.

Rifles were retreating back under heavy fire. We could see them falling as they tried to reach us. I knelt beside Lieutenant Warren and tried to attach a tourniquet above the stump of his right arm but he died before I could finish the knots.

"Sir, we 'as to go, sir!" my orderly called out. "Colonel Galbraith's orders, sir. We're to fall back from the ravine."

I only learned after about the layout of the Maiwand Valley battlefield, about the choices made by our commander Brigadier General Burrows to press out beyond the ravine's natural berm, how our 2,500 men were outnumbered ten to one. At the time I was only aware of soldiers dying around me, of the hateful howls of the approaching Ghazis, of too many wounded needing my attention all at once. I did my duty then, such as could be done with so little time and so many injured, and have paid the debt in nightmares and broken nerves since. It was a bitter price, but a fair one to preserve even a few lives.

"We must go, sir!" Murray insisted. "Look! Look down there!"

'Down there' the Afghans had poured up from another damned wadi to the south, from cover we had not suspected, and now swarmed to flank the 66th Foot. Our line was more of a horseshoe, with the Rifles and the Bombay Grenadiers strung out and exposed. We were perhaps doing more damage to the enemy than they to us, but they could afford to lose three men for every solider they took from our ranks.

Even as Murray and I looked on, the two companies of Jacob's Rifles broke, fleeing back towards us with no order, leaving the whole of the 1st Grenadiers exposed to be cut down. Our remaining retreating artillery was overwhelmed and captured. The remnant of the fleeing Rifles crashed into the left wing of the 66th, disrupting it to fatal confusion.[4]

"Now, sir!" Murray roared in my ear. "Back to the village. There are many more wounded there. You're needed, sir."

He forced me away from Warren and the other no-hopers, back towards

---

4 The Battle of Maiwand on 27th July 1880 and the subsequent British retreat to Kandahar, during the Second Anglo-Afghan War, was accounted a terrible defeat for the British and Indian troops. Almost a thousand Empire soldiers were lost, and Watson's 66th Foot Regiment, "the Berkshires", lost its colours (as a result of which, colours were no longer taken on active service). Ayub Khan's victory was costly though, with between 2,500 and 3,000 Afghan losses.

Rudyard Kipling wrote of the battle in 'That Day', *Barrack-Room Ballads* (1892):
"There was thirty dead an' wounded on the ground we wouldn't keep -
No, there wasn't more than twenty when the front began to go;
But, Christ! along the line o' flight they cut us up like sheep,
An' that was all we gained by doing so."

the ruined remnants of Khig.

Even in my dream I flinched as the Ghazi advance patrol broke out before us. The fire from their cheap Jezail rifles rattled around us. Two men close to me fell, but then our soldiers dropped on one knee and returned shots in good order. I drew my service revolver and joined in the fight, but I do not know if my shots went home.

At that moment a fire exploded within me, the agony of a metal ball passing through my body. I dimly realised that I had been hit, and then I lost all thought or hope.

I awoke, not over the pack-mule where Murray had slung me for the ragged retreat, nor in the overcrowded base-camp hospital at Peshawar, nor sweating in a bunk on the *Orontes*, invalided home a ruined wreck, but in the tangled sheets of my bed in the attic of 221B Baker Street. It took me a moment to recognise the new surroundings, and to realise that the voice that had cried out in fear and awoken me was my own.

There was a tap on my door. "Doctor Watson?" Sherlock Holmes enquired. "May I enter?"

I reached for a glass of water on the bedside table and managed to sip it without my trembling hand causing a spill. "Of course," I told my visitor. "Come in."

It was after one in the morning but Holmes was still dressed. Indeed, he wore an outdoor coat as if ready for an expedition.

"I am taking a stroll," he advised me, as if he had not heard my shout or recognised my weakness. "It is a fine, clear night and I have some errands to which I must attend. I wondered whether you would appreciate a constitutional?"

My bull-pup, curled in his basket, perked his ears and sat up eagerly, deducing in his own canine way that a walk might be forthcoming.

"Errands?" I enquired. "Concerning your work."

"Indeed. I should be pleased to hear your opinion of the matter in which I am engaged—if you will consider what I tell you bound with the same ethics as you hold information about your patients."

"I have already offered that assurance, at our previous adventure," I promised Holmes. "But…"

The wounded, wearied veteran in me warred with curiosity and an unaccountable desire to keep on fighting.

Holmes flicked me an appraising glance. "Did I mention that more than one person's happiness may depend upon the outcome of my foray tonight?"

I dressed, found my hat and cane, called my dog, and followed Sherlock Holmes out into the night.

❋❋❋

We walked the quiet streets towards the river, almost alone except for a beat constable who tipped the rim of his helmet and greeted Holmes by name. For his part, Holmes said nothing to me as we passed down towards Westminster Bridge. I had expected and dreaded his diagnosis of my night-time disturbances, but he made no reference to them.

When he did break the silence, it was about something entirely different. "On Saturday the 16th of January this year, Miss Agnes Shipton of Old Compton Street was to be married to one Daniel Cordy, a journeyman whitesmith with Bodmin & Venter of Dean Street. The pair were childhood sweethearts. Cordy and Miss Shipton had grown up together in her father's house since Cordy's parents had died when he was eleven. However, Daniel Cordy did not turn up at the church on the happy day."

"He jilted her?" I responded. "A breach of promise."[5]

"So it appeared. The matter has become complicated since, as Miss Shipton had rather thrown her bonnet over the wall ahead of her wedding day, and is in the family way."

"You are hunting her missing groom?"

"I would not normally involve myself in a sordid marital absconding, but there are some notable features attached to this case. Mr Henry Shipton, the young lady's father, was doubly upset, since Cordy was, as he put it, 'Like a son, even before 'e wed our Aggie.' Father and daughter alike were afraid that some accident had befallen the lad. Adding to that suspicion was that the absent groom packed no clothes or other belongings before he disappeared, and left behind a much-treasured only portrait of his late parents, along with a cigar tin in which his savings were stored."

"That would be unusual if he had bunked off in the usual way."

"There was another surprise, a telegram," my walking companion told me. "A missive arrived on 14th February from Mappin, Webb, and Co. of Oxford Street, the jewellers,[6] dispatched to know why Cordy had not

---

5 Reneging on a contract to marry was a civil tort offence in England at the time of this story, laying the responsible party liable for compensation, technically known as "heart's ease".

6 The venerable firm of Mappin & Webb began in Sheffield in 1775, opened its Oxford Street, London shop in 1860, and grew to be a significant international firm in the first half of the 20th century, known for its fine silverwork and watchmaking. The house created

appeared to take up his employment there as one of their silversmiths."

"He had a new job waiting for him?"

"And a substantially better one than his present position. Workers in fine silver are paid far more than workers in tin or other base soft metals, and Mappin's are reputed for employing only the best. His salary would have been more than double what he received at Bodmin & Venter's, an excellent wage for a newlywed fellow looking to settle and start a family. Yet he had spoken no word of the offer or of his acceptance of it to Miss Shipton or her father."

"Or to his present employers. I assume the delay in taking up the offer was for him to work out a four-week notice on his previous position?"

"When they were approached about the matter by Mr Shipton, the representatives of Bodmin & Venter expressed surprise and dismay to learn that Cordy had intended to leave them. Indeed, Cordy was in line for a promotion at his present company, who felt him a valuable member of their staff."

"I suppose a young buck might still get nerves on the day of his wedding and simply up and run, throwing his whole future away," I allowed. "Did he offer any such indication of doubts to those who knew him?"

"None of the young couple's friends could offer any explanation for the disappearance, or suggest where Cordy might have gone. His employers were equally baffled, since he had a good record and reputation with them, and was known as a talented and hard worker who would doubtless have risen in the company. 'A very deft hand at miniature figurines, and a regular proper artist,' was the testimonial they rendered."

"Were the police consulted? Was a check made on the hospitals and mortuaries?"

"A report was made to the local station, though I doubt it would have been taken too seriously. Young men run out on girls every day in our sad city, and there are boats always ready to take on an extra hand no-questions-asked, setting forth to every corner of the Empire and then round the globe. If there had been a body or any sign of foul play then things might have been different, but there was not. Nor had any London hospital received the young man, alive or otherwise."

"The poor girl. Agnes. She must have been distraught. Especially given her condition."

Queen Victoria's Jubilee necklace, which she designated as an heirloom of the Crown. Mappin & Webb was granted its first royal warrant (official permission to advertise that a firm produces goods for "a royal court or certain royal personages") in 1892, and today holds warrants from Queen Elizabeth II and Crown Prince Charles.

"She did not discover that souvenir of her missing fiancée until a month later. At the time she simply could not comprehend why her supposed life-mate had disappeared. Even his best man shed no light on the matter. So then Henry Shipton contracted the services of a private enquiry agent."

"To no avail," I guessed.

Holmes held up a finger. "Here is the first point of distinction, Dr Watson. This investigator called back the day after he was engaged and returned Mr Shipton's fee."

"Is that usual? To refund a client if there is no success?"

"I have never known any debt-and-runner man to do it before. Nor to give up a per-diem rate so quickly. A second investigator proved similarly recalcitrant in staying on the case, but at least recommended that the Shiptons might come and speak with me."

We reached the Embankment and looked out over the Thames. A fingernail moon glittered in a clear sky, so rare for foggy, smoky old London town.

"It is now more than three months since the failed wedding," I noted. "Surely the trail has now gone cold?"

"Somewhat. But two other features of interest have come to light since the time that Cordy vanished. There was a second disappearance, that of Cordy's best man, Howard Dulcimer."

"Another one? How soon after?"

"On March 1st, just a few days after Miss Shipton discovered her pregnancy."

"He was not thinking of the old custom that the best man must step in and marry the bride if anything happens to the groom?" I snorted.

"It is too early to theorise. I prefer to make such judgements based upon firm data. You observed my methods in the sad affair of Jefferson Hope's revenge. Dulcimer was also an employee of Bodmin & Venter, not one of the whitesmiths who carry out their commissioned work but rather a sales clerk in their public showroom. He was not so well regarded, having been chastised and docked wages on occasion for tardiness and having been disrespectful to management."

"Who told you this?"

"I interviewed both Mr Bodmin and Mr Venter individually, as well as verifying facts with the shop foreman and senior sales clerk. I prefer to avoid hearsay, except as a means of understanding the bias with which the speaker imparts his news."

We strolled upstream, our way lit by the novel electric lamps that had replaced the gas mantles these last three years.[7] My Afghan nightmares blew away in the mild night-breeze, replaced by the concerns of Miss Shipton and her family.

"You said there were three odd features, Holmes," I prompted him. "What was the other?"

Holmes was ready for the question. He dug deep into his coat pocket and produced a silver coin, no more than seven-tenths of an inch in diameter, which he handed to me. "This was hidden beneath a loosened floorboard under Cordy's bed. What do you make of it?"

I examined the object. "It's French. A fifty-centime coin. Shiny and new. One side depicts a woman's profile—Liberty, I suppose, with a small star over her head. The inscription at the rim reads 'Republique Française'. On the reverse is written '50 Cent.' and the date of issue, and the motto 'Liberte, Equalite, Fraternite.'"[8]

Holmes snorted. "But the unique thing, Watson, the clue that convinced me to take this case, the reason for our midnight foray! Look again. Look carefully!"

I reviewed the coin in my palm once more. A fifty-centime piece was common enough, worth about four shillings.[9] Although lacking the elegance and authority of a sterling coin it was still a substantial bit of minting and...

"Holmes!" I called as I saw what he had expected me to notice. "This coin is dated 1882! Next year!"

My companion's eyes twinkled in delight. "Splendid, isn't it?"

"Do the French print their currency in advance?"

"No. Here is a coin that will not exist for another eight months, doctor, concealed in the lodging of an absconded groom!"

---

7 Victoria Embankment was the first street in Britain to be permanently lit by electrical lights, with the first twenty lamps placed in 1878 and extended to fifty lamps by 1879. However, the experiment was judged too expensive to continue and in 1884 the gas lamps were restored again.

8 The obverse also includes a small-print credit 'E.A. Oudiné F', the name of celebrated sculptor and medal-maker Eugène-André Oudiné (1810-1887), who in addition to designing IIIe République coinage has works displayed in the Tuileries gardens, Jardin du Luxembourg, the Louvre, the Invalides, and Versailles, and who is sometimes termed 'the father of the modern medal'.

9 50 French centimes in 1881 had roughly the consumer buying power of U.S. $5 today, but amounted to a generous daily income for a working-class labourer (who might earn as little as a twelve centimes or a sterling shilling a day) in an era when food and rent were significantly proportionally lower.

I reviewed the 50-centime piece with renewed interest. "So this is… what? A forgery?"

"Certainly that," Holmes agreed. "Here, compare it with this coin, the 1880 minting. Look at the moulding of the leaves on Liberty's headpiece, and on the laurel wreath on the tails side. See how they do not quite match? And the small printing of the engraver's name, how the proportions are not quite right? This is not only a forgery, but a poor one."

"There is also a notch on the rim of the 1882 fake," I spotted.

"That was entirely my doing, I'm afraid. I took a small sample for chemical analysis. You recall the smells that permeated our rooms yesterday and earned me a rebuke from Mrs Hudson? I was verifying the composition of the coin in your hand."

"Not silver, then?"

"Not in any great quantity, though an admixture is necessary to give the zinc, nickel and other ingredients the right sheen. The weight is slightly off too, point one-nine-one ounces rather than point one-nine-four, but not sufficiently for anyone but an expert to notice."

I tried to follow how this impacted upon the affairs of Daniel Cordy. "The missing youth was a tinsmith, talented enough to be offered a position at a prominent silversmiths. Could he also have been a forger, carving out moulds for coiners who made this facsimile? It explains why he might disappear suddenly, if he suspected he was discovered. Or a falling-out amongst thieves?"

"Perhaps. I expect there to be more to the story, however, and tonight I intend to discover it. Would you care to accompany me?"

Our walk had taken us to the seedier end of the riverbank, past Waterloo Bridge and New Blackfriars Bridge, then into the narrower streets behind the waterfront wharves off Upper Thames Street. I judged us not far from St Paul's Pier and Queenhithe Dock, though not yet approaching Southwark Bridge.

It was now past two, but there was still life and movement on these routes. Clusters of sailors and shoremen drifted between the lit-up taverns and music houses, men waking with girls who should have known to be home long since, boisterous drunks tottering, and sly fellows who kept to the shadows. I was glad that Holmes and I carried our walking canes and that I had my bull-pup with us. I began to wish that I had unpacked that tin box in which I preserved my service Beaumont Adams, which I had set aside in relief that I might never need it again.[10]

---

10 The Beaumont Adams revolver was the standard British Army handgun from 1862 to 1880, favoured because of it was the first true double action firearm (cocked by either the

Holmes took us down a side-alley that had no identifying street sign. We passed half a dozen dark doorways, one of which was occupied by a passionately-embracing couple, and came at last to a low entrance down three steps. A rap from Holmes's cane-handle won us admission to a low sawdust-floored cellar where eighty or ninety toughs and a few men of better quality were gathered round a sunken square.

At first I thought the drinking den to be a venue for cock-fighting or dog-and-rat matches, but as we pressed past the trestle that served for a bar and through the heaving throng I apprehended that the pit served as a bare-knuckle boxing ring. Two squashed-nosed brutes were staggering around each other as the spectators goaded them on to further injury. One of them had an open gash over his left occipital that was bleeding down into his eyes.

"What is this place?" I muttered to my guide. "Why are we here?"

Holmes made a covert gesture towards a fellow in brash tweeds who was stood on a three-legged stool close to the ring, clutching a cigar in one hand and a cash-box in the other; some kind of organiser, bookmaker, and master of ceremonies, it seemed. "There is Lemmy Clement, our host, who possesses an intimate knowledge of the dark dealings between Smithfield and the river. He will likely not know where to find our forgers – not the ones we specifically wish to locate – but he will undoubtedly know someone who does."

"We are here to question him?"

"We are here to win the information from him."

A roar went up from the ring as the bloodier of the two combatants went down to a haymaker left hook, leaving his swaying opponent to be supported by his fellows as he strutted the ring in triumph. Money changed hands.

Clement spotted Holmes. "You! Again! When are you going to learn?"

"I already know plenty, Lemmy," my companion assured the seedy tout. "Have I not demonstrated it on five occasions now? Must I offer a sixth instance?"

"Yer luck won't 'old out forever, laddie. But if you don't need yer teeth no more and you want to liven the night for these lads round the ring, yer welcome to step in and take your drubbing."

"He wants you to fight?" I realised. "Holmes…!"

"I have been here before, Watson," my new friend advised me. "Each

---

hammer or trigger) and delivered a hefty 54 bore, .422-calibre bullet. It was replaced by the Enfield mark 1 as the army's weapon of choice the year that Dr Watson was pensioned out.

time I have left triumphant. The sweet science is another study of mine, one I take as seriously as all others. But having, as our host suggests, 'pushed my luck' in depriving the audience of their expected bloodbath on several visits, I felt it prudent to bring along a second to watch my back. If you would be so good?"

Clement was calling to the rear of the room, where a giant of a man sat on a bench with a female companion across his knee. "Emil! Set the lass aside and come an' grind up a victim. This 'ere's the buck who put down Orville and the Mincer, an' made a monkey o' Long Tod, come back to try again. Show 'im the error of 'is ways!"

I looked in horror as the fellow rose. "He must be six-foot-six if he's an inch," I warned Holmes.

"Yes. A Russian émigré by his hair and tattoos, earning a day-living at the docks. Today he was carrying molasses. He has spent some time in prison, where he acquired the half-healed scar on his upper left bicep, but has been released for around nine months now. You need not look so startled, doctor. Mere observation and elementary interpretation make his history an open book."

"To you, perhaps, Holmes. I only see a huge fellow coming to thrash you."

"Then you miss the obvious. See how the knuckles of his left fist have more scarring than his right? He favours that attack. His weight is mostly on his right leg, through, so he will prefer to lunge off that foot. His left ear is the more cauliflowered, suggesting a weakness in his guard from a transverse position. Furthermore, he will likely be distracted by my hands and not keep a telltale watch upon the centre of my body-mass."

I could see that Holmes had made a study of combat, but I was still uncertain of his chances against the Cossack colossus.

"Before we begin," Holmes told Lemmy Clement, "there is the matter of our wager. I propose the same terms as before. I will hazard five pounds; but if I prevail then you must tell me what it is I wish to know. On this occasion the datum I seek will be in regard to a coining racket that was recently seeking to recruit a skilled forger in silver. Who wanted such a fellow and for what job? That's my fee."

"*If* yer win," Lemmy insisted. "Which you won't, on account of Emil knocking yer brains out!"

Holmes passed me his coat, jacket, and even his shirt, and wrapped such bandages around his knuckles and wrists as the meagre rules of the establishment allowed.

"No gouging, no teeth, and naught below the belt," the swarthy fellow who served as referee announced. "Three taps and you're yielded, ten-count and you're done. No 'elp from the audience please, and nothing thrown into the ring. Are both you sports ready?"

Emil took his corner, his mad eyes grinning behind that bristly cloud of Russian beard. He finished his bottle of stout and tossed it behind him, then gestured for Holmes to come on. My comrade dropped lightly into the opposite angle of the sunken pit, flexing his toes and moving featly.

The referee lowered his scarf and the vast Cossack lurched forward, much faster than I had anticipated. One expects men of his bulk to be slow, clumsy, but he was anything but, closing the gap to Holmes in an eye's blink. The crowd's throaty cry rose like an animal roar.

Holmes scarcely moved, shifting his head aside just enough that Emil's killer punch whistled past, then responded with a quick one-two to solar plexus and Adam's apple. Emil grunted as he flew past, and crashed into the slatted side of the arena. Holmes dropped back as the giant swung round and lashed again. He sidestepped two blows and deflected a third before placing his own knuckles square on the soft cartilage of the Cossack's nose. I heard the snap of nasal septum, and Emil's Russian oath.

Holmes ducked right down, avoiding a bearhug grasp that might have crushed him, and responded to Emil's cheating by sweeping out a foot to hook Emil's left leg from under him; as my companion had discerned, his opponent favoured weight on the right.

Emil clambered to his feet, bleeding freely from his broken nose, but otherwise undeterred. He spat a wad of blood and came in again, slower and more cautiously this time. I recognised his strategy, to pummel Holmes back to the side of the ring and catch him there unable to evade. That way strength, not dexterity, would settle the fight.

I would have called to warn Holmes, but things were moving too fast. I saw him fall back as the Cossack wanted, but just as it looked like he might be cornered, he feinted, swinging his left hand out and opening his fist to show outstretched fingers and a naked palm.

Then I remembered what Holmes had predicted about the giant's attention. In the fraction of a moment while Emil's gaze was on is adversary's left hand, Holmes rose on his toes and delivered a rattling right hook under the Russian's chin. Such was the force of the punch that it staggered even so huge a combatant for a second, and with that chance Holmes set to work with a series of precise, devastating, and perfectly-calculated attacks. Each was delivered in rapid succession, bludgeoning

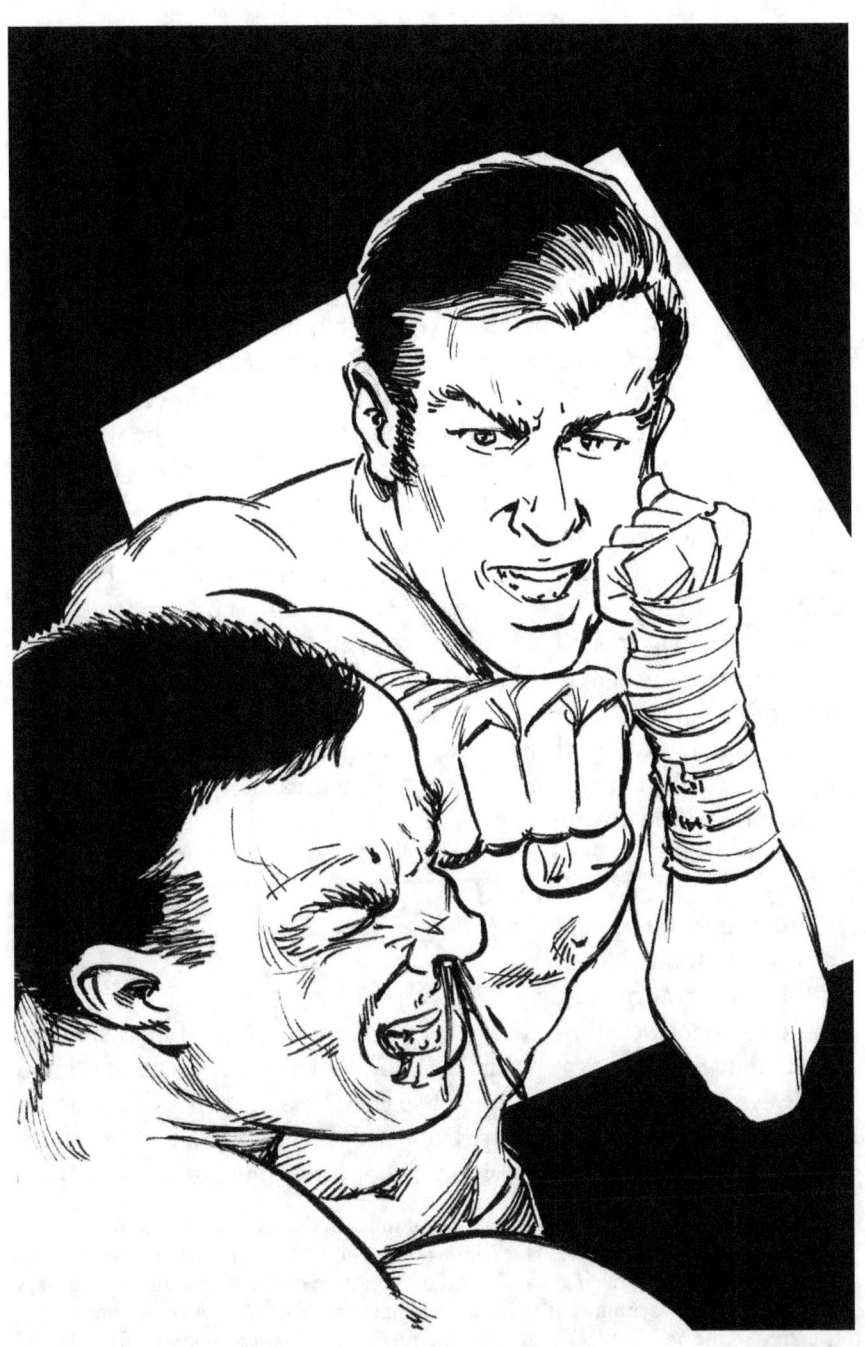

.... his own knuckles square on the soft cartilage of the Cossack's nose.

Emil about the ears, in the gut, over the kidney, on that shattered nose again, left cross, right hook, left hook, uppercut, body barrage, until the huge Russian reeled, uncertain from whence the next attack might come, perhaps unknowing even of where he was any more.

Holmes's haymaker lifted the Cossack from his feet, bounced him off the side of the pit, and dropped him face-first onto the matted straw.

The crowd, which had momentarily lapsed into shocked silence, broke into a resounding cheer.

Holmes climbed out of the ring to rejoin me and reclaim his belongings. Emil had never once laid a hand on him, except when Holmes had deflected. "There is a strategy for dealing with larger men who are accustomed to rely upon their bulk and strength," he noted clinically as he wiped his knuckles. "When one's opponent is also inebriated and given to telltale signs of his intended next assault, the outcome is inevitable."[11]

Some of the men in the crowd who had lost money on the fight looked as if they might have wanted to continue the fray themselves, but Holmes's salutary skill and my own presence with a sturdy bulldog at my side paused them long enough for us to reach Clement.

"Damn yer," the fight host told Holmes as we cornered the fellow. "I was sure Emil would do for yer."

"He did not," my friend answered. "Now pay up! Who has been seeking out a fellow skilled in carving silver moulds with a view to a little coining? It might have been any time since Christmas."

"Yer probably know all the usual 'ands by now," Lemmy answered sullenly.

"This would be someone new they wanted, someone with a fresh eye and a steady touch."

The fight arranger shrugged. "No one's coming ter mind. No honestly, guv'nor, I'm not welching. I'd 'ave 'eard if there was a call for anyone like that. I might even 'ave expected it. Yer know that old Crowther's gone blind in one eye now, and the other 'un not so good? 'E's been the go-to man on-and-off since Victoria was a lass. Dubberidge is in pokey, and 'Viscount' Jack Spencer dropped dead right on 'is figgy pudding last Twelfth Night

---

11 Holmes's martial acuity is mentioned several times in the Canon. He is confirmed as a trained boxer in 'The Adventure of the Gloria Scott' (*The Memoirs of Sherlock Holmes*, 1893). In *The Sign of Four*, the prize-fighter McMurdo with whom he had fought three rounds says of him, "You might have aimed high if you had joined the fancy." Watson proclaims in 'The Adventure of the Yellow Face' (also from *The Memoirs of Sherlock Holmes*) that "He was undoubtedly one of the finest boxers of his weight that I have ever seen." Holmes's skill in the ring is one of his more demonstrated talents, quite apart from his mastery of the obscure unarmed combat method of Baritsu.

—a right shock that was for his poor old missus. So the surprising thing is that there *'asn't* been a hunt for a talented up-an-comer with a touch for larcenous sculpting."

"Who's setting up an operation then?" Holmes persisted. "Someone taking premises for a little after-hours minting."

"I can't 'elp yer. Coining's not what is was, not with banks weighing their deposits now, and the Royal Mint putting on milled edges to stop clipping, and such precise moulds that it makes it a right pain to copy. And the peelers are getting too damn good at finding the yards. It's not like yer can 'ide smelting, not in London town."

A thought occurred to me. "Holmes, it may be too dangerous and difficult to reproduce British coinage now, but foreign currency, stamped-out here and shipped abroad..."

"Indeed. And the absence of new endeavours or recruitment drives is evidence in its own right."

Clement evidently felt that he had not given value for money. In his own way he was a chap who paid his debts. "I don't know as I've been able to 'elp much," he confessed.

"Well, one other thing, then. Howard Dulcimer—does that name mean anything to you?"

"Dulcimer?" Lemmy frowned, then grinned. "Why yes it does. When I 'eard it before I said to myself, joking, 'Dulcimer – that name should ring a bell!' So I remembered it, like."

"The hammered dulcimer is a stringed instrument, like a zither," Holmes pointed out. "No bells at all."

The fight promoter's face fell. "Really? Well, fool me, then, I suppose. But that's 'ow I remember 'earing the name. No, *reading* it, on a ledger from a cove that was trying to sell me 'is debtor inventory. 'Snagger' Fenwick, it was, who wants to retire from the lending game on account of 'is lumbago. He was down 'ere four, sixweeks back trying to flog 'is list to me. But there were too many duffers on it 'oo'd never repay, not even if yer broke every kneecap between 'em. And too many 'ad up-an'-vanished, like that Dulcimer."

I did a quick calculation and realised that the best man must have already disappeared before Mr Fenwick had initiated his retirement plan.

"What kind of debt did Howard Dulcimer owe?" Holmes enquired.

"Don't recall the exact amount," Clement objected. "I was only scanning down the list, yer see, when 'is name leaped out. It'd be five quid or so—a fair bit for a bloke of 'is station, but not that out of the ordinary. I reckon 'e'd seen Snagger was on to 'im and would be sending the lads round, so 'e'd 'opped it."

"Do you take on many such client lists, Lemmy?" Holmes probed. "And if so, for what backer?"

Our host stiffened, maybe even evinced a flash of fear, and shook his head. "I've paid up for yer one way or another tonight, squire. I reckon yer should be on yer ways now. Don't you?"

Holmes tipped his hat to Clement and we made our departure.

✳✳✳

"What now?" I wondered, as we made our way out of the dockside backstreets, making a brisk pace towards St Paul's and Ludgate Hill. "If the fellow you had hoped might have the key had failed you, then…"

"No, his testimony was of use, Watson. Eliminating possibilities whittles us down to the probable and then to the actual. Think! If there is a foreign coining operation happening in London, but no secret locations where such things could be minted within the city boundaries, that leaves two other options. What are they?"

I drubbed my wits into action. "Either the mint is outside London, or it is a known place in the metropolis."

"Good. And if it was outside the city, how might Cordy have acquired that remarkable futuristic coin to hide under his floorboard?"

"So it was likely local to him. He took no days off on which he might have travelled?"

"He had requested a week's leave after his wedding. There were arrangements made with Miss Shipton's great-aunt who runs a bed-and-breakfast lodging at Brighton for the couple to visit there for a honeymoon. Otherwise, Shipton was at work six days a week, serving all the extra shifts he could in order to save up for married life."

We followed Fleet Street through the Strand, our footsteps echoing in the still night. We passed under the shadow of the Law Courts and cut along narrow Wych Street onto Drury Lane. An occasional late carriage or hansom cab rattled past, but otherwise London slept; except for us, Sherlock Holmes and John Watson, treading on, seeking justice.

"Cordy must have been one of the counterfeiters," I decided. "How else might he have come by the coin he concealed?"

"I can think of a number of scenarios," Holmes replied. "Perhaps the most likely is that the coiners showed him the sample. 'Can you do better than this? Make something more realistic?' Whether he agreed or not, somehow he pocketed the poor fake and hid it where he thought no-one would find it. Perhaps it was an insurance policy, a way of implicating those who sought to draw him in if they did not go away?"

"If so, it didn't work."

"It set us on, did it not?

"What about Dulcimer, then? Why did he flee? Was it to do with Miss Simpson, or 'Snagger' Fenwick, or something else? Did Cordy have the coin from him?"

"I doubt that Dulcimer's liabilities to Mr Fenwick represented the whole of his sum of debt," Holmes estimated. "On the other hand, it seems unlikely that a predatory lender such as 'Snagger' would have allowed a mere shop clerk to run up such a tally without expectation of a windfall payday."

"Might 'Snagger' have done something unpleasant to a defaulting Howard Dulcimer?"

"If he had, then Dulcimer would not still be on the debtors list he attempted to offload. And Snagger's only reason for harming a debtor would be as a warning to other defaulters. Secrecy would not benefit that."

Belatedly it occurred to me to ask, "Where are we going now?" My knowledge of our capital, though adequate, was not the equal of Sherlock Holmes'ss; but we did not appear to be walking a direct route to Baker Street.

By now we had weaved our way through to Seven Dials, heading directly for Soho. "The Simpsons live on Old Compton Road," I recalled. Our route was taking us very near there.

"We need not walk quite so far that way," Holmes instructed me. "Moor Street, Queen Street, Green Street, and onto Dean Street will be the shortest cut."

I was amazed at Holmes's grasp of London cartography, and said so.

"Why, a London hackney carriage driver must memorise every street," Holmes told me. "There are classes, and an examination. I have taken both."

"Bodmin & Venter's premises are on Dean Street."

Holmes nodded at my deduction in satisfaction and approval. "There are enquiries I intend to pursue with them."

"At four in the morning? Will their offices not be locked up until eight-thirty?"

"But their tin-forges may work all night, especially if they have enough orders. Or one particular order."

A concern assailed me. "Holmes! Apparatus designed for the smelting and moulding of tin might be adapted to the pressing of other metals!"

"And no new site for illicit coining has been noted by the dockside demi-monde?"

"But... Bodmin & Venter is a respectable establishment. If management knew..."

"Doctor Watson, it is hard to see how management could not, if their moulds, presses, and cutters were being utilised for illegal purposes. But we cannot be sure without primary evidence. Hence our visit."

I matched Holmes's long determined strides along the empty pavement. We turned right at the Royal Soho Theatre, and there was the ornate three-storey frontage of the tin-works, surmounted by a large public clock. The offices and showroom frontage were unlit.

"Deliveries to the rear, I fancy," Holmes told me, ducking down a service alley and boldly testing the wooden inset door on the larger archway gate. That the latch was down did not slow him for an instant. He slipped out a blade that I had not known was concealed in the end of his walking cane, and slid it between door and jamb to slip the catch. Then Holmes was inside the yard, looking around.

I followed him like a man in a daze, caught up in his purpose, determined to see what might happen next. A summons for trespassing, most likely.

The cobbled delivery yard led to sheds on one side and a stable opposite them. At this hour both sets of buildings were closed up, though chinks of light shone from the lamps left to light the horses, and perhaps for the grooms who slept in the loft above. Directly across from us, concertina shutters had been folded back to expose a small forge and benches of die-cutting apparatus. A dozen men laboured there, stoking the furnace and shifting a bath-sized crucible on chains to heat the contents.

"Forgers?" I whispered to Holmes.

"For all we know they might be printing out tin soldiers. We require a closer inspection."

"We cannot summon the police?"

"Indeed not. Apart from anything else, if Cordy or Dulcimer are captive on the premises, a raid might imperil their lives." Holmes cast about and spotted a double-doored floor-hatch much like a coal chute in one corner of the yard. "This way."

The cover was fastened with chain and padlock, but I was unsurprised by then when my companion produced a pair of instruments from his cuff and sprung the lock.

"You have an unusual set of skills," I noted.

"I am attempting to furnish myself with all the necessary assets for my chosen profession," Holmes told me. "It is a work in progress, but fortunately this lock was a crude and simple mechanism. The shady fellows from whom I learned such a talent would consider it a mere bagatelle."

With the padlock gone, the trapdoors lifted to reveal steps down under the factory. Holmes found a hand-lamp on a hook just inside the passageway, which we lit to guide our deeper intrusion.

The short corridor was built of old brick, of a vintage beyond the modern works above. Much of the foundation of London is reused from what was there before, back to the Middle Ages and time immemorial. There were three doors, all secured with rim-locks.

Holmes first checked the room on the right. He made short work of the tumblers.

A barrel-roofed vault vanished off beyond the light of our lantern. Row upon row of wooden crates were stacked against the walls. A serial number was stencilled on each container, but there was otherwise no text to identify contents.

"Let's have one of those down and the lid off, Watson," Holmes declared. We heaved a box off the top of the nearest pile. Its weight betrayed its contents before the chink of coin as we set it to the ground conformed things.

The lid opened on a straw-padded tray of fresh-minted 50-centime pieces, all dated for the year to come.

"There must be five hundred coins here," I calculated, "and three trays under that. A thousand francs! This box is worth almost forty pounds!"

"If the coin was real," Holmes reminded me. "But see, two thousand coins a box, seven boxes in a stack, say one hundred and sixty stacks in this cellar… approximately £44,280 at present exchange rates, I fancy."[12]

My jaw dropped. "This is forgery on a grand scale! An industrial scale!"

Holmes admitted it. He strode across the corridor and threw open the second door to reveal a similar horde stored there, albeit with some unused space for additional boxes.

"We have the evidence now!" I exclaimed.

"And reason enough for Cordy's disappearance," Holmes added. "However, we may progress that matter by examining the final door here, the one that has a heavier-duty rim-lock—a lock which has a keyhole only

---

12 A little over $5.4 million in modern U.S. currency.

on this side. Keep watch."

He set to work again with those instruments of his, springing the tumblers so that we might enter the final chamber.

A young man looked up blearily from a pallet, his eyes blinded by our lamplight. He had a three-month beard and a pallid complexion.

"Daniel Cordy, I presume," Holmes addressed him. "You are late for your wedding!"

The prisoner stared at us with incomprehension. "Who are you? You... you're not with Venter?"

"We're here to rescue you, man," I told him. "Your bride and her father sent us."

"Agnes!" Cordy's face screwed up in anguish. "She's all right? Not harmed? They said, if I didn't do the work they set me, that..."

"She is concerned about your whereabouts, distressed by your absence, but that is all," Holmes answered. "Well, she is also carrying a four-month child of yours, so I imagine you might wish to go to her."

"A child!" Such a mixture of emotions raced across the young man's face, blurred into jerky shock and a tentative smile, before returning to horror. "If I leave, then they will kill her. Kill both of them—and her father, all of them!"

I gestured for him to follow us. "All the more reason to leave now, so we can summon the police and expose this operation." Then I noticed that a chain around Cordy's ankle affixed him to a staple on the wall, as if he was a hound fastened to his kennel.

Holmes was already moving in to tackle the lock. I kept an eye on the corridor behind us and saw as the trapdoor through which we had entered was wrenched open.

"We are discovered!" I warned.

Holmes left off his endeavours on Cordy's fetter and joined me at the doorway. "We should have realised that the coiners would be bringing their new pallets of half-francs down into their storage spaces as they were cooled," he chided himself. "We observed the factory at work. The rest was only a matter of logical deduction. I am becoming versed in the knowledge and techniques required for my occupation, but I see that I still require some experience in their practical application."

A shout went up from men at the entrance. "Oi! There's intruders! They're in 'ere!"

A quartet of porters set down their coin-boxes and hastened in to confront us. Holmes hefted his cane, sliding out the blade at its tip. I held my own walking stick ready as a baton. Side by side we blocked the doorway to the still-shackled Cordy.

"Watch out," the prisoner called to us. "They are brutal, desperate men, in the pay of a ruthless one!"

"What did they do to Mister Dulcimer?" Holmes asked, but he kept his eye on the advancing thugs.

"Howard! They killed him! They killed him in front of me!"

The matter had progressed, then, from kidnapping and counterfeiting to murder. A night stroll to quieten the ghosts of Maiwand had become an encounter as dangerous and potentially lethal as our frantic retreat from Jezail fire and Ghazi artillery.

I had wondered, after that desperate retreat with the Afghans nipping at our heels, with their woman unmanning what captives were taken and their forward riders ripping through our wounded as they limped for refuge, as I bled out, and the question seemed not if I should die but in what manner, whether my nerve was broken forever. Would I baulk in the face of danger should I ever face it again? Did my nightmares reveal that my courage was shattered, as crippled as my body by that hellish ordeal?

Now the fight was upon me again, but a joy surged within me as I felt my spirits rise to the battle. I stood shoulder to shoulder with Sherlock Holmes and knew that, though I carried the wound of my experience, my self was intact. I carried also the strength that my trials had won me, and I held the line beside my friend.

Holmes spared me one discerning glance and smiled in grim, approving understanding. "Our strategy will be superior to that of Brigadier General Burrows, Doctor Watson," he promised me.

When they saw our arms, the bravos held back. Another fellow appeared, a foreman by his cheap waistcoat and collar. He was certainly in charge, for he was armed with a Remington Navy Revolver, which he aimed at Holmes.

"Drop your sticks, whoever you are, or I shall kill you now."

"Now or later, does it matter?" Holmes replied, seemingly indifferent to the threat. "Why should I believe the killers of Howard Dulcimer?" I saw my companion's eyes flick over the foreman, doubtless collecting a thousand details that might be of use in somehow besting our adversary.

"Do you imagine we came here without telling anyone?" I challenged the Bodmin & Venter employees. "I expect two-score of armed constables will be along in a very short while. And using firearms for criminal acts, that's a guaranteed hanging offence."

The foreman did not look disconcerted, though his subordinates betrayed some concern. "Mr Venter can take care of all that. You have no idea what you have stumbled into. Powerful men are behind this, powerful enough to bid the coppers come and go as they please. Now, last warning: drop your weapons or I fire."

Holmes carefully stood his sword-cane against the corridor wall, so I set my walking stick aside also. When my bull-pup growled at the intruders I went to one knee and secured a firm hand on his collar.

"Inside the cell," the foreman ordered.

Holmes passed me a look urging my compliance, so I retreated into Cordy's prison and took station close to the chained-up smith. Holmes paused at the doorway and leaned there to address our captors. "You may tell your employer that Sherlock Holmes is his unwilling guest; that I now understand the full nature of the enterprise being conducted on the premises of Bodmin & Venter; that the observations I have made can be made again by others; and that without instruction from me to cover the trail I followed, the conspirators in whose employ you operate will certainly be located and confined. Whatever immunity your masters believe they might enjoy will evaporate quickly enough when this affair is aired in the light of day and on the presses of the broadsheets. Communicate that to those you serve—quickly."

"There is no need to pass such a warning," a new voice from outside the hatch called down. Another fellow entered the corridor where the foreman and his henchmen had us trapped. By his dress he was a gentleman, of perhaps fifty, with a trimmed moustache and sideburns and silver rings on his fingers.

"Mr Edward Venter," Holmes identified him. He had interviewed him before. "Does your partner Bodmin know of your company's sideline, or does he merely prefer not to enquire too closely into the additional income line on your accounts sheet?"

"Bodmin covers the more public side of our works," Venter replied. "Who are you really, and why are you trespassing on my property?"

"My name is Holmes, as I told you when you lied to me on our previous encounter. This is my colleague and confidante Dr Watson. We are here as private citizens concerned with public justice in the matter of the murder of Mr Howard Dulcimer and the abduction of Mr Daniel Cordy, along with associated crimes and a conspiracy to destabilise the Third French Republic."

Venter's expression shifted at the final element of Holmes's statement. I too was surprised to hear such an allegation. "What do you mean by that?" I asked my companion.

"The advance date of the coins is the indicator," he explained to me. "They are being prepared in bulk, in readiness. What do you fancy the effect that a hundred thousand pounds-worth of false currency would be on the struggling French economy next year? Especially if it became known that so much of the coinage was debased? This is not intended as a financial fraud, Watson—it is a coup."

Venter nodded, proudly. "It is a strike against a corrupt and criminal regime. For more than ten years now, the so-called *La IIIe République* has systematically destroyed France, has ignored the pleas of its people and the better classes to restore the rightful rule of benevolent monarchy. For ten years the feeble Chamber of Deputies and Senate have jawed about putting a king back on the French throne, until the political system that was established only as a temporary stopgap has made itself permanent. Small men saw their chance for power and took it."

It was eleven years since the disastrous Franco-Prussian War and the capture of Emperor Napoleon III, the unification of Germany and its claim of large tracts of France as compensation.[13] Since then the provisional government had settled into an actual one as Venter charged, and French attention was focused on revenge against the Germans and on territorial ambitions in Africa, not on internal debates about a restored monarchy.

"You are talking politics," I told Venter. "We are speaking of murder."

"So am I!" the businessman snarled. "The murder of a nation, as well as the silent, sneaking executions of those who would protest it. In the days of Thiers[14] we were satisfied to wait for the state to right itself. Under Magenta[15] we expected that our day had come, but the old man did nothing!

---

13 The war of 1870, which ended so disastrously for France and led to the rise of Otto von Bismarck and the unified German state is considered a significant cause of World War I. In its aftermath the Third French Republic dealt with internal uprisings, the loss of many French colonies, and significant economic hardships, but in the last quarter of the 19th century reforged the nation towards the *belle époque* and occupied significant new territories during the Rush for Africa. However, the French never forgot the sting of their defeat by the new German Empire or the losses of Alsace and Lorraine, and their appetite for a new territorial war with Germany led to their enthusiastic approval of military action in 1914.

14 Marie Joseph Louis Adolphe Thiers (1797-1877) was the first elected President of France between 1871 and 1873.

15 Patrice de MacMahon, 6th Marquess of MacMahon, 1st Duke of Magenta (1808-1893) was the President of France from 1873-79. Since he was a member of the aristocracy, monarchists had great hopes that he might forward the restoration of the Crown, but MacMahon remained resolutely neutral in his elected office.

Now France is ruled by the fanatical Grévy[16] and all debate is silenced. Only firm action will save the Garden of the World from republican ruin!"

"Your foreman boasted that you had powerful backers," Holmes noted. "Your endeavour is supported by many monarchist émigrés, no doubt. Perhaps also by such nation-states as would prefer a change of regime in France, or might simply profit from political turmoil or economic difficulties there. I doubt that even a coining scheme of this magnitude could accomplish the overthrow of the present state, but I suppose fanatics have no time for considered estimation."

"Your judgements are irrelevant," Venter insisted. "You have trespassed where you do not belong, and you will pay for it."

"You have broken British law on British soil," I told the businessman. "It is you who will regret your actions."

Venter was confident in his victory. His men roughly searched us, confiscating even matches and penknives, and pushed us roughly into Cordy's prison cellar. The door slammed on us, and I heard that heavy rim-lock turn to fasten us inside.

"That confirms that Venter too has masters to whom he reports," Holmes considered. "He cannot simply do away with us. He must obtain instruction."

"They will kill you though," Cordy cried. "Just as they did Howard!"

Holmes turned his attention to the captive. He prised those lock-picks from his cuff again—only now did I apprehend how he had managed to divert our searchers from discovering them—and set to work on Cordy's ankle-cuff. "Explain how you came to be involved in this affair," he instructed the captive. "Dulcimer brought you into it, did he not?"

Cordy blinked in surprise. "Why yes! How did...? When I was to marry, I was concerned to have enough money to make a good home for Agnes. We might have gone on living with her father, of course, as we has always done, but eventually we hoped to have a home of our own, with room for.... She is truly with child?"

"I have heard it from her own lips," Holmes assured him. "And the physical evidence is now incontrovertible."

---

16 François Paul Jules Grévy (1807-1891) was the third President of France from 1879-87, and the first who was an avowed republican rather than a declared monarchist. He was one of the "Opportunist Republicans" who dominated French politics in the 1880s, and passed the 'Lois scélérates' ('villainous laws') that restricted the freedom of the press in an attempt to halt anarchy. He initiated school reforms across France but is best remembered for presiding over France's controversial last colonial expansion era. He was forced to resign from office after a scandal where his son-in-law was found to have sold Legion of Honour awards for cash.

The father-to-be stared bleakly at his shackle. "And me not there, and her thinking I abandoned her like that! She will never know, for there's no escape from here. She will be forced to live in shame, and our child a bastard. She will think..."

"Your account," Holmes reprimanded Cordy.

"Yes, of course. Well, Howard knew I was trying to earn all that I could. He hinted that there was a way I could earn more at Bodmin & Venter's, more than I might get simply from working extra shifts. He had fallen in with their plans for coining, you see. Howard was always short of money, and his debts were becoming considerable."

"Venter had already tried his coining scheme, but he lacked a silversmith of sufficient skill to create adequately convincing moulds," Holmes suggested.

"Yes. There was some old chap they called on, apparently, but his eyesight was going. His casts were just not good enough to pass."

"Old Crowther," I said, recalling Lemmy Clement's account.

"Howard brought me a coin to look at, asked if I might make a better version than the crude copy he had with him. I said no. I'm not a forger. I never would, except..."

"We shall come to that," Holmes told him. "You retained the poor facsimile."

It occurred to me that our captors had not retrieved that coin from Holmes's pocket when they had emptied the other contents.

"I slipped it away when he wasn't looking, and hid it. I thought perhaps I might need some lever to protect me."

"Did you tell anyone about the offer?" I wondered.

"No-one. Who could I say anything to? I thought it best to quietly find other employment. And I did, at an interview with Mappin, Webb, and Co.—a dream job!"

"Until you gave notice to Bodmin & Venter, Ltd.," Holmes surmised.

"Yes. That was when they seized me, locked me here. The day before my wedding!"

"Did they force you to make those better moulds then?" I hazarded.

"I wouldn't. Not then. They kept me here and they... they hit me, but I'm not a criminal. I'm not. But then Howard got to asking questions, trying to find what they had done with me, and they brought him in too. They brought him right over there, in that corner, and they... they..."

Holmes could doubtless read the old brown stains better than I could, but the signs of sprayed blood were unmistakable.

"Then they said they would do for Agnes too," Cordy went on. "I knew they would. I couldn't resist any longer."

Holmes bobbed his head, as if satisfied that theories he had formulated were properly validated. "They kept you because they had other work for you to undertake, Mr Cordy. You have prepared other templates?"

"A twenty-centime piece and then a one-franc coin. I do not think they have yet begun production on those. Next I am to prepare a two-franc sculpt."

"There is yet some time before 1882."

We waited in the cellar while the clamour outside diminished. From the heavy footsteps it seemed that more boxes were being added to the coin stores. After thirty minutes or so the noises ceased and we heard nothing more. The illicit work was done for tonight and things were being cleaned up before a day shift took the place.

I stirred. "We cannot remain here as passive captives. We must act before the lamp burns dry. We must attempt to break down the door." Had the door included a keyhole on our side, Holmes might have been able to jog the mechanism with his lock-turning tools. As it was, we would somehow have to overcome a stout two-inch thick portal and whatever guards waited outside.

Cordy's gyve sprang loose. Holmes regarded his work with satisfaction. "Are you set to leave, Mr Cordy? There will be an element of danger."

"I'll do anything to get to Agnes and see her safe," the young man promised.

"Very good. Watson, you open to door and I shall go for the nearest guard."

I was baffled. "Open the door? There is no way to reach the lock. I can attempt to break through but..."

"The door is not sealed. I used irony to thwart the lock."

"I don't follow."

"When I was leaning on the jamb, I pushed our 1882 half-franc into the rim-hole where the lock-bolt goes into the doorframe. Hence the bolt did not settle in to secure the door. You will find our way unimpeded by that hefty lock. Ready?"

I smiled at my friend's cunning. One must not rise early to outwit Sherlock Holmes but remain vigilant all night!

I flung the door back. The villain who had been leaning on it toppled inwards and sprawled on the floor. Holmes leaped over him to engage the foreman who also kept sentry, grappling with the fellow before he could

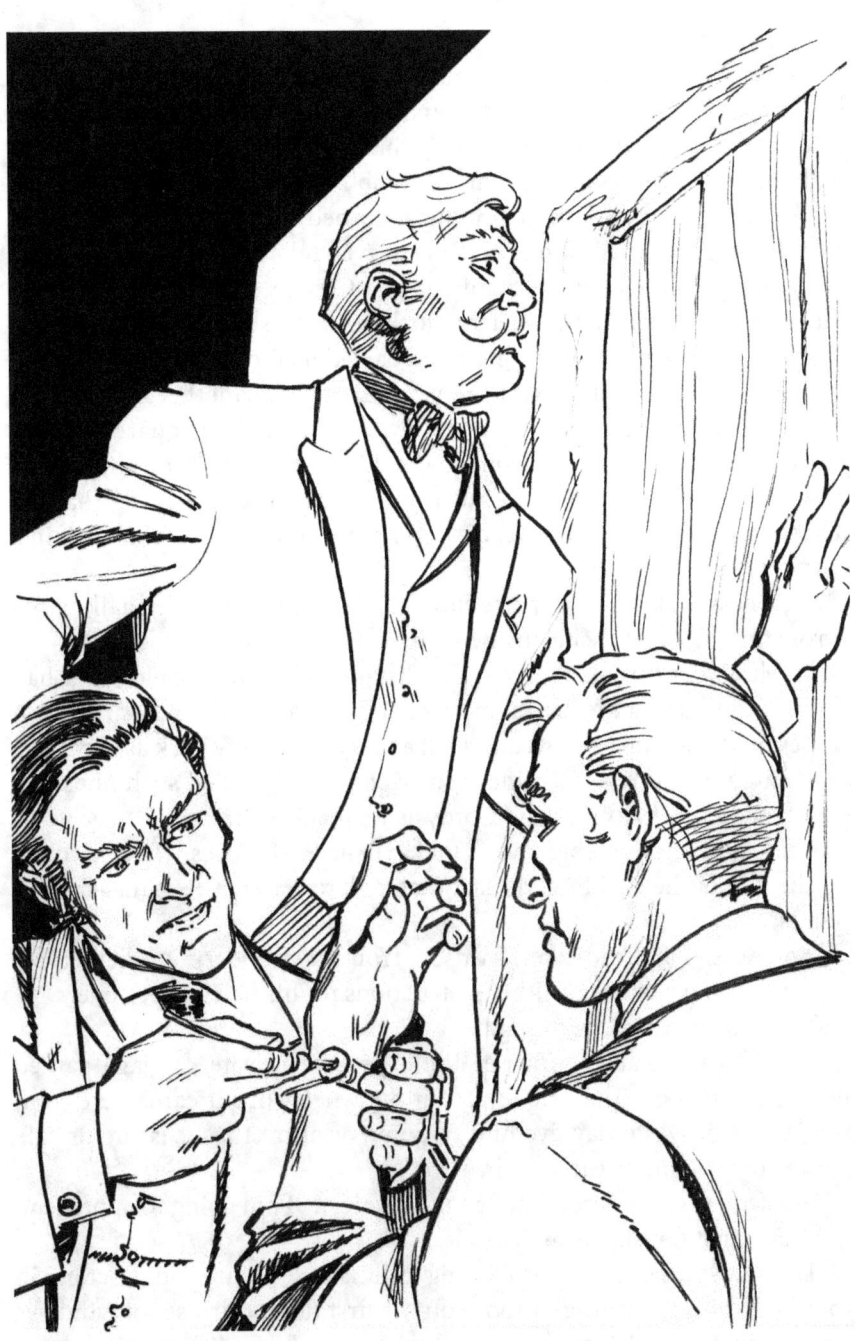

Cordy's gyve sprang loose.

draw his pistol again.

Since I had the other thug at my feet, I dropped a knee down across his throat and administered a dubbing I felt I was long overdue to bestow somewhere. My bull-pup, excited by the action, sank his teeth into the malefactor's leg and worried him like a rabbit.

The foreman was no Emil. Holmes downed him with a blur of blows, so quickly that the fellow had no time to even take a breath to call alarm.

We dragged the downed criminals into Cordy's cell. Holmes retrieved the impossible coin and used his lock-picks to seal the felons in. He checked the foreman's Remington and passed it across to me.

We reached the hatch into the yard. There was another guard there, but he was looking outwards, watching over the lading square. Holmes hooked the sentinel's legs from under him, tumbling the unfortunate down the steps with his skull rattling on each rung. I checked that the fellow was unconscious not dead, and Cordy and I dragged him to sit in a corner under the steps.

"Boldness is our best defence now," Holmes told us. "We shall march across the yard as if we belong here."

It felt as dangerous covering the distance over the cobbles as it had walking the ridge at the dry ravine, wondering if at any moment an unseen sniper might end one's existence. I felt a prickling on my back as if a Ghazi marksman was aiming his rifle at me right now. I stuffed such nonsense away and flanked Holmes and Cordy as we made for the exit.

Then I saw another objective. "Hold," I called to Holmes. "That staircase up the side of the building, doesn't that look to lead to the management's offices?"

"So the signage indicates, Watson. You are wondering whether Mr Venter is still up there, awaiting instructions for his helpless prisoners."

"Yes. Do you think he might be?"

"Look to the stables. You see the expensive private carriage parked beside them? From the dried mud on the wheel-rims it came here from the West End yesterday evening. We may venture that it is the private conveyance of one of the site's owners."

"So Venter is still here." I hefted the revolver. "I am going to apprehend him. He must not slip away."

Holmes studied me, as if making a decision. "Very good, doctor. Go to his office—you see the lit room on the first floor, third set of windows along? Simply hold him there until my return." He flicked me a small smile. "We are having a memorable stroll."

"After this I may be able to get some peaceful sleep."

Holmes continued with Cordy for the exit gate. I turned aside and took the external stair to the business offices.

I had not died at Maiwand. I had taken a wound, but wounds can heal. Lieutenant Watson of the 5th Northumberland and the Berkshires was no more, but Doctor Watson of Baker Street was alive— and awake!

The door into the back offices of Bodmin & Venter was not fastened. I progressed without interruption or delay through the darkened general room and past a clutch of juniors' chambers, counting off doors until I came to the one painted with the name 'Mr T. H. Venter, Director'. There was lamplight behind the frosted glass panel.

I knocked and was bidden to enter. The man behind the desk looked up and saw his captive bearing on him, armed and prepared.

"You are a traitor and a killer," I told him. "Keep your hands on your desk and remain silent. The police will be along shortly to end your plot."

His face paled. "You do not understand. My backers…"

"Confess yourself to Scotland Yard, sir. I have no interest in your defences for kidnap or murder."

I heard through the thick window-glass a distant but shrill blast of a police whistle. Holmes had summoned reinforcements.

Our stroll was over.

This stroll.

※※※

"I imagine an examination of Bodmin & Venter's accounts will prove of significant interest," Holmes mentioned as we tucked into a much-deserved late breakfast from Mrs Hudson's tray. "Fortunately, the political embarrassment and further enquiries are not our concern."

"All we need do is turn up to the delayed wedding of Miss Agnes Simpson to Mr Daniel Cordy," I agreed.

That happy reunion had been effected soon after the police had appeared in force at the tin-works and Inspectors Gregson and Lestrade had taken command of the scene. The joy of the happy couple (Cordy and Miss Simpson, that is; one would never accuse Scotland Yard's pre-eminent detectives of delight in each others' company) was complete and immediate. Holmes's satisfaction came from unravelling a mystery, but my sense of accomplishment was from seeing those young people reunited for a future together.

"You are not deterred at having a fellow lodger who has now twice dragged you into unpleasantness?" Holmes checked, suddenly hesitant.

"There is such a thing as too quiet a life. An invalid who hopes for recovery must exercise to recover his faculties."

"I had hoped as much. As I said, I am still assembling the assets I require to excel in my chosen vocation. It is becoming clear that one such asset is John H. Watson."

"Should my assistance be required on some future investigation, I trust you will not hesitate to mention it."

"Such an investigation will most likely occur."

We consumed our breakfast and considered the future.

WHERE DO WE GO FROM HERE?

A HOLMESIAN REFLECTION FROM I.A. WATSON

On an unspecified day in early January 1881, Dr John H. Watson entered the chemical laboratory at St Bart's Hospital to meet Mr Sherlock Holmes. Both men were seeking affordable rooms and agreed to lodge together at the upstairs flat at 221 Baker Street. Of such meetings are iconic literature made.

A Study in Scarlet, the account of Holmes and Watson's first case together, was issued to the public in *Beeton's Christmas Annual* for 1887 and as a book the following year; it was extremely well received. Literary agent Arthur Conan Doyle was encouraged to provide another example of Sherlock Holmes's abilities. *The Sign of Four* debuted in *Lipincott's Magazine* for February 1890, and thereafter short story accounts of the detective's investigations appeared regularly in *The Strand Magazine*, beginning with 'A Scandal in Bohemia' in the June 1891 issue.

However, Holmes's "extremely interesting case" detailed in *The Sign of Four* took place over four days in September 1888 (according to most standard Holmes chronologies), and his memorable meeting with 'the Woman' Irene Adler was in October 1887.

Quite some time had passed between Holmes and Watson's 'origin story' and their later published exploits. In the interim they had become firm friends, and although Dr Watson remained amazed by Holmes' acuity he was no longer dazzled by it. The initial discovery period as the two men found an equilibrium had long since passed.

Later Canon entries filled in a few of the gaps. In 'The Adventure of the *Gloria Scott*', Holmes tells Watson of "the first [case] in which I was ever engaged", usually dated around autumn 1874. He deciphered 'The Musgrave Ritual' in October 1879. There are passing references to at least fourteen cases that are likely to have been pre-Watson, including the famous matter of "the *Matilda Briggs* and the Giant Rat of Sumatra".[1]

---

1 Mentioned in 'The Adventure of the Sussex Vampire', *The Case-Book of Sherlock Holmes*, 1924)

But the earliest Canon investigation where Watson accompanies Holmes after *A Study in Scarlet* is accounted to be 'The Adventure of the Speckled Band' in April of 1883.[2] The next was 'The Resident Patient' in October of 1886.[3] In short, there is no account via Arthur Conan Doyle of Holmes and Watson's early time together once they have solved the murder of the unpleasant Enoch Drebber.

This absence naturally bothers Holmes completists. Our modern inclination is to expect 'the full story', including the early days of our cast as they develop the relationships into which they eventually settle. We live in the age of the flashback, the 'character arc', the retrospective continuity. The Canon's silence on the initial partnership of Holmes and Watson is a source of frustration.

Holmesians have been trying to supply answers for a long time. Theories abound, including biographer W.S. Baring-Gould's proposal that Watson was actually absent from England for a prolonged period from January 1884-86, tending to the last days of his alcoholic brother and meeting his first wife. But for all the discussion on Holmes's "missing year" between the conclusion of 'The Adventure of the Bruce-Partington Plans' on 23rd November 1895 and 'The Adventure of the Veiled Lodger' around eleven months later,[4] or his absence after the Reichenbach falls, it is these neophyte days of which the least is definitively told.

Contemporary editors working on Dr Watson's copious but not always organised notes have assayed some accounts which may be of utility. I.A. Watson's summation of Holmes's March or April 1882 encounter with 'Spring-Heeled Jack' is presented in *Sherlock Holmes Consulting Detective* volume 7.[5] However, it is rare that Holmesian scholarship tackles the very earliest exploits of the Baker Street partnership.

One cannot help but wonder, though. We are very familiar with Holmes and Watson's first adventure together. Its details form the template for all the stories that come after. But what about the second adventure? The third?

Hence the present account, painstakingly recovered from the neglected historical documents of the Watson estate and offered as an insight into

2 Collected in *The Adventures of Sherlock Holmes*, 1892.

3 Collected in *The Memoirs of Sherlock Holmes*, 1893.

4 Recorded in *His Last Bow* (1908) and *The Case-Book of Sherlock Holmes* (1927) respectively.

5 *Sherlock Holmes Consulting Detective* vol 7, Airship 27, 2015, ISBN 10: 0692387196 ISBN 13: 978-0692387191

a fascinating formative time for the world's foremost detective and his 'faithful Boswell'.

I.A. Watson
Living in the past
October 2018

✳✳✳

I.A. Watson - has recently been awarded his third Best Pulp Short Story award in the Pulp Factory Awards, for his final contributio to his *The Legend of Robin Hood* omnibus. This is relevant because pulp stories—Sir Arthur Conan Coy'ls serial and series periodical works included—are gradually being rediscovered as a literary form. I.A. Watsons accounts of Holmes (recovered from notes of John H Watson's, naturally) are examples of the popular format and appear in all fifteen volumes of Sherlock Holmes Consulting Detective and elsewhere. He has also written the novel *Holmes and Houdini.*

Other recently-shortlisted fiction by I.A. Watson include *Bulldog Drumond: On Poisoned Ground, Bulldog Drummond: Disaster Zones*, and short stories from nine of the Consulting Dective volumes.

A full list of I.A. Watson's published work, with free stories, exceerpts, and articles, is offered at:
http://www.chillwater.org.uk/writing/iawatsonhome.htm

Sherlock Holmes

in

"The Moriarty Obsfuscation"

By
Gary Lovisi

"Aye, I've never been so damnably perplexed!" the man mumbled to himself as he left the building that housed the venerable official police headquarters of Scotland Yard.

The wide, grand city of London was a bustling cosmopolitan center of the British Empire that year of 1895, but to the man who mumbled to himself in abject frustration as he walked The Strand and other glorious byways of the magnificent city—none of which he took notice of at all now—for his conflicting thoughts were twisted into a miasma of frustration and dire dread. For a monster was loose in his city and he needed to bring him to book.

Inspector Alec MacDonald of Scotland Yard, newly raised up to a lofty status in the department was terribly dismayed and despondent. Even though no less a detective than the great Sherlock Holmes himself had bestowed upon him the respectful nickname of "Mr. Mac", yet MacDonald did not now enjoy that acknowledgement of his friend's vaulted consideration of his talents. These had been outlined by Watson in his chronicles of the Holmes case, "The Valley of Fear". For now, MacDonald was engaged upon a case that he could not prosecute to his satisfaction—even though he was sure he knew who the criminal was. It was proving most frustrating.

MacDonald ignored the wonderful sights and sounds of Greater London as he walked the streets from Scotland Yard to his room near The Strand. He took no notice of anything or anyone, for his mind was transfixed upon his latest case, a vile act where a young boy had gone missing. The inspector feared for the worse. It might just be the terrible ending he feared, but he swore it would not be—if he had anything to do about it. He refused to accept what years of police experience told him, that the boy was dead—murdered by some foul man who took the child's life for whatever terrible reason.

The boy, Thad Harris, a good lad from a good family, had suddenly gone missing days ago. MacDonald knew only too well now at this late date what that meant. The boy met foul play but the police had no proof of anything yet, no body, no evidence of a crime—but he did have a suspect. Words from trusted informants assured him of this fact. But the inspector's frustration grew when he realized he did not have any proof to arrest the scoundrel—much less to bring him to book at the assizes. It was a nightmare, the young inspector had struggled with the particulars of this case for the last few days since the boy had first gone missing.

It had all occurred in this manner.

Five days before, young Thad Harris had been waiting for the Midtown horse drawn tram as he did every day at that early time in the morning. The boy was going to his public school far from his home in Central London. That particular morning the tram had been running late, and a second car had been dispatched along the route, following closely behind the first car. So the driver of the first tram saw the young lad, but knowing his car was running late to schedule, and pressing to make up some time on that schedule, had passed by the lad. Passengers on his car also saw the lad, and some begged the driver to stop and pick up the boy, but the man continued on his route in an attempt to make up on his lost time.

The next tram came by in the space of five minutes, but it also passed by the spot where the boy waited—*because by then the boy was no longer there.* The boy was nowhere to be seen. In fact, it appeared to the police later that young Thad Harris had simply disappeared into thin air. There was no evidence present of any foul play, nor any blood found.

Alerts were sent out to all local constables. The boy's parents were horrified, there was a great commotion by all of London to seek out the lost boy. Days passed and there was no information or evidence to be had. The case had struck a solid wall and MacDonald was at a loss as to what to do.

The thoughts swirling in the ace detective's head caused a collision of ideas and theories, from dark imaginings to more pedestrian reasons for the boy's disappearance. Perhaps there was some simple explanation for the missing boy? Perhaps he had just run off? Maybe he had even went on some young lad version of a holiday? But no, MacDonald had spoken to the parents, the neighbors, the boy's friends and teachers at his school, and there was no reason for him to run away. It was most unlike the lad. That left more nefarious reasons for the boy's disappearance, some of which the inspector did not want to overly dwell upon, for he knew well the dark heart of some men and the treachery of the criminal element. Nevertheless, he realized that he must face these facts and do all he could to resolve this case.

Inspector MacDonald took the matter to his superior at The Yard the next day. Inspector Lestrade was not overly helpful nor very supportive. The diminutive older man had the appearance of a weasel, with ferret-like eyes, a coarse grim mustache, and a look upon his face that seemed to make him appear to be perpetually annoyed. MacDonald was sure the appearance told the truth of the inner man, but he was MacDonald's superior at the Yard so deference to his rank and moods must be made. And truth be told, Lestrade while unimaginative—as Mr. Holmes always spoke of him—was not a bad fellow. He was honest, and he did have a certain bull-headed determination when on a case—for good or ill—and he did care.

"Just solve it, MacDonald! Somehow you must solve it. And quickly! This is becoming a hot potato among the politicians and it needs to be closed soon," Lestrade demanded. It did not seem to matter to him how it was solved, or who was brought to book for the crime, so long as someone was arrested soon. MacDonald revolted at that manner of working a case, for he had other ideas. Better ideas?

"Aye, I wish I could solve it immediately, but there are too many problems and I have only one witness and she *din nae* see much!" MacDonald stated in his thick Scotish Aberdeen accent. His accent always came out more forcefully when under times of stress, or anger, like now.

"Then look to other ways, as your friend Mr. Holmes might well instruct you. 'Mr. Mac' he calls you, with some fondness and even respect I am sure," Lestrade shook his head. The great Holmes had never shown *him* such respect and he was quite jealous of the fact. And MacDonald was also younger, even though he did show promise as an top flight investigator.

"Aye, there is something I plan, but I need to run it by you to get some of our men onboard. Are you willing to hear me out and try something… well, a bit different?"

"All right, MacDonald, least I can do is hear your plan, and if we put it into operation I hope for your sake that it works."

"I hope it does as well," the young inspector replied carefully.

※※※

Inspector Alec MacDonald had all the men in place the next morning. The two manikins had had set up he had borrowed from Amberson's large clothing shop on Saville Row. He had had the devil of a time persuading the owner, Mr. Hadley, to part with two of his most human life-like manikins. They were of a young boy of about Thad Harris's size and age, and another of an adult man of the size and age of the man an early morning witness on the tram had told the police she had seen when the first tram had passed by the lone boy. The man at that time had been seen down the street, quickly walking towards the pick-up spot for the first of the horse drawn trams.

"You really think this will work?" Lestrade said dubiously as he stood next to MacDonald, across the street from the tramway route. He was working a case of a recently murdered constable in the same area, and that pressed more upon his mind now.

"It may, Lestrade, it just may. I am hoping that it will jog the memories of some of the people hereabouts."

"I think not. No one cares, MacDonald, and no one notices, I am afraid," Lestrade offered grimly, from his own long years of experience.

"There I believe you are wrong, sir. Some people do care and some do notice and all we need is one of them to come forward and tell us what they have seen," MacDonald continued with a confidence in his voice that he did not exactly feel deep in his bones.

"But will they? I think not. I think this manikin play is just that, a rather amusing, even innovative attempt to find a key witness, but I do not believe such—theatrics—will avail you anything on this case."

"And yet you approved my plan?"

"Yes, I did. I will approve anything that might bring this case to closure, MacDonald, even your starry-eyed ideas and theories. I think you have been too much involved with Mr. Sherlock Holmes over the years and influenced by his wild ideas on criminal investigation. While I admit, his methods may sometimes be interesting, they are not as we like to see things done here at the Yard. Take care, my young friend. While I give you that Mr. Holmes sometimes comes up with interesting information that occasionally helps us here at the Yard, he and his consulting detective ideas can never be a replacement for us, the official police," Lestrade said knowingly in a firm tone.

"Aye, I agree, Lestrade, but he has his uses, would you not agree?"

"Yes, he has his uses," Lestrade reluctantly admitted, but he did not elaborate on how many times Holmes had pulled his arse out of the fire and closed cases for him that he could never have closed on his own. "Now what of this plan of yours, MacDonald?"

"Simple really. I have placed the two manikins in the exact areas of the street on the tramway route at the time the Harris boy went missing. I have dressed each manikin in the clothing they were wearing upon that early morning. We know the clothing and colors that the boy wore. The man, our suspect, is another matter, but we have that one witness, who told me the man looked 'rough'. So I have made him up to appear that way."

"And then what? The locals will just come around and ask a lot of questions," Lestrade stated. "Annoying questions."

"Aye, there will be some of that to be sure, but also it may jog the memories of some of the locals. Not the home owners here, who are rather well off—but their domestic help. The people who work here lead lives that do not often change, they live each day the same as the next and the previous. I am counting on that aspect of their regularity. The same people pass by the same street, the same time of day. It can be relied upon like clockwork. The same people take the same tram to come here, at the same time, at the same location every day. Someone had to see something."

"Perhaps," Lestrade reluctantly admitted. This entire plan seemed to be a fiasco in the making, right out of one of Mr. Holmes's wild schemes. Lestrade could see plainly where MacDonald had taken his influence from, but regarding the complicated politics of the Yard, it appeared the young inspector may have bitten off more than he could chew on this particular case. This fiasco could sink his career if he was not careful. Lestrade shook his head, he did like the dour young Scot, but the two inspectors were fierce competitors at the Yard and they had a history of disagreements and sometimes difficulties in cooperation.

"So what do you think?" MacDonald asked his superior, as his eyes scanned the two manikins standing across the street, and the two Bobbies standing beside them. They were there to instruct passersby why the manikins were on display—which immediately grew some curiosity among the locals—and to ask if any of those passing by remembered anything that might help in the case of the missing Harris boy.

"This plan does not seem to be bearing any fruit," Lestrade acknowledged impatiently after some time had passed. He was afraid he was wasting the time of two of his constables on some type of trivial forlorn hope, that might have better been used on the murder of Constable Sanders.

"Aye, it may take some time," MacDonald reluctantly admitted. Then one of the Bobbies who was speaking to a young woman near the adult manikin called out.

"Inspector MacDonald, I think you need to talk to this one!"

MacDonald bolted across the street, with Lestrade following right behind him. From their observation position they went to the Bobby and the woman. She was a young woman, obviously Irish, one of the many working women who did all manner of jobs in the houses of the upper classes in this area.

"Mable Gaylor," the young lass told the Scot.

"Yes, Miss Gaylor," MacDonald began in a friendly manner. "And what is it that you remember seeing on that morning when the wee tyke went missing?"

"The man… The Man that walked towards the tram—and the boy. I saw them plainly. I was seated in a tram being drawn towards the stop by two horses. I saw the man and the boy when the tram made the turn up Uxbridge Wells, but when it came down the street to the usual stop, the boy was gone—and so was the man. I recall that at the time as being somewhat odd."

Lestrade looked at the woman carefully, "Exactly what did you see?"

"That is all, Sir," the young lady replied.

MacDonald nodded, "Can you describe the man or the boy?"

"Well, they look very much like the two store dummies you have placed upon the street here. That is what drew my attention now and why I have come forward. They are positioned in the same location as I remember them being that morning. I noticed them because I remember noting how rough the man looked, and then I noticed the young boy all alone. He should not have been alone at that time of morning. The boy wore bright clothing, a red shirt, a bright blue cap. I imagine it was his school cap."

"You are most observant," MacDonald stated, thinking it through. "Can you describe the man more closely?"

"Well, like I say, he was rough, a street tough of some kind. I sees the like of them in me neighborhood all the time. Someone to stay away from," the young lady replied meaningfully.

MacDonald nodded knowingly. He had what he wanted, and now what he needed. He carefully withdrew four small charcoal sketches from his vest pocket that he had had an artist make up of his suspect, and three other men, that looked very similar in appearance. His suspect was the image of a rough man, a street tough whose violence was known in certain criminal circles and she chose him straight away. MacDonald's suspect! MacDonald held out the small drawing that clearly showed the man's face. He asked her once again, to be sure. "So this is the man you saw, Miss?"

The young lady gasped fearfully, "By God! That's him! That's the man, I'd swear it."

"You'd swear to it?" MacDonald asked carefully.

"Yes, I would."

MacDonald looked over to Lestrade, "Well, it is the man who I thought it was."

"Yes, well it may be him, but how do you get him with no evidence, no body? You know we checked him first thing, after your informant pointed him out to you. He has an alibi. For now, he is untouchable as far as the law goes," Lestrade replied.

"Well, like I say, he was rough, a street tough of some kind."

MacDonald sighed, "I know, and therein lies the rub, for sure."

"We have put a 24-hour detail of Yard men on him, but the deed's done, the boy is gone, or dead. The body is hidden or lost. You'll never find what you need to solve this, MacDonald. Too bad for you...and his family, of course."

MacDonald's face grew red with anger and in his thick Aberdeen accent he proclaimed, "Well, I'll *nae* accept it, Lestrade. I'll bring this man to book, if it be the last thing I do!"

✳✳✳

Inspector Alec MacDonald brimmed over with consternation and frustration. This latest case, the missing boy, Thad Harris, presented many problems, none of which he seemed able to solve. What had happened to the boy? Was he even still alive? MacDonald did not know, though he feared for the worse. No body had been found, no evidence of foul play had been discovered at the scene where the boy had gone missing. There was no blood evidence anywhere in the area as well. It was a conundrum worthy of his friend, the consulting detective, Sherlock Holmes. However, while the dour Scot from Scotland Yard respected the methods of the man he considered the master detective—MacDonald did not want to call in his friend on this case. Not just yet. He would try to solve it himself first. If he could. After all, he believed he was sure who the culprit was, a rough, tough thug and East End career criminal who went by the bizarre name of Shadow Noneya. It was a strange name to be sure, perhaps some form of alias? He did not seem to be a foreigner, so it did not seem to be a foreign name. Or perhaps it was? He wondered about that name, where it came from, or what it meant, if anything.

A trusted informant had told Inspector MacDonald that a man with the unlikely name of Shadow Noneya had done the crime. He had had this Noneya fellow followed day and night since the boy went missing, but to no avail. The man never gave any indication of his crime—or any crime. MacDonald found the man's room and he himself tossed his crib for evidence. There was nothing. The man seemed to be a petty crook, involved in many things, though none of them seemed to be of the level where he could have him arrested and put away for years—nor did anything indicate he had any involvement in the Harris boy's disappearance. But MacDonald knew the game being played here, this Noneya was a bad one, but little known outside of a small circle. He was a fellow who seemed to be up for anything and while not possessing professional criminal tendencies, was much valued as a thug. He was most widely known as a solid safecracker, but only using strong-arm tactics. He was also prone to fly into violent rages and could be extremely dangerous, especially when inebriated. Had this man abducted the Harris boy? If so, why? Had he killed the boy? Or perhaps, had he just been in the right place at the right time—or the wrong place at the wrong time—when the boy had gone missing and he really had nothing to do with the missing boy, as he said? Well, every criminal said he did not do the crime. MacDonald was beginning to doubt his witnesses and informants, and his superiors at the Yard. Inspector Lestrade in particular, no longer believed in the theory that Noneya had done the deed.

MacDonald sighed and spoke softly to himself, "Aye, it be a most confusing puzzle, one worthy of Mr. Holmes, but I shall solve it, if it is the last thing I do."

MacDonald's determination was growing, even as his doubts were also enlarging. Was he on a wild goose chase? A wild goose chase, while the real culprit was getting away! That thought galled the dour Scot as much as the crime itself.

"Where are you, young Thad Harris?" MacDonald whispered to himself. "What the hell happened to you?"

Inspector Alec MacDonald, "Mr. Mac" to the great Sherlock Holmes, shook his head in frustration. He knew what he had to do. He had to solve this case, and do it in the manner of the Great Detective, using the careful procedures that he had learned from Holmes over the years. The boy must be found—either alive, or his corpse—but he must be found and the case solved with the culprit brought to book for his crime. As far as MacDonald was concerned, that would be made to happen, so he steeled his nerves, drew upon his solid Scotish determination and made himself ready to track down this Shadow Noneya and find the evidence of this crime. For he knew the fellow had to be his man. He knew that it would not be easy to get the man, but he was ready, willing, and able to carry out his investigation to wherever it led him. To the end.

MacDonald relied on the evidence given to him by his informants and now by the Irish gal who had positively identified the sketch of Noneya as the man seen near the tramway when the boy went missing. She had picked him out of a group of four similar sketches MacDonald had made up. There was no doubt in his mind that the young woman was telling the truth, the shivers of her body when she saw that sketch of Noneya made certain of that. She was terrified of the man. And he was a quite terrifying fellow in appearance. Nevertheless, MacDonald had to concede that Lestrade was correct, the man had an air-tight alibi, so while Lestrade urged MacDonald to look elsewhere, the dour Scot doubled-down and knew he had to investigate even deeper into this Noneya fellow.

With this in mind he brought in the venerable Constable Lowery to aid him. After explaining the case, he asked the constable, "I need your help."

"So what do you make of this Noneya?' Constable Lowery asked of the Scot when the two talked over the mystery over a couple of pints. Lowery was an older officer, and while he had never achieved detective status at the Yard, he had seen and done a lot in his long career. His advice was valued by MacDonald, and he often worked with the inspector.

"Dangerous, for sure, and certainly capable of abducting the lad, or... killing him?" MacDonald stated firmly.

"I agree, a bad 'un for sure. He is a lone wolf, but I have heard he's always had pretensions of working for one of the big gangs here in London. They won't have him though. They don't like him much. He's too violent, unpredictable, so they seem to keep him at arms length. He has no gang connections, though he wants them dearly."

"So he wants into the big gangs, does he?"

"Yes, very much I may add, but they don't seem to want him much," Lowery replied.

"Interesting," MacDonald stated thoughtfully.

"Yes, but why would he take the boy in any case—or kill him?"

"Aye, that's the part that's eating into my craw. You know the type, he may be someone who...well..." MacDonald did not want to go into details, but Lowery knew what he meant.

"I think not, not this fellow, but who can truly tell," Lowery stated, then allowed a determined nod of his head. "But I'll tell you something, there was also the murder of a constable hereabouts a few days before the lad went missing. Constable Able Sanders, well liked, well respected. It is supposed that he had come upon a robber who was working one of the better homes hereabouts. Constable Sanders came upon the robber and confronted him, who stabbed him to death in the early morning as he left the house. Then he made his escape."

"Yes, that killing was terrible," MacDonald replied. He did not know Constable Sanders but he felt bad for the man and his family. He knew Lestrade and others at the Yard were furiously working the case. However, he had not thought of connecting the two crimes until now. Was it possible?

"Yes, it was truly tragic," Lowery added in a soft tone.

"How close to this spot did it happen? What time of day? Any witnesses?" MacDonald asked curious now.

Lowery checked his notes, "It was nearby here for certain, and occurred two days before the boy went missing. It was early morning, and as far as we know there were no witnesses to the constable's murder."

"So tragic," MacDonald said in a soft thoughtful voice. "Tell me, what did this robber steal?"

Lowery thought, scratched his head sagely, then nodded, "I believe it was some kind of safe job. The owner of the house had a safe that was said to have some minor valuables, possibly some jewelry and cash. The safe was pried open with a crowbar, strong arm work, and the contents were taken."

"The jewelry has not shown up for sale in any of the usual places?" MacDonald asked curiously.

"As far as we know, nothing has yet shown up on the black market," Lowery added.

"As expected, he, or someone else, must be holding back on selling the swag," MacDonald stated. "I'm even more sure this Noneya is our man now, he is said to like breaking into safes, but I've had him followed and watched with no leads. I've personally searched his crib, nothing has shone up."

"Yes, Inspector MacDonald, the man is an uncanny fellow and it will take some uncanny plan to trap him and bring him to book," Lowery told his chief. "He may suspect he is being watched, or like most criminals, of a paranoid mind."

"Aye, that may be the case, but I will do what needs to be done. Will you help me trap this monster, Constable Lowery?"

"For sure I will," Lowery replied proudly. It was another chance to work with an inspector he respected and partner upon a case that needed to be solved. Lowery had a young son at home almost the same age of the Harris boy and he also wondered if the murder of Constable Sanders could be connected to this missing boy.

※※※

"Then we'll bring him in, question him, and see what we can find out," MacDonald stated to the constable. "You with me on this, Lowery?"

"Yes, of course, Sir, but where do we find him? I have heard he has gone missing himself now."

"Indeed, he seems to have slipped through a crack in the floor like some wily cockroach," MacDonald said in evident frustration. It was obvious the thug had known he was being followed and looked at carefully by the police. So he had gone to ground and was now missing.

That did not alarm MacDonald overly. The inspector and constable made all the necessary inquiries. They talked to every snitch, rat and roach they knew. They borrowed the resources of other constables and Yard men. They threw a net that went wide and deep to touch every informant they knew. And finally, when it appeared that Shadow Noneya had disappeared as cleverly as had young Thad Harris, they hit pay dirt.

It was in the manner of a friend, of a friend, of a constable who worked the gritty East End. It was an area that had a certain pub, one said to be frequented by many scoundrels. Noneya would be a patron of such a pub. So MacDonald and Lowery headed to the place as soon as possible.

The place was a dive of the worst proclivities, a real den of thieves. It was hidden on a back street so that if you did not know it was there, you would miss it entirely. That lent it a most interesting aspect.

As Inspector MacDonald and Constable Lowery entered the den, the place turned suddenly quiet, and fully half of the patrons of the establishment quickly got up from their seats or stools and left the pub without one word, but with many a foul look at the two coppers.

Lowery looked askance at the inspector, "Charming place, eh? This type can smell a copper a mile away, I'll wager."

"Aye, just the sort of place that—look—and there he be!" MacDonald pointed to a rough looking customer seated with his head in his hands as he gulped down the rot-gut raw alcohol served in this vile establishment.

The man the two coppers were seeking did not move as the two policemen approached his table. The man was alone, and by now most of the pub's patrons had left the place or moved artfully well away from where the two coppers were going.

"Shadow Noneya?" MacDonald asked in a booming voice as he stood firmly in front of the slumped down man. He was ready for anything from this wily fellow.

"Who wants to know!" the man growled back in slurred speech, took another hit of his drink, but he did not look up to see who it was who had addressed him.

"Inspector Alec MacDonald of Scotland Yard."

"Oh, you again!" the man slurred his speech loudly in a defiant and disdainful manner. "I told you all I knows. I knows no more!"

"Yes, but you *din nae* tell me your real name. It is not Shadow Noneya, and I am sure you have a long criminal track record hereabouts."

"You have me all wrong, inspector."

"I think not," MacDonald shot back. "So give me your real name."

Noneya looked up at the inspector and the constable who had accompanied him into the pub and gave them a twisted wicked smile. "That's for me to know and for you to find out."

"And we shall find out, we have no worry on that score my cheeky fellow. Or perhaps you should worry. Worry very much, I be thinking. There's a murder charge I could easily put upon you."

"Why, you can't push on me! I gots my alibi, I do! The old woman saw me, she be a right proper old bird too, and she said she saw me walk away plain as day. And I did! You have nothing on me. Now leave me be!"

"No, that is not going to happen. I think we'll be taking you back to the Yard for more questioning," MacDonald stated in a grim hard tone.

Noneya gave the inspector a nasty look.

"Now stand up, allow my man here to frisk you, and come along peacefully, or it will be the cuffs for you. You'll *nae* get a fairer deal for taking you in for questioning," MacDonald urged. He gave the man a moment to get himself up from his chair and table. The pub was almost empty now. The publican hid behind the stout planks of the bar. The place was deathly quiet.

"No, I think not, inspector," Noneya blurted out in anger. "I's gots me rights! I knows them rights! I's got an alibi, I do. The old bird. She spoke up for me, no matter what that young Irish git on the tram might have told you. Sure, I knows all about her, your secret witness, she be. Well, she's wrong, and so is you! Now be gone! I'll not be going with you anywheres today!"

Constable Lowery smiled with grim anticipation as he withdrew a stout wooden cudgel from his belt. "Should I use my talents to persuade this vile puke to give himself up and come with us to the Yard peacefully?"

A grimace came to MacDonald's face. He had thought of pushing Noneya, and Constable Lowery was surely fully capable in that area of persuasion, but something the man said struck the inspector as quite interesting.

"All right, Noneya, or whatever your true name might be," MacDonald stated in a gruff Aberdeen accent. "I'll *nae* be taking you in to the Yard today. However, I will see you soon, you can make book on that. Come on,

Lowery, let's leave this den of filth, the very air here is fetid."

Constable Lowery put his cudgel back on the latch upon his belt with some regret. If anyone needed a bit of firm persuasion, he was convinced that it was this drunken criminal fellow, who he looked at with a stern promise. "Oh, well, we'll meet up with the likes of you again. And perhaps then the inspector and I shall not be so polite and accommodating. Have a good day you crooked bastard."

MacDonald tamped down his anger at the turn of events and looked full into the face of Noneya and growled, "And tell me this, what kind of name is Noneya anyway?"

The man looked back at the inspector with a twisted leer and just said as bold as could be, "None ya damn business!"

Constable Lowery mumbled some words that sounded like 'vile puke' and then held back the inspector, whispering, "Not the proper time, and not the proper place for that now."

MacDonald reluctantly agreed.

Noneya just laughed and could not resist adding, "And you can both goes to hell!"

The two policemen held their tempers and left the pub. They breathed with relief when they hit the cool clean air outside of the place on the street.

"A tough and nasty bloke for certain," Lowery stated.

"Aye, a bad 'un for sure," MacDonald agreed as the two walked away. He wondered what the man meant by his words about his name. Could it be true? The inspector already had his next plan in mind, and it centered on the old lady that Noneya used as his alibi. There was something not right there. He was sure of it. There had to be. And he would find out what it was, and that might well break open this case.

✳✳✳✳

She was elderly, maybe even ancient, but she was a most tough, opinionated and sharp old bird. She did not suffer fools, nor police, lightly. She seemed to put both in the same category.

"You back again!" She told MacDonald as she looked at him carefully with open disdain. She did not like to see coppers at her home again with their annoying questions. She did not like the look of the constable copper that was with the inspector either. However, Constance Mullens did not have any choice in this matter and she knew it, so she allowed the two coppers into her rooms and led them to seats in a living room where they could question her. It was the same room where the police had questioned her days before. It had a large picture window that looked out broadly upon the street with a clear, unobstructed view. It was from her seat in this room, by the window, looking outside, where she had said she had seen Noneya walk away from the boy who had been waiting for the tram. Her eyes were good, sharp and focused, perhaps even better than MacDonald's own weary eyes, he feared. That did not bode well for his case. He needed to question this woman more—and more closely.

"I need to ask you further questions about the man you saw that day the boy went missing," MacDonald began in a friendly manner.

"Always more questions," she responded bitterly, not hiding her annoyance.

"I know you spoke of what you saw to me already, and to other police, but I need to ask you if you saw anything else, anything you are not telling us because you may believe it is not necessary or you think it to be inconsequential."

The old lady laughed at that. "I told you and the Yard men all I know, all I saw. I know no more, and I saw no more."

"Aye, 'tis as you said, yet there is something missing in your testimony," the inspector added.

Constance Mullens' old leathery face flared red with anger. "What do you mean? You accusing me! How dare you!"

"Of course not, Mrs. Mullens," MacDonald was quick to respond, to assuage her rage. Was it faux rage? He was sure that it was. "You are not a suspect, for we already have one."

"And from what I have been told, my testimony clears him," she muttered.

"Aye, it does, but it does not make sense as it conflicts with testimony we have from a young working woman who was riding the tram that very day and she clearly saw the same man. She identified him positively."

"So? She is wrong, or mistaken," the old lady insisted.

"Why is *she* mistaken or wrong—and not *you*?" Constable Lowery added, chiming in for the first time.

The old lady just shook her head.

"A boy's life may be in the balance," MacDonald reminded her.

"And I told you all I know, all that I saw," the old lady replied.

Inspector MacDonald nodded, allowed a grim little smile, then added, "Mrs. Mullens, you are a widow, are you not?"

"These ten years past, though what that has to do with your questions I can not understand."

"Then I shall get to the point," MacDonald continued firmly. "What is your connection to this man, the man who goes by the name of Shadow Noneya?"

Constance Mullens looked visibly flustered, grew nervous, her eyes darting from the face of the inspector to the constable and back again. MacDonald knew his question had hit a nerve. He was determined to dig further.

Constable Lowery could not resist a smile, for he knew the game was up now. He had seen this look upon the face of many a suspect in his long years of working for the Metropolitan Police. However, he said nothing yet, for this was MacDonald's case to pursue as he chose.

MacDonald did not miss the cue either; he nodded slowly, thinking it through. So there was a connection!

"Who is this Shadow Noneya? You know something about him. What is it?" the inspector asked firmly.

"I know nothing," the old woman spoke up plainly, but both men could see she was lying now.

"I think not. I think you know quite a bit. I suggest you spill it to me now or I shall have Constable Lowery here put you in cuffs and take you to the Yard for further questioning. You more than likely will spend your evening, and perhaps some days, in a cell in our Metropolitan Police head-quarters. Overnight, perhaps more than one night, instead of remaining here in your very pleasant home this evening. It is up to you Mrs. Mullens. Tell me what I want to know."

Inspector MacDonald waited, patient, he knew she was thinking over her options. They were severely limited and there was no real choice. She would never accept a night—or nights—in jail to protect the likes of some-one like Noneya.

"Oh, all right, if it will keeps me out of gaol. I knows the bloke a bit, but only through my late Mr. Mullens," she stated carefully with a sly wink. "It was many years ago. My Mr. Mullens and he did some early work together, before he passed on."

"Criminal work you mean," the constable elaborated.

"Of course, what other kind is there?" she replied simply.

MacDonald allowed a smirk of disgust at her response but did not verbally comment, instead he told her, "Continue. So who is this Shadow Noneya?"

Constance Mullens just laughed, "I almost peed meself when I first heard the name. As I said, I knew him through my Mr. Mullens about a dozen years back. Back then he went by the name of George Turner, but he used many names to throw off the coppers. It appears he's done a good job of it."

"So you lied," MacDonald stated.

"Yes—no! I mean…" she stammered, then carefully the old bird toughened up. "I did see him on that day the boy went missing, I was not lying, but I did not see him go over to the boy—but…"

"But—what?" MacDonald demanded.

"There was a second tram that appeared almost immediately after that pulled forward by a team of horses."

"We know about that. That was the second horse-drawn tram that was added to the rout and followed closely behind the first tram that was running very late," Constable Lowery stated.

"Yes, that was it, I think." the old lady replied. "In any case, the second tram was one of the new double-deckers, and it blocked my view from the window here. So I saw George Turner walk down the street, but I never saw him go near the boy."

"So your alibi for him is not as solid as it first appeared," MacDonald said with a knowing smile.

"Well… I could not really see clearly…"

"Your view was obstructed, so your alibi for him is suspect," MacDonald added.

"Say what you will about it," the old bird replied.

The inspector now changed tack. "So Shadow Noneya is George Turner?" he said to the old lady.

"Yes, among other names he also uses," she replied in a low tone.

"Quite the career criminal," Lowery stated gruffly.

"Yes, quite," the old lady replied with a bit of pride in her knowing smile.

"M'am, your morals are seriously askew!" Lowery insisted annoyed.

MacDonald quickly stepped in, "Tell me something, Mrs. Mullens, what does the name he is using mean? If anything?"

The old bird laughed, "Shadow Noneya, yes, George was always an inventive bloke for sure. I knows that Shadow was the name of his beloved dog."

"A dog!" Lowery stammered.

The inspector nodded, caught his constable's eye, he would test her now. "And his last name, Noneya? When I asked him about it he told me it was 'none of ya damn business.' Is that correct, Mrs. Mullens?"

The old bird tittered her laughter, "Yes, none of ya damn business, copper! That is George Turner all the way," she admitted. "Now you have what you need, so now you can leave me be."

"We can very well arrest you, Ma'am, withholding evidence, lying to the police, being it could be a murder case, things could go hard on you…" Lowery warned her.

"No, you won't, I told you what you want to know, Inspector." she replied, not acknowledging the constable at all. She knew who made the decisions here. "I am an elderly widow, I told you all I know and that's the God's honest truth."

"Hah!" Lowery grumbled softly. He was sure she was holding something back.

"Well, then Mrs. Mullens, the constable and I will leave you be now. Thank you for your time," the inspector replied and the two men left her home.

✳✳✳

Once outside on the street MacDonald and Lowery walked away from Mrs. Mullens home thinking over what they had learned.

"Well, at least we found out the true name of this Noneya fellow," the constable stated, allowing a slim grin of victory.

"Aye, but that's not the key element we learned here today, Lowery," MacDonald told him in a careful and sharp voice. "We would have eventually discovered Noneya's true identity and all his various aliases, he's got a long record and he's very much in the police files. Somewhere. He could not hide his true identity from us for long. What concerns me more is Mrs. Mullens statement, she did see Noneya there, but she did not see him approach the boy."

'Yes, but that was because she said her vision was obscured by the passing of the second tram on the street outside her window," Lowery stated carefully. "That means he could have approached the boy. It is a weak alibi, all things considered."

"Aye, her vision from her window was either obscured by the tram as she told us, or she is lying to protect that man. In any case," MacDonald reluctantly had to admit, "his alibi while weakened, still holds. He was never actually seen with the boy."

"Nonsense, you know it is a false alibi!"

"Both you and I know that it his alibi does not hold water with us, but in a court of law," MacDonald reluctantly had to admit to his constable, "it could save him from conviction. In fact, I suspect that no crown prosecutor will even pursue such a case under these circumstances. Something else is needed here, Lowery. Something else, something more."

"But what could that be, inspector?" the constable asked with some regret.

"What, indeed? It must be something new, and bold, and something that will work to convict this George Turner, this damnable Shadow Noneya,' the inspector replied tamping down his frustration. "We must find the boy!"

"And do you know what that course of action might be, inspector?"

"Not yet, Lowery, not yet, but I will find a way," MacDonald stated with firm resolve. He would bring this George Turner—this Shadow Noneya to book for this crime—this murder—for he was sure now the man had killed the missing boy. He would solve this case, if it was the last thing MacDonald ever did as a Scotland Yarder, he would get this man.

❋❋❋

The disreputable man seated alone at a table in the corner of a notorious East End pub continued his drinking and thinking. He had a lot to think about, and he had drunk a lot of the cheap rot-gut alcohol served in this nefarious establishment. He was let be by the other denizens of the disreputable pub, a most malignant place to be sure, a den of thieves and cut-purses, thugs and even killers.

The man who went by the name of Shadow Noneya these days paid no attention to anyone or anything in the pub, but everyone stayed well away from him. They all knew he could be a most dangerous man when the evil power of strong drink was upon him.

"Bring me another bottle of your best slop!" Noneya shouted to the harried publican in a low ominous growl that brooked no delay. "I have a lot of drinking, and a lot of thinking, to do."

Noneya burped loudly, his head weaved drunkenly before he was able to steady himself on his chair. He was in distress. Angry. They were trying to connect him to that missing boy business again. 'They' being the damnable coppers, but especially in the person of a particular inspector from Scotland Yard. He was always nosing around. Noneya was sure that inspector—a dog-faced dour Scot by the name of MacDonald—did not believe a word of his story or accept his alibi. Not one word! The copper was nosing around where he should not be nosing, and he would not stop.

Noneya did not like that, but he did not care over much yet, for he was sure he would not be connected with the missing boy. He was sure of it. There was no evidence. But that didn't lighten his mood at all. What bothered him most was that his association in this missing boy case had made him untouchable by the powerful mob organizations he yearned to work for.

The truth was that with all the vile, nasty, despicable things he had done in his life of crime, he could not believe that this one crime should bring the focus upon him and now bring such heat down upon him so that it could be that one missing boy might be his undoing!

Noneya knew that was all bollocks, but that is what he was thought of by those whose approval he sought out the most in the organized criminal world. Untouchable.

He took another swig of the deadly brew, knowing if the coppers didn't kill him, this poisonous swill surely would. He grew angry, he had stolen some cash and jewels out of that safe in that posh home over a week ago, and the next day had fenced the baubles to Larry the Snake for practically nothing at all. It galled the thief. For Larry was connected and followed rules imposed upon him by the criminal organization he worked for. Larry followed the rules, and imposed them on Noneya and his swag. It galled the thief in him that he could not get more for his ill-gotten gains—not that he wouldn't have drunk it all up in any case—but it annoyed him that he was shut out of the organization and all they could do for him when he sold stolen swag. Other thieves and robbers who were in the organization received a much higher pay off on any stolen goods they forwarded to the mob. Also, they received considerable protection from the law. Noneya was angered and insulted that he did not rate these considerations, for he yearned for a bigger pay off and protection for his work. He threw an empty bottle at the wall of the pub, the glass shattering into a hundred pieces. The violence mirrored his anger.

"Hey, you! Stop it!" the pub owner shouted out from the safety of behind the bar, but he did not come out to confront the man who had thrown the bottle. He was not that foolish.

"Hurry up with another bottle!" Noneya barked in slurred drunken rage.

The publican froze, for while he was afraid to bring the new bottle to the enraged man's table, he feared not to do so as well. It was then that a rough stranger who had just entered the pub took the bottle from him asking, "I'll bring it to him, if you're not minding me to do so."

"No, no, not at all," the nervous publican said from behind the bar with a deep sigh of relief as he pushed over the new bottle to this brave

...it could be that one missing boy might be his undoing!

stranger. The publican had never seen this fellow before but he could spot a rough tough one for sure, for this one appeared to be a very dangerous man, much like the man at the table. He watched with fear as the man approached the seated customer and placed the new bottle on the table in front of him. The publican feared there might be a fight, a regular donnybrook or worse, but instead the man calmly sat down with the man at the table and the two seemed to be speaking in soft tones he could not hear. He looked away, perhaps better not to hear anything at all concerning these two, such was the credo of his pub.

Shadow Noneya looked up as the man approached him, noting he was bringing a new bottle of booze. He knew the man was not the publican, or a waiter, but another wily tough such as he was. The newcomer was scarred and bruised, hard-boiled and had the eyes of a criminal and the smile of a murderer. Noneya respected that and liked him straight away. Now this is the type of bloke he could appreciate.

"Name is Sam Emory," the newcomer stated when he had sat down calm as could be and passed over the full bottle. He did not ask to sit down; he did not say anything else.

Noneya looked over at him again, nodded in a drunken stupor, took the new bottle, pulled out the cork and poured his glass full. He took a deep swig, growled, and then took another swig. He did not pour a drink for the newcomer who had brought him the bottle. He did not care. The fact that he had allowed the man to sit at his table at all said quite enough.

Sam Emory nodded, took the bottle, and without asking poured himself a drink and downed it like a pro.

"What's your name?" Noneya asked finally, as if he was now just paying attention to the newcomer. Perhaps he was.

"Sam Emory, I told you, and what's your name?"

"I'm called Shadow Noneya," he slurred his words.

"You have the look of a tough character who can handle himself in any situation," Emory told him straight away with a hard twisted grin. "I can tell. I can tell talent when I sees it. I be like that meself. It appears you an' me gots a lot in common, I presume. We both likes doing jobs, taking chances, making a big pile of dosh."

Normally, Noneya would give such a rogue his walking papers, with a hard shot to the head, but this fellow intrigued him. This fellow was a tough criminal, much as he was. He liked that. He respected that. It had been a long time since he had had a partner, and he saw this fellow as a possible contender. He had worked with a partner years ago when he had worked with Mullens, so he was thinking maybe it was time to get together with a new partner. For it seemed that was what this bloke was proposing. Otherwise, why would such a sharpie approach him? A partnership opened many possibilities. Such a move would double the spoils because of bigger jobs. Maybe this thug had some contacts with one of the organized gangs and could persuade them to take him in? Which was the real dream a criminal like him wanted now in his life.

"I have my plans," Noneya replied.

"I'm sure you do, but I have bigger plans, like I told you, I recognize talent. I could use a talented man like you. And you could use a big increase in the dosh you make for your efforts. What do you say?" Emory asked him. "Interested?"

"Keep talking," Noneya stated without emotion.

"I gots me some connections, I does. I'm in firm with an organization, you know what I mean?"

"Yeah, I knows what you mean," Noneya replied clearly interested now.

"Well, I'm thinking we could work some jobs together, make a pile of cash, do good work. We'd do better together than you or I would do on our own. Two such men could do bigger jobs, the more the cash for both of us."

"Sam Emory, you say your name is?"

"Yes, Samuel Emory I be, my usual haunts ain't around here but I be known in the right circles. I be looking for what me boss calls 'opportunities'. You get what I'm telling you?"

"I get it, but you do look familiar to me, somewhat."

"Forget that, forget what you see, get it? Just think about the dosh. Do you like the quid?"

"Sure, I like it plenty."

"Good, then you and I will partner up and do some work together for my boss. You game?"

"Sure, I'm game. I'm game for anything."

"That's fine. That's what I likes to hear. We'll have our first job tonight."

Noneya responded with surprise, "Well that's fast."

"That's the way the boss likes things done."

"And who's the boss? What's the organization?"

"Concentrate on the jobs we do, and we'll see what comes of it. You game? If you do good, you will soon know more, and may even earn a spot in the organization."

"I told you I'm game."

"Then welcome to the organization Shadow Noneya. Here, have another drink, then we'll be on our way to do our first job together."

"What is it to be?"

"Ask no questions, but know this, if you play your cards right, you can be a part of something big. Really big, you know what I mean?"

"Yes, I know what you mean."

"Good, then finish your drink and we'll be on our way, and say nothing about any of this to anyone, upon your life."

Shadow Noneya nodded, finished his drink quickly on one gulp. A new partner, a new job, and a new organization. Things were definitely looking up.

※※※

It was a straight out robbery. Simple, really. A quick jump and grab. They took the man down fast in an alley. Quietly. No violence. Sam Emory had insisted on no violence and his partner went along with it—he would do anything to get into the organization. The victim had some cash, which Emory freely gave to his partner, which improved Noneya's mood considerably. What Emory had robbed the man for was not the cash at any rate; it was for the bag of diamonds he had secreted upon him.

"Blymie! Look at them glittering baubles!" Noneya spoke in awe when his partner showed him the stolen gems later on. "I'm keen on getting my cut. We done good work this night."

Sam Emory, whose real name was not Sam Emory, nodded, but did not turn over the gems to his partner, not even his half of the loot. "Sorry, mate, but these all goes straight away right to the boss. You can keep the cash; that should be enough for you, for now."

"Yeah, but… I mean, the cash is a good score, but them diamonds…"

"No. Sorry mate. They goes to the boss first. Later, when they get cut and sold off, you and I will get our share," Emory told him firmly. "That's the way the boss works. You either takes it or leaves it. He does things his own way, the smart way, and you'd be smart to keep to his plans. Never fear, we'll get our cut."

Noneya nodded reluctantly, then offered a slim grin, "I guess this bit of work tonight will put me in good with the boss?"

"You're in like a champion with this haul—if you does as you is told. And the fact that you held off and did not hurt—or kill—the victim, is a big plus for you. With the boss. He doesn't like needless violence. Or sloppy work, so keep that in mind."

"I will, I will. We done good work tonight", Noneya said with pride, then he looked closely at his partner.

"What's on your mind," Emory asked, noting his new partner was looking at him very carefully now.

"So Sam Emory it be now?"

"What do you mean by that?" real menace in his voice.

"I seems to recall another fellow with your hard looks working this end of London under another name, some years back."

"Oh, you do, does you?" Emory replied carefully, a serious dangerous tone to his voice now.

"Yes, I does. It was years ago, but he was sent away, he was. Prison. He had another name then, but I can not recall it."

"Well, before you get all uppity about names, let me tell you something Mr. Shadow Noneya—if in fact that be your own real name—and I knows it is not! If you wants to get into all that, then go for it, but I would advise against it. You know a man uses a name not his own, for his own reasons. I do—and I presume so does you! Mayhaps we should just leave things there better left unsaid, and concentrate on doing jobs and making cash? The boss does not like too many questions either—"

Noneya nodded, knowing his new partner was right after all. The name a man used for his work was his own business and no one else's.

"All right," Noneya replied accepting the situation. After all, the night's work had gone well—in fact, better than expected. He had a pocket full of cash, nearly a hundred quid. Good money. And he and Emory had a big pay day in the future coming from the sale of the stolen diamonds. Things was definitely looking up.

"You solid with all this?" Emory asked carefully, testing the waters, no doubt.

Noneya smiled a twisted rictus of delight, "Right as rain, my friend, right as rain. When do we do our next piece of work?"

"That's the spirit! Soon, very soon. The boss does not like any grass to grow under the feet of his men. There'll be something very soon, and I'll let you know tomorrow," Emory told him bluntly.

"Sounds right to me. So the boss considers me one of his men?"

"On my word, but he is happy with you, so far, and if things go well on the next job, he may want to have one of his captains meet you and bring you more deeply into our organization. You up for that?"

The career criminal smiled with pleasure at the promise. The words were like manna to his ears, his dreams seemed to be coming true; an affiliation with a serious organized criminal gang was his most fervent desire. It meant more dosh, bigger pay outs, and what he wanted most—protection from coppers while he did his work. No doubt about it, things was looking up. And dead coppers and missing boys would soon be a thing of the past and no longer any concern of his.

"I'm ready. You call on me tomorrow and I'll be ready for another job done for the boss."

"Well, that's the spirit! I'll see you at the pub, in the afternoon. I'm sure we'll have another job for tomorrow. Meanwhile, have a drink, get some sleep and be at the pub in the early afternoon."

"I'll see you tomorrow, partner," Noneya laughed.

"Good, then I will leave now and I will see you at he pub on the morrow. Good night to you, partner, we did some good work this night, and the boss will be most appreciative." Emory stated.

Shadow Noneya grinned wolfishly. It appeared he was on the way in— or would soon be in—a proper criminal organization. He left Emory and walked to the pub for a few celebratory drinks before he hit the sack for the night. Who knew what the next day would bring, but for the first time in a long time, Shadow Noneya was looking forward to tomorrow.

✳✳✳

Tomorrow came sooner than Shadow Noneya would have believed. He was early to the pub the next day, eager to find out what the next job would be, and eager to get in good with this organization. He sat at the table guzzling down some more rot-gut swill, as he saw a figure come over to his table. He expected it to be Sam Emory, his new partner and gang emissary—though it seemed a bit early for him—but he was surprised to see that it was that nosy Scotland Yard Inspector MacDonald once again. Now what did he want? Noneya growled menacingly but knew the powers that be whom he wanted to impress would look askance if he used violence on any copper, much less an inspector from The Yard.

Noneya sighed, took another drink and waited.

"You back again," he growled. "You turn up like a bad penny, you do."

"I'm here to tell you that I shall get the goods on you, Shadow Noneya. Or should I call you by your true name, George Turner? See, I know all about you now. You'll not hide any longer and I will close this case of the missing boy one of these days, and you'll face gaol for it, if not the rope, I am sure."

Noneya rubbed his neck and swallowed with some difficulty. Usually the coppers did not bother him overmuch, he ignored them and he certainly did not fear them, but this copper was the overly insistent kind. Relentless. The never-give-up kind. The big dog that takes a big bite that never lets go. He had to admit he was worried about what this inspector might find.

"You knows a lot it seems," the criminal stated looking evil eyes at the dour inspector who met his gaze and returned it with a most disconcerting stare. The criminal looked away. This was getting serious.

"I know enough, and I will find out more" MacDonald told the fellow. He did not sit down at the table, but stood over the man, looking down upon him as if he was addressing some type of foul offal. The criminal did not like the implication. It rattled him.

"I told you all's I knows, inspector," Noneya replied calmly, he was trying to keep calm, he knew he had to keep calm—or at least appear that way. Normally, in his old days, he would have ambushed such a pesky copper and give him a shiv in the guts for his nosy behavior, but now—with the organization uppermost in his mind, and probably watching his every move—and knowing their style—he knew this called for a lighter touch.

"Yes, and you do have an alibi," MacDonald added with a smirk.

"Yes, surely I do. A right fine alibi it be, too," Noneya added with a foul grin. Maybe he had bested the coppers after all? For if they really had any evidence against him he would surely be in cuffs and marched away to a jail cell by now. The inspector did not seem to be so inclined, and he was alone, not coming at him hard with a brace of stout Bobbies. So maybe they had nothing on him? What difference did it matter what they 'thought', so long as they had no evidence? They could prove nothing!

The inspector told him, "Your alibi is weak."

"But it will do," Noneya stated boldly.

MacDonald ignored that remark. "All right, Noneya—or should I say Turner? In either case I will be keeping an eagle-eye on you. Sooner or later you will slip up, and some evidence will turn up. I will find it. Then you will have an appointment at the assizes."

"Not me!" Noneya shouted in defiance, but he was not so sure about his future with this tough copper on the case. He watched with fearful apprehension as the Scotland Yard inspector gave him a deadly look and then stormed out of the pub.

Noneya took a deep breath. He had not been arrested, so they had nothing on him—maybe? But? But, what? *What* was the fact that he had

had enough of this man hounding his tracks? This Scotland Yard inspector was becoming a major problem and would have to be dealt with. But how? He could not just kill the man outright—much as he wanted to do so—and was capable of doing. That would never work with his new associates if they found out—and he had a feeling that they would know all about it as soon as it happened. And their punishment for such a deed would be far more severe than any justice the police or courts would ever meet out to him. No, he knew he was in a precarious pickle of a problem and he needed help. The organization might just be the answer.

"Why so grim?" the voice of Sam Emory spoke to him suddenly from in front of his table. He had not even realized his new partner had entered the pub so transfixed had his thoughts been upon that nosy copper and what he might turn up.

"Things be on me mind," Noneya replied noncommittally.

"Sure, we's all gots our little secrets, don't we?' Emory stated with an evil leer.

Shadow Noneya did not reply to that.

"So what's the news? Do we have another job?"

Sam Emory sat down at the table, pushed over a new bottle of poison, poured a glass for Noneya and himself, and said, "Here, drink up, we have another job."

"That's good news," Noneya stated, drinking down the fiery liquid.

"I'm going to make you a rich man, Shadow Noneya," Emory told him as he downed his own drink with a satisfied growl. "My, that swill is rough!"

"So what's the job?"

"A sweet one for sure. A quick and easy one for the likes of us. A lorry loaded with crates of high-grade Scotch. It sits just down the street a ways. We finish our drinks and then go to it. It's just down the street a bit, and it's all been set up beforehand with the lorry driver, so there'll be no problem. We just walk over, and then drive it away. What could be simpler?"

Noneya could not believe how easy it sounded. "That simple, eh?"

"When you works for the organization and works for our boss, things be like that," Emory stated with a wicked leer.

The two thugs finished their bottle, left the pub and then walked five blocks down the street to where a horse and wagon were parked outside another pub. The wagon was full of wooden crates.

"All prime drinking goods," Emory told his partner. "Come on, get up here with me and we'll drive it away."

"Now?"

"Of course."

"Just like that? Just drive it away?"

"Yes," Emory replied with a sly grin.

"So it is as easy as that, is it?" Noneya continued, astonished.

"It be as easy as that, partner. You're working for a serious organization now. They have ways to control things, if you know what I mean."

Shadow Noneya nodded, surprised and astonished at how easy the theft appeared to be. It proved to be even easier. All set up for them. The two men drove the lorry to the other end of the city, where they turned it over to another driver. Minutes later that driver and lorry were gone, and Emory handed his partner another bundle of cash money. "For your part in this little job, mate."

Noneya looked at the bundle; it must have been a hundred quid, in small bills, a fortune for such quick easy work.

"Is it always like this? With the organization, I mean?" Noneya asked delighted at the large and quick pay off.

"Sometimes even better, partner," Emory told him. "You done good on these last two jobs. You got a firm hand, that's good. Look, there's a big score coming up, something really big, serious money, you want to be a part of it?"

"Sure, you know I do. I'm up for anything."

"Good, I knew you had the pluck for this kind of work, but know that this job ain't like the others, it's special. You'll have to meet one of the captains who work for the boss to be approved for it."

"Who's that?"

"One of the captains, the boss has a few. The Colonel. The Doctor. The... well, anyway. You will meet with the one who goes by the name of The Doctor, this time," Emory responded carefully. "You game?"

"I damned well am!"

"Good, then I will meet you at the pub tomorrow and take you to see The Doctor. I will explain to him how you want to do more work for us. He never speaks, only listens, only you and I will do the talking, unless he wants to ask you a question. Understand?" Emory explained.

"A Doctor, The Doctor, is he a real doctor?"

"You're not listening to me, mate, you do not ask any questions, you are the one answering the questions—and offering explanations. You see, The Doctor, reports directly to the big boss."

"So who is this big boss? Who or what is the name of this organization?" Noneya asked curious. He wanted to know who it was he was working for now.

Sam Emory looked at his partner hard, then nodded, speaking softly, "Guess it does not matter much at this point to clew you in on some things."

Noneya waited patiently.

Emory looked around carefully. No one was close by. No one could hear his words.

Sam Emory moved in close to his partner, placing his lips close to the man's ear. Then in a quiet whisper he uttered one word. A name, that was it. But it was enough.

Noneya looked at Emory and silently repeated the name in a fearful whisper, "Moriarty?"

"And you thought he and his organization did not exist, that he was just some rumor, and not real?"

"Yes."

"And that is exactly what he wants everyone to think, so keep that in mind if you are keen on living a long life," Emory warned.

✳✳✳

The next day, Shadow Noneya was seated at his usual table at the East End dive of a pub where he usually drank his swill. This day he was far less drunk than usual. Emory had impressed upon him the night before that it would be a severe mistake to be seen drunk when he was taken to meet with The Doctor. The Doctor was the right-hand man of the big boss, Mr. M., and he did not like drunks.

So Noneya remained seated, sober, waiting, nursing a drink, wondering what was to come. He did not have long to wait before Sam Emory came into the pub.

Emory was dressed better than usual, it was obvious he had made an attempt to clean himself up and look presentable.

Noneya realized he should have done the same. This was an important meeting.

"You ready?" Emory asked.

"Waiting and ready," Noneya replied, getting up from the table and walking over to his partner who waited for him to approach.

"Good day for you today. You have a chance to get in with a serious organization. Make the most of it," Emory said, looking at him hard, "and do not bollocks it up!"

"I will not."

"Remember, The Doctor is the representative of Mr. M. So makes a good

A name, that was it. But it was enough.

impression. Ask no questions. Only answer my questions. Remember, The Doctor will probably not do any talking, he will not ask you anything. I will ask the questions. He will just listen. You answer—and you must answer truthfully. No lies. No deceptions; that is important, understand?"

Noneya nodded, accepting the ground rules. Then Emory led him out of the pub and down the street, up and down more streets to an open area of the city with small homes. They were single-family dwellings attached to each other with doorways that opened upon the street.

"He uses this building sometimes," Emory explained. "Come on now, follow me."

Emory checked his pocket watch. It was just at noon; Noneya could hear Big Ben far away chiming the hour.

Emory next produced a key and unlocked the door to the house, and he led his partner into the place, down the front hallway, into a large back room that was empty but for a desk and chair at the far end of the room. Seated in the chair at the desk was a well-dressed man, a real toff by the look of him, with a bushy moustache. He was dapper and trim, with sparkling sharp eyes, but he did not say a word, not even acknowledging their presence. Noneya had never seen him before, but he was impressed.

"I brought him as instructed," Emory told the mysterious man known as The Doctor. There was no reply.

Emory nodded, "Then I'll get to it. This is Shadow Noneya who has done some good work for us lately. He wants to be a part of the organization, and is asking for bigger jobs. He is capable."

Noneya looked at The Doctor, who did not reply or even seem interested. He was just there filling a seat at a desk, in an otherwise empty room, in an apparently empty house. It was all very mysterious to the criminal who more than anything wanted into this organization—and what it offered.

Sam Emory looked over at his partner, "The organization has certain rules for members. You must tell the boss the truth in all things before he will take you on—if you lie—you die. Understand?"

Noneya nodded, but so far The Doctor had not asked him a thing. So there was nothing to lie about. Not yet.

Emory went on to explain, "They want to know the truth—everything—about your past. The big boss does not care what you have done or why you did it, he does not care how heinous or vile it was, but he must know the truth. All of it. Understand?"

Noneya nodded once more, carefully, for he better than anyone knew he had bad things hiding in his past. Some of them very bad and fairly recently hidden.

"Tell The Doctor, beginning when you were doing your first job, all the criminal actions you have been involved in. Tell us up to the last year. Begin now," Emory ordered.

Shadow Noneya swallowed hard, then he began speaking, starting in his youth, talking up a storm of crime and illegal acts: some bad, some terrible, too many to detail, but he was not asked for detail on these older crimes.

Two hours later, Emory asked him, "That takes us up to the last year you must recount. These are the most important, the recent crimes, still outstanding. Is there anything in these crimes that could cause you trouble?"

Noneya thought of that nosy Scotland Yard inspector and the missing boy. Yes, there was a problem. He didn't know how to answer.

"You have a recent problem?" Emory repeated the question, sensing his partner's unease.

"I... I may have...something recent, yes, a nosy inspector trailing me."

"I see," The Doctor spoke up now for the first time. "Mr. M. will want to speak to you in person about this recent problem. A Scotland Yard inspector is serious, but it is nothing that our Mr. M. can not handle. An appointment will be set up. When you see him you must tell him the entire story—and the absolute truth. Only the truth. You should know that Mr. M does not care what you have done or why, but he must know all the details to see if he can fix them to see if you are to be allowed to join his organization, and to receive his protection. There is no other way. Emory, bring him tomorrow at noon. Mr. M will meet with him then."

Then The Doctor got up and quickly walked out of the room without another word and was soon gone.

Sam Emory playfully punched Noneya in the arm, "You're hiding something, eh? I can tell. Then again, we're all hiding something, eh? You'd best come clean tomorrow with Mr. M. It's a life and death situation for you now. Mr. M. can take care of it, he's a problem fixer! He's got The Yard in his pocket. You'll want to clean yourself up a bit too, to meet him, mate!"

The two men left the house and headed back to their East End haunts. Emory left Noneya at the pub, then set off on his own.

Noneya was alone now, he could not drink, he had no thirst for drink as he was busy thinking of all the hidden truths he held within his mind.

The fact that he would have to come clean about his recent criminal actions disturbed him immensely, but he knew he did not really have a choice if he was to be allowed to join the organization. Mr. M! *Moriarty!* The name was a legend, a rumor, a word that instilled fear in the London underworld. And now he was going to meet the great Moriarty himself. Shadow Noneya was in a fearful way and knew he was not going to sleep at all that night. He had no idea what tomorrow might bring but he was ready to take the next big step in his criminal career, and he'd better not blow it!

❊❊❊

The next day Sam Emory met his partner and escorted him to the meeting place with the organization boss, Mr. M.

"This will be a posh place, not like the other. His Majesty loves the good life and you'll want to get in on it," Emory told Noneya as they took a hansom cab to an exclusive section of London and a very well-known hotel. The place reeked of wealth and power. Noneya was suitably impressed. Emory escorted him upstairs to a private suite of rooms.

"Be on your best behavior here, I warn you, and be sure to tell him the truth in all things, no matter how inconvenient to you it may be," Emory warned.

"I understand," Noneya whispered, highly impressed by the majesty of the place, the high living and wealth he saw strewn about. This is what he wanted.

"Then come on, it does not pay to keep Mr. M waiting." Emory led his charge into the richly appointed hotel suite, through a succession of wondrously furnished rooms, the playground of the wealthy and powerful for sure, Noneya noted with excitement and anticipation. If only he could just get in with an organization like this and do work for Mr. M., then all this could be his too—and his problems with the police solved as well.

The sitting room was large and well appointed with expensive furnishings. Emory led his charge into it and closed the door behind them. Now the two men were alone with Mr. M.

Noneya stepped forward, beckoned thusly by the impressive figure seated at the other end of the room, a tall, aesthetic, almost cadaverous well-dressed gentleman, with fiery eyes and a hard look to him.

Sam Emory took a step backwards out of the way, but he did not leave the room. He had not yet been dismissed, so he stayed and stood inconspicuously behind his partner. Silent.

"Come forward," the man, certainly the big boss himself, the man known as Mr. M., or Moriarty, ordered his visitor.

"Yes, sir," Noneya replied with as much respect as he could muster. He moved carefully forward, not knowing what to expect.

"So you want to join my organization?" the man asked him in a firm tone.

"Yes, sir."

"Do you know who I am?"

"Yes, sir."

"Who am I?"

Noneya though fast here, he would not be so bold as to say Mr. M., or especially not Moriarty, so he just took the wisest course. "You are the boss."

"Your boss," the man replied, "but you can call me Mr. M."

"Thankee, sir," Noneya replied, then realized something. "Sir?"

Moriarty looked at him with deep snake eyes. Most disturbing. "Yes?"

"Does that mean I am in the organization, sir?"

"Do you want to join us?"

"Oh, yes, very much so, sir."

"Good, I can always use a good man. I have heard good things about you from Mr. Emory there," Moriarty said calmly with a nod of his head, then he looked at the man before him with a grim look. "However..."

Shadow Noneya suddenly grew very nervous.

"However, there are certain problems we have with you that need to be cleaned up before I will admit you. Do you understand?"

"I think so, sir."

"You think? So you are a thinker, are you?"

"I meant no disrespect, sir."

"Noneya, not your true name, no problem. I know all about you, and your long criminal career. Quite impressive. You told my agent, The Doctor a full history—but you left out your most recent activities. Why did you do that? You will recount them to me now, all truthful and with full facts and details."

Noneya had not been fully truthful and grew fearful now as he stood before this man who was known as the most terrible criminal mastermind in all of London.

"I have some problems with a Scotland Yard inspector who is nosing around me for something I never done."

"Never done? I think not!" Moriarty told him in a fierce tone bordering on dangerous anger. Noneya grew more fearful. "The truth shall set you free. I want the truth!"

Noneya shivered, realizing he was at a turning point in his life now and he dared not fail.

"Now is the time for truth, Mr. Noneya. You must now be entirely truthful with me if you are to join this organization. Tell me every detail of your recent crimes—you know which ones I mean. I want to know the reason that Scotland Yard inspector is after you. If you are entirely truthful and tell me everything, then I can help you make it all disappear. I have contacts in the Yard, even in Whitehall, so I am able to make certain crimes be erased from the record, evidence can disappear, but you have to tell me the truth and give me all the facts and details. Here. Now. You may begin."

Noneya nodded, he had not wanted to divulge the truth of his recent crimes but if he had to tell anyone, it would do him good to tell his new crime lord the details so as to get the protection he needed from the organization.

"Scotland Yard is after me," Noneya told his master now.

"Tell me the truth and I can make that go away. I care not what you have done, or why you did it. I care not how heinous or vile your crimes were. After all, we are all criminals here. What I need is the truth to fix things. Admit it all here to me now and you shall find me a most generous benefactor. For instance, are you aware that the Scotland Yard inspector you mention has recently found a compelling piece of evidence in his case? He is busy closing the net around you."

Shadow Noneya looked up shocked by this knowledge. What evidence? Not the body? Surely not the body? He looked at Moriarty for some explanation. The man's face was as immobile as a stone, indicative of absolutely nothing.

"No, not the body. Not yet. One of the boy's shoes has been found," the crime lord said simply. "Sloppy work—or bad luck—could be bad for you."

Noneya was fearful now; he felt the walls closing in on him and realized he was sweating profusely. He also realized that he needed the protection offered by Mr. M and his organization now more than ever.

"All right, I admit it, I done it."

"Done it? Done what exactly? Give me every detail and fact about what you have done."

Noneya nodded gravely, wiped the sweat from his face. It was cool, even cold in that room with the windows wide open on a balmy London Autumn day, but he was sweating, almost soaked to the skin.

"I killed 'em both, I did. I stabbed the constable, and when I realized that the boy was a witness, I came back later and killed him too."

"The missing boy, Thad Harris?" Mr. M asked quickly.

"Yes."

"Good, that is good. So tell me all the details. How did it happen? Where is the body of the missing boy?"

Shadow Noneya fidgeted uncomfortably, he wished he could chug a bottle of rot-gut swill right now to give him nerve, but he knew that would not happen here. He had to be careful that he did not mess this up—for he now thought he realized why his partner, Sam Emory, was standing so silently behind him. Could be his partner Emory might become his executioner if he failed to answer Mr. M's questions to the crime lord's satisfaction.

"Sir, the lad saw me kill the constable after I robbed the safe in a house nearby. The constable was right there and saw me when I came out of the house with the swag. He called me over to question me, it was early morning, I thought no one was on the street. I had to kill him. I shived him. He died instantly and I got away. I only realized later that a young boy had seen my deed. I saw him waiting for the tram two days later and took him away. I killed him and placed the body in a canvas bag that I weighed down with cobblestones. Then I dumped it in the water off the quay."

"Where exactly is the boy's body?" Mr. M. asked.

Shadow Noneya told him.

"Mr. Emory, send The Doctor to check his story and then have him report back to me. We will wait here. It should not take long," the crime lord stated.

Sam Emory called in the man who Noneya had met the previous day as The Doctor. The two whispered together for a moment and then The Doctor left the room.

No one spoke.

A timepiece on the mantle struck the hour.

Time passed.

Shadow Noneya was terrified. He stood in front of Mr. M. like a condemned prisoner at the assizes. He had told the truth, but he still hoped that after so many days the boy's body was where he had placed it. If not, he was in serious trouble.

More time passed and the hours grew.

No one spoke. There was nothing to say. They waited. Patiently.

Finally after three hours the man known as The Doctor came into the room.

"Yes?" Mr. M. asked him.

"We have found the boy's body," The Doctor reported with a strained tone.

"Excellent," Mr. M. replied the one word with just a hint of victory in his voice.

The man who called himself Shadow Noneya wiped the sweat off his face. "So everything's good now, right sir?"

"Yes, exceptional," Mr. M. told him with a slim grin.

Noneya finally allowed a grim smile of satisfaction and victory. He had done it! He was safe and he would now become a full member of the most serious criminal organization in London.

✳✳✳

"And now," Moriarty said with a stark look to Noneya, "we get to the rest of it."

Shadow Noneya nodded, expecting some good words to announce his entrance into the organization.

"Mr. Mac," the man known as Moriarty called out in a loud firm voice, "I believe it is time for you and your men to make your appearance."

There was a long pregnant silence and then Scotland Yard Inspector Alec MacDonald, accompanied by Constable Lowery and a brace of stout London Bobbies suddenly entered the room.

"We heard it all, clear as day, Mr. Holmes," MacDonald stated as he instructed his men to confine the suspect and place him in cuffs. "Shadow Noneya, George Turner, you are now under arrest for the murder of Metropolitan Policeman Able Sanders, and for the abduction and murder of the boy, Thad Harris. Your plan worked perfectly, Mr. Holmes."

"Mr. Holmes? Sherlock Holmes? No, it can not be. I have heard that name," Noneya cried out in terror.

"Sherlock Holmes, it is," the man who had passed himself off as Mr. M., or Moriarty admitted with a triumphant leer.

"No! This can not be! I am to join Moriarty's gang! I told you the truth, I gave up the boy's body," Noneya shouted, looking directly at the man who had passed himself off as the legendry crime lord.

"Moriarty has been out of the country these last few weeks on some major criminal activity, no doubt," Holmes explained with a cunning leer. "I am Sherlock Holmes and I took his identity to trap you into giving up the evidence Inspector MacDonald needed to bring you to book for your crimes. You proved most cooperative in our little ruse."

"This cannot be!" Noneya sputtered, enraged that he had been tricked and realizing what it meant for him now. "Get these cuffs off me!"

"Shut up!" Constable Lowery growled as he made sure the cuffs were secure and tight.

"Sam! Sam Emory, you're my partner. Get me out of this!" Noneya pleaded.

"Sorry, mate, you see, I work for Mr. Holmes. My real name is Shinwell Johnson, better known by some as Porky."

Holmes added, "And this gentleman—The Doctor—is in fact my friend and associate, Dr John Watson. You are quite properly done in, Mr. Noneya, and unless I am very much mistaken, there is a rope that shall no doubt be awaiting you in the future for your crimes."

"Aye, you are correct, Mr. Holmes. He's done for now, he is," MacDonald spoke up with pride, allowing a tone of victory in his voice. "Constable Lowery, take him away."

"Come on you lousy puke!" Lowery said as he took the man away.

"This case is now closed," MacDonald stated with firm resolve. "I thank you once again, Mr. Holmes, and you as well, Doctor Watson, for your help. And you, too, Mr. Johnson."

"You can calls me Porky, Inspector."

"Well you did a fine bit of work there," MacDonald stated to the re-formed criminal.

"Porky is one of my secret weapons against crime, Mr. Mac," Sherlock Holmes said with pride. Porky smiled at the praise.

Suddenly the voice of Shadow Noneya was heard in the background as he was whisked away by Constable Lowery and the Bobbies. "You tricked me! That is not fair! You lied to me!"

"No, what you did to that poor boy, and my constable, was what was not fair. Now you shall pay for it!" MacDonald shouted back in anger at the man as he was taken out of the room, his Scottish blood was up. "You wanted to join a criminal organization, now you shall. There are plenty of criminals where you are going!"

Noneya shouted back, "It is not fair, I was tricked!" Then his voice diminished in the distance, his last words were, "I was supposed to join the organization!"

Sherlock Holmes and Doctor Watson, with Mr. Mac and Porky could still hear the man's angry voice lessening in volume as he was taken down the hallway and out of the hotel to lockup. Then he was gone and there was sweet silence.

※※※

The sitting room at 221B Baker Street contained Sherlock Holmes and Doctor Watson, and with them were two guests, Scotland Yard Inspector Alec MacDonald, and reformed criminal Shinwell "Porky" Johnson.

"I want to thank you once again, Mr. Holmes," MacDonald said with a soft voice. "I *din nae* want to trouble you with this case at first, but I was at my wits end to put this man away."

"That is quite all right, Mr. Mac. I was happy to offer some assistance," Holmes replied. Watson did the honors of pouring each man there a generous glass of a barely passable brandy.

"I knew it had to be him from the beginning, as a trusted informant told me," MacDonald went on to explain. "Early on, the Irish lass identified him for sure, but his alibi from Mrs. Mullens made things complicated."

"Well it is all settled now for good," Holmes stated. "And you, Porky, did an excellent bit of play acting by leading the swine to the trough, so to speak, and even Watson played his part well, in our little drama. By the way, Mr. Mac, your manikin ploy was little short of brilliant!"

"Thank you, Mr. Holmes. I took a page from your book there. I said to myself, what would you do in a like situation?"

Holmes allowed a smile.

"Well, it was most difficult for me, Holmes. When I knew what he did to that young boy—and the constable of course—I could not deny your request. I hope the man pays dearly for his crimes," Watson stated, taking a stout pull at his glass of brandy.

"Fear not, Doctor, he shall," Porky replied.

MacDonald nodded, "He abducted that poor boy, and killed him in cold blood. I knew it and I just had to find a way to prove it. Mr. Holmes made it all possible."

"Well, he sunk himself with his own words," Watson added. "We all heard it, and he will not get off this time."

"No, he shall not," Sherlock Holmes said. "I find it rather ironic that with Moriarty away—I noticed this two weeks ago when certain of the more complicated and intricate crimes in London seemed to cease—so with him away, I saw no reason not to borrow his identity. Just me sowing a bit of confusion and obfuscation among the criminal classes...and

Morarity. As this Noneya never had anything to do with Moriarty, or his organization, it proved rather easy to have Porky here lead him on. I had them do a couple of pretend crimes together to cement their partnership, so then I could have him brought before me where he would have to admit all his crimes in order to join the organization he so much desired to become a part of."

"And he went for it like a rat to cheese!" Porky stated with a wide grin. "I knew he would."

"And that gave me the evidence I needed," MacDonald allowed.

"Right, Mr. Mac, we had him just where we wanted him," Holmes replied with a thin smile of victory.

"Well, Mr. Holmes, I must be off to see our prisoner rightly in gaol, but I want to thank you once again, for the boy, and for his parents," MacDonald stated with a firm nod of his head.

"I thank you for bringing the case to my attention, Mr. Mac. A most satisfying conclusion, I must admit," Holmes said with a wily grin.

"Here! Here!" Watson chimed in.

"Then I'll be leaving you now, Mr. Holmes, and good luck to you," MacDonald told him.

"Mr. Mac, a most interesting case," Holmes told the beaming Scotland Yard inspector with a rare smile of satisfaction. "You never fail to come up with something first rate."

Inspector MacDonald nodded to Holmes allowing a wide grin as he walked out the door.

"And I will be on my way as well," Porky stated, offering a respectful nod to Holmes and Watson.

※※※

When their two visitors were gone, Watson walked over to his friend, "You know, you made a most convincing Moriarty, Holmes."

"Yes, I believe I did. I have been studying the fiend for many years, Watson," Holmes admitted with a sharp voice, then he offered up a slim grin. "However, what surprised me was your fine play acting as The Doctor. Why, Watson, I never thought you had it in you. I believe you could pass muster as a rather convincing criminal, if you ever had the conviction."

"You told me how to act."

"Yes, I did, and you fell to my directions like a duck to water. You made a most convincing criminal," Holmes told his friend.

"I do say, Holmes, that is rather a bit much, even for you," Watson said somewhat indignant, even offended. "I see no reason for you to insult me. I did the best job I could under very trying circumstances."

"And you acquitted yourself most ably, Watson. Why, if I did not know better, I would have believed you to be one of Moriarty's most dangerous henchmen! Colonel Moran himself, could take pointers from you."

"Really, Holmes, you can be insufferable at times!"

"Oh, Watson, you are rather touchy tonight. Pour me another glass of that passable brandy and we will go out for an early dinner to celebrate Mr. Mac's closing of this most distasteful case."

"I am with you there, Holmes," then Watson added with a glint in his eye, "but I must say again, you proved a most convincing Moriarty—one wonders that you would have made an adequate criminal yourself."

"Good old Watson," Holmes chided with a thin smile, "Had I the desire, I would have made a most excellent criminal. England should be overjoyed that I did not take that route. As you have noted before in your chronicles of our adventures, it is most fortunate for this community that I am not a criminal!"

THE END

SHERLOCK & MR. MAC

As have many of you, I have enjoyed the original Sherlock Holmes stories by Arthur Conan Doyle my entire life. I have also had the pleasure and, indeed the honor, of writing some Sherlock Holmes pastiche stories and novels, as well as many non-fiction articles about the Great Detective. My stories have appeared in various book anthologies, as well as *The Strand Magazine* and *Sherlock Holmes Mystery Magazine*; and so far, one book published by Airship 27 Publications, *Sherlock Holmes: The Baron's Revenge*. That novel is a sequel to the popular story Arthur Conan Doyle wrote about one of Holmes's most famous cases—with one of his most deadly villains, that being Baron Gruner in "The Case of The Illustrious Client". Another of my Holmes stories, "The Adventure of the Missing Detective" was nominated by the Mystery Writers of America for an Edgar Award. So Sherlock and I have a long relationship. I have always very much tried writing my stories in the style and manner of Doyle. I consider them tributes to Holmes and Doyle.

This new tale features Scotland Yard Inspector Alec MacDonald—Mr. Mac—as Holmes fondly calls him in the novel, *The Valley of Fear*. MacDonald was the one Scotland Yard detective who was respected by Sherlock Holmes. In this latest outing of Mr. Mac, (a previous 2-story book with Mr. Mac and Holmes was published in 2017 by Stark House Press as Black Gat Book #11), I have followed in the footsteps of Doyle himself by basing a Holmes story on a true crime case. Doyle did this himself in his background story concerning the Scrowers that formed the basis of *The Valley of Fear*. Unfortunately, like most true crime cases that form the basis of a fictional crime story, the real story is often far more brutal and shocking than the fictionalization. Sadly, this case fits that pattern perfectly.

As unlikely as it may seem, "The Moriarty Obfuscation" is based on that actual murder that occurred in Australia in 2008. The genesis of this story came from my wife, Lucille, who is a true crime buff and was horrified by a true crime podcast titled "Casefile" (episode 54), in which it appeared that a murderer not only got away with his crime, but was recruited by a powerful criminal gang that would protect him from prosecution. She was so affected by the circumstances that she brought the facts of the case to my attention.

It was a truly brutal crime and I have lessened its effects in my Holmes story, but I have kept the brilliant police work intact—which proved to be key and truly amazing. Due to excellent and innovative police work by an Australian team of detectives, the police came up with the evidence to solve the crime and put the murderer behind bars.

The basic facts of the true 2008 Australian case concern the abduction and murder of a 13 year-old boy named Daniel James Morcombe by Brett Peter Cowan, a career criminal who called himself Shaddo N'unyah Hunter. This insidious brutal murder of an innocent young boy would not have been solved without the Australian detectives putting into operation what was originally a Canadian police procedure called "Mr. Big".

"Mr.Big" is an undercover police technique created by the Royal Canadian Mounted Police where there is little forensic evidence and they need cooperation from the suspect to get a conviction. The daring Australian detectives formed a team in 2011 that put this plan into operation, making their target buy into what he thought would be a protective criminal gang—something he had always wanted to be a part of so he could be protected. However, in order to become a part of the gang, the killer had to give up all his secrets to the leader—and he did! That leader, and all members of the "gang" were undercover detectives whose diligence worked. As a result, Cowan was soon taken into custody after he gave up the evidence of his crime. In the true case it would lead to prison for the murderer, just as it did in my Holmes story.

I wanted to write this story to highlight the brilliant and daring work of the Australian police who caught a brutal killer, and at the same time be respectful of the memory and the family of Daniel Morcombe. My purpose in writing the story was to pay tribute to the exceptional police work—which was worthy of Sherlock Holmes himself.

Those of you who would like to find out more information can contact the Daniel Morcombe Foundation, Inc. in Australia, or access their website at: Danielmorcombe.com.au, to learn how to keep kids safe, for education about this important subject, or to make a donation to support their good works.

GARY LOVISI is the author of various stories that have appeared in Airship27 books over the years, including such quintessential pulp characters as The Moon Man, The Crimson Mask, The Purple Scar and The Phantom Detective. His latest books include *The Secret Adventures of Sherlock Holmes: Book Five* (Ramble House), and the forthcoming, *Sherlock Holmes & Mr. Mac* (Stark House Press, Black Gat Book #11), as well as his popular 2012 Holmes novel for Airship27, *Sherlock Holmes: The Baron's Revenge*. He is a Mystery Writers of America Edgar Nominated author for his Sherlock Holmes story, "The Adventure of the Missing Detective." Lovisi has also written three books in his Jon Kirk of Ares series, a sword and fantasy series inspired by Edgar Rice Burroughs' John Carter of Mars books; with two new books in the series: #4 *The Mind Masters*, and #5 *The Time Masters*. To find out more about Gary Lovisi and his books check out his website at www.gryphonbooks.com or visit him on Facebook.

Sherlock Holmes

in

"The Disappearance of Mr. James Phillimore"

By
Dexter Fabi

In musing over the cases that I have previously written of Sherlock Holmes, I find a collection of these that were worthy of mention but heretofore yet untold. It is with a considerable sense of obligation that I here detail the case of the disappearance of one Mr. James Phillimore, late of the exclusive and high society neighbourhood of Grosvenor Square of London. These papers of Holmes's untold cases are held at the Cox and Co. Bank at Charing Cross in my own dispatch-box under my name, John H. Watson, M.D., and have been of tantalizing interest to the reading public since I had mentioned them in passing in *The Problem of Thor Bridge*.

Since Mr. Phillimore is still known to be missing from this world and a sufficient amount of time has passed, I can now tell the story of his disappearance and why Holmes and I had to keep it a secret up until now.

The last that anyone had heard of or seen Mr. James Phillimore is when he stepped back into his house upon a rainy morning to gather up his umbrella. He was never seen in this world again.

First, I feel it incumbent upon me to describe Mr. Phillimore's importance and why the public is so intent till now on hearing about this case.

Mr. James Phillimore was a traveling stage magician and circus man who had performed in many shows in the United Kingdom and America. It was when he was about twelve years of age that he had received his first book as a gift from his parents on the subject of Egyptology. He had then run away from home to join an expedition for the digging season of 1885 in Luxor, Egypt, in the Valley of the Kings. In the digging season of 1890, he had found the tomb of a pharaoh of the 20th dynasty of ancient Egypt. Though the tomb had been robbed once in antiquity, it still harboured a great wealth of artifacts of irreplaceable value. The Egyptian government had declared it a crime to smuggle antiquities out of Egypt. Yet, Mr. Phillimore was said to have trafficked in all the antiquities that he had found and therefore had robbed what was left of the royal tomb's contents. Some of them he kept for his own personal collection. After his illegal trade in Egyptian artifacts from the newly discovered tomb, he was a well-made man in London, quite celebrated. His exploits and adventures in finding the tomb on the west bank of the Egyptian town of Luxor were well accounted in the London papers of the day.

Of his estate when he left this earth, it was distributed according to his last will and testament, with all of his money going to his son, Hartley.

A statue of Anubis made of solid gold and worth a king's ransom was also bequeathed to his son, Hartley. An idol of Osiris in a combination of gold and silver was bequeathed to his half-brother, Henry. Regarding his personal collection of Egyptian antiquities, the Egyptian government had attempted to seize them all when learning of his disappearance. The British government had stepped in and did not want to set a dangerous precedent with the returning of Egyptian antiquities from England to Egypt. The British Museum has the Rosetta Stone, which Egypt had wanted since the time of Napoleon returned back to their homeland, but it has been kept here in London. The collection of Mr. James Phillimore twenty or so years after his disappearance went on display in the British Museum. They are now held in safety by the British Museum and protected, and this is also why I can now tell all about what had happened back then.

I was reminded of the whole affair when walking with Sherlock Holmes during extended hours at the British Museum when we had passed the Egyptian collection of Mr. James Phillimore, now disappeared for more than twenty years after he had gone to fetch his umbrella from his house. It was now the the autumn of 1915.

"Watson, ah, my dear Watson, this does bring back memories. I feel as if they are flooding me at the moment," he said as he laid his hand onto the museum glass and regarded the collection with close scrutiny.

There among the display were four canopic jars, jars which held the internal organs of one who was to be mummified. Also there were the wrapped mummies of an ibis, a cat, and a small crocodile. The glint and allure of gold and silver was everywhere in that cramped space that held the Phillimore collection. The British Museum had taken care to not label the treasures as from the estate of the missing James Phillimore, nor to even refer to his name in any of the placards next to the artifacts. The display cases holding the treasures had only a single plaque indicating that this group of Egyptian historical objects were from the British expedition to the Valley of the Kings of 1893.

An obsidian knife from the Nubian region, which is present day Sudan, was there. It was with these knives that ancient Egyptian embalmers had cut into the abdomen of a deceased body to remove the internal viscera, with each of the four jars holding in turn the liver, intestines, stomach, and lungs. Papyri of the ancient Egyptian Book of the Dead detailed the rituals and chants that were needed for the deceased to pass into the afterlife before the judgment of Osiris in the Hall of Two Truths. The Opening of the Mouth ceremony, which the priests performed during the preparation of the deceased to enter the Underworld, was shown in various sets of rare papyri in the secret Phillimore collection there in the British Museum.

Other Egyptian treasures on display were rare New Kingdom jewelry of pure gold, lapis lazuli, and carnelian. More shimmering objects included an idol of Isis in pure electrum, writing implements for a scribe of the Egyptian God of writing, Thoth, and a wooden model of a solar barque boat that would bring the dead on a journey into the afterlife. In rare ebony was a statue of Set, a God of Murder who had killed and dismembered his own brother, Osiris, and scattered the pieces around Egypt and even into ancient Byblos in what is now the Levant. Also there in the Phillimore collection were deeply veined alabaster jars, scarabs of hematite and faience, golden armbands, and a gilded throne bedecked with turquoise. There were more treasures found in this clandestine and rich collection that the museum had tucked away from the main lines of foot traffic.

Of all the patrons visiting the museum to-night, we no doubt knew that it was only the two of us there that knew the import of this collection and why the British Museum had not properly labeled the origin of such riches.

"Watson, I do think it is time you chronicle the tale of the disappearance of Mr. James Phillimore, now that an adequate amount of time has passed," Holmes barely whispered as his eyes were dazzled with the treasure of pharaoh Sethotep.

My readers will remember that this case had not been uncovered for the public for the space of twenty some years now, and there was good reason to, as will be detailed in this narrative. For one thing, the reader's mind may leap to the Egypt's Supreme Council of Antiquities wanting to take back all of Mr. Phillimore's contraband relics. Another reason may be to cover up a scandal within the family. There are many possibilities.

It was on a blustery and rainy evening that Holmes and I were enjoying the warmth of a fire in his consulting room at Baker Street. Puffs of blue smoke had clouded the room from Holmes's pipe, infusing the area with a sort of dreamlike quality. I was busying myself with the London papers and finding not much of note to tell Holmes. This was early on in 1893, about twelve weeks into the disappearance of Mr. James Phillimore.

Mrs. Hudson was clearing up the tea things after wanting to bring us some warmth on a chilly night when we heard the ring on the front stair.

She had gone to see who the caller was and immediately led up a soaked visitor all in tweed.

Holmes and I had beseeched our visitor to sit down in the chair reserved for all who had come to us seeking help.

"I can see that you have been about in Queen Mary's Garden in London and that you have no doubt had some of the best pastries in the city," indicated Holmes to our guest.

"Why, what the deuce?" our damp visitor had responded softly. "But, how?"

"Regent's Park has the only garden in London or the immediate vicinity that holds the saffron crocus, or known by its scientific name as *Crocus sativus.* From this species is harvested one of the rarest of spices, saffron, and you do have a scent of saffron about you. Further, I can see that you have written out the directions to Regent's Park which holds Queen Mary's Garden. The directions are partially sticking out of your pocket but I am familiar with the route and end destination since it is such a frequent tourist attraction. But you are no tourist as I can tell from your Londoner accent. You have partaken of the fine pastries nearby the garden, which a visitor to the gardens usually does. These pastries by Mrs. Jennings are known to be among the finest pastries in all of England, indeed of the United Kingdom, and only sold near the area of Regent's Park. Also, it is customary of Mrs. Hudson to ask any of our guests if they want anything for snacking, and you had declined, since Mrs. Hudson would have brought these things immediately before you had sat down before us."

I had become used to these immediate deductions of Mr. Holmes by now, the cold sight readings of which he was so noteworthy.

Our visitor, exasperated from all the truth Holmes had extracted, decided to stay quiet in the midst of such deductive reasoning power.

Mrs. Hudson had stoked the fire higher and implored our soggy guest to sit right near the hearth in order for him to dry himself out. He had brought no umbrella.

After some shivering, preliminary talk about the London weather, and a gradual drying about of his entire person, he launched into the reason of why he had come here.

"Mr. Holmes, your renown is quite unassailable. You are one of the most famous detectives to grace the annals of crime and you have solved the most baffling of cases."

Holmes puffed on his clay pipe and took some more of the tobacco from his Persian slipper.

"For the past twelve weeks, my father has unaccountably disappeared. It is the most baffling of things to ever happen in my lifetime.

"You see, I am the son of the renowned archaeologist Mr. James Phillimore, the discoverer of Sethotep's tomb in Egypt. My name is

Hartley Phillimore, Ph.D. in Egyptology from the University of Oxford. My father had discovered the lost tomb of a previously unknown Egyptian pharaoh of the 20th dynasty. This pharaoh was short in his reign, reigning for only eight months according to the inscriptions on his tomb walls. He had preceded the great Ramses III and is not to be found on the official Kings Lists of Egypt since he was an adherent of a heretic religion.

"My father was always an adventurer—he loved to travel to exotic and foreign lands and found great pleasure in acquainting himself with the most unusual kinds of people—contortionists, sword swallowers, snake charmers, stage magicians, and the like. In fact, he was a stage magician himself before deciding to run away from the family to seek fame and fortune in the Valley of the Kings in Egypt.

"He had first visited Egypt as an apprentice to the renowned French archaeologist, Dr. Gustave Janvier, during the digging season of 1890. It was here that he communicated to me by letter one night that he had a lead on what possibly was a previously undiscovered royal sepulcher in the city of the dead known as the Valley of the Kings. It was hinted that there may have been a pharaoh who had reigned for a short time before the ascendancy of Ramses III and he had known this. The letter says that he was in the area of the Ramesside kings, which was the correct area to find the hypothetical Sethotep's grave.

"What led him to believe that he had found Sethotep's grave was that there were rocks that were descending from a digging area and he had also found some shards of clay jars which tomb builders would write upon. On one of these clay jar shards was the cartouche of an unknown king. James had saved this shard and kept it to himself, not letting Dr. Janvier know anything about it. Indeed, no one had known about it besides me.

"Once my father James was in Cairo, he secretly brought the pottery shard to an American library where he found a book to decode what the cartouche said and whose name was within it. A cartouche is a long oval that holds within it the name of a pharaoh. For my father to find a cartouche on a pottery shard in the area where Sethotep was rumoured to be buried caused great excitement for him. Yet, he didn't want to share his secret discovery with the world just yet. He wanted sole credit and he wanted the fame that it would automatically bring him if he were to discover the tomb mostly intact and unrobbed.

"James had confirmed in the American library in Cairo that the cartouche held the name of the Egyptian pharaoh that he was seeking— Sethotep. The name of Sethotep is translated to 'the God Set is Satisfied,' indicating that the evil God of Chaos and Murder, Set, is pleased. No doubt this pharaoh was an adorer and worshiper of the god Set.

"My father had gone about in the middle of the night when the regular expedition was asleep in their tent city to excavate near the area where he found the pottery shard and the falling rocks. He excavated by himself with two local Egyptians and came upon the tomb of Sethotep.

"Inside, he found riches beyond imagining. The tomb had only been robbed once in antiquity. Most of the inner treasures near the sarcophagus of Sethotep were still there in their shining glory. The tomb walls were in a state of wonderful preservation, their colors still quite vibrant.

"He did not share his discovery with the world but successfully kept Sethotep's tomb a secret for two years and he and the two Egyptians with him had enriched themselves by selling the contents of the tomb on the underground antiquities market. After two years, the two Egyptians that he had hired had leaked the information about the discovery of Sethotep's grave with the Egyptian press after all of the contents of the tomb were used up by all three of them. The three were now wealthy beyond compare, but from there, chaos had descended. It was three months after the two Egyptians had shared the discovery of Sethotep's tomb that tragedy had struck in the form of a murder-suicide. This murder-suicide of the two Egyptians had exposed the fact that the two and James Phillimore were profiting from illegal antiquities trading from the grave of Sethotep. First the Egyptian journalists had picked up the story, and then the rest of the world. James, my father, was at first vilified by the Egyptian press but then later held reluctantly as a local hero for finding a previously unknown pharaoh's tomb. The Egyptian treasures from Sethotep's tomb that he had sold on the underground market in Britain and France were mostly irrecoverable by anyone after the discovery of the tomb and the murder-suicide of the two Egyptians. Yet my father James was now in London and living a wealthy life after his trafficking of illegal Egyptian artifacts.

"James Phillimore was, of course, barred from ever entering Egypt again. He could never go back to the tomb of Sethotep. The Egyptian government had banned him for life. The tomb of Sethotep is currently controlled by Egypt's Supreme Council of Antiquities and the Egyptian government and is now under restoration and preservation until it can be opened to the public as a tourist attraction.

"James was both reviled and admired in the Egyptian papers while the British papers held him in the utmost regard. He was now the shining star of the Egyptological world. Claiming Sethotep's tomb was one of archaeology's greatest discoveries of the 19th century, the British press had put him on a pedestal. The French press was more wary in glorifying James. Since James was under the guidance of their archaeologist, Dr. Gustave Janvier, they claimed that it should have been France's achievement rather than the achievement of someone subservient to the eminent archaeologist. They reviled him as a mere stage magician and had emphasized that he had no qualms about breaking the law and running an underground antiques business that served to profit him and only him while giving no credit at all to his mentor, Dr. Gustave Janvier.

"The love of Egypt runs in our family line. I was always interested in ancient Egypt and now have a doctorate in the subject. I have given papers and lectures on late Ramesside Egypt and have visited Egypt twice. The government there always accommodated me before but now will not allow me anywhere near the tomb of Sethotep. Indeed, I too have been barred from visiting Egypt because I have a strong resemblance to my father.

"It has been twelve weeks since my father has disappeared. He simply vanished after going back into his house in Grosvenor, a well-to-do district of London, to seek his umbrella for a rainy morning. Of his whereabouts, no one can account for. His maid and butlers have said that he had entered his study to retrieve his umbrella where it always was, but why he should shut the door, the staff at his home had no reason. It was unlike him to shut the door to his study if he was to simply retrieve his umbrella and go back outside into the torrents of rain. But there it is. By the time the authorities had broken down the door, all they had found was his dried footsteps and a missing umbrella. It seems as if he had just vanished from the world.

"I have not heard from him, and it is now twelve weeks, very unlikely of him to not contact me at all. He was wont to telegraph me with what he was recently up to and to express excitement at me becoming an Egyptologist in the formal sense. We are a religious family of the Anglican Church and in the weeks leading up to his disappearance he stopped visiting church services, where I would usually see him once a week. I did visit my father once at his home and smelled strange incenses being burnt and he looked much thinner than usual, much paler. Since his disappearance, I have not heard anything. I have looked in every place where he is usually to be found and have not turned up anything.

"It has been twelve weeks and I have come to you, Holmes, to help in this plight. I fear for my father, Mr. Holmes. Just the history of his involvement with Egypt and what he did to secure a fine lifestyle, I know there must be someone out there who would want to wish him ill will."

Listening to all of this, I could tell that this was a problem that Holmes thought would be of possible interest to him. For one, young Mr. Hartley Phillimore had said that he had first contacted Scotland Yard and Inspector Lestrade and they had made no heads or tails of the situation. Mr. Hartley Phillimore had also contacted the Egyptian government and no one of Mr. James Phillimore's description had entered Egypt. Egypt was keeping a close eye on James Phillimore and anyone who had looked like him in order to bar them from entering.

Usually people visit Holmes when they have exhausted all other options. It was timely then that young Mr. Hartley Phillimore had visited when he did because the scene of Mr. James Phillimore's vanishing was still nearly fresh.

It was then that we agreed that we would visit the scene of Mr. James's vanishing on the morrow and seek any evidence or clues as to where he had disappeared to. Till then, Holmes contented himself with looking up all of the persons involved in his Continental Gazetteer, that beneficial encyclopedia of his that had information on prominent persons.

✳✳✳

Inspector Lestrade of Scotland Yard had soon come upon the scene of James Phillimore's vanishing when he learned of Holmes's visiting.

"Holmes, we had already searched the area for evidence, and nothing remains to be discovered. The Yard has already searched everything here."

"Hullo, what's this?" Holmes asked as he neared the desk of Mr. James Phillimore.

The detective closed in curiously on the surface of the desk.

"Ah, but you have not found this, Mr. Lestrade," said Holmes with some mockery, carrying up to the light a morsel between tweezers.

It was a slip of papyrus with Egyptian hieroglyphics on it. It was found within the ashtray on Phillimore's desk.

"Hmmph," he had replied to Holmes's impertinence. "Capital, Holmes. But I want to know, as I'm sure your new client wants to know—how does a person just vanish from a locked room? And why get an umbrella if he is to make a show of vanishing?"

"That is what we are here to find out, old friend," said Holmes, trying to patch up for his rudeness.

"Take this room and really look at it," followed Holmes. "No windows, only one means of entrance, a double-doorway which was locked shut at the time of Mr. Phillimore's disappearance. The doors were locked from the inside, not locked from the outside. No chimney or fireplace. No means of exit or entrance besides the locked double-doors. To-night Watson and I will search this entire room for any more evidence that may be pertinent to the case. I must admit, it is a highly intriguing one."

Lestrade had taken his leave after Holmes had confirmed that nothing was taken from the room while Scotland Yard had performed their investigations. Lestrade had said that everything was exactly the way it was found at the time of Phillimore's disappearance.

We had been on task all through the night and into dawn looking through that locked room of the vanished antiquities dealer. We had found a scrapbook of all the articles in the British and other presses that praised his finding such an important Egyptian tomb as Sethotep's. The room was dominated by a deep and expansive carpet. There were an incredible lot of books in this study. Most of the books were on various aspects of Egyptology, a multitude of books on the process of mummification, the afterlife in ancient Egypt, and the history of ancient Egypt. Holmes started to look into the books that were there. I paged through all the books, which had taken up most of my time, and found no slips of paper or hidden communications. We had both looked for any other means of entrance and exit besides the front double-doors and found that the only way anyone could enter or exit was through those very doors. There were no secret passages or hidden compartments. It seemed as if the fellow just dissipated into air.

It was the middle of the night and Holmes had questioned all three of the staff, the maid and two butlers. They all verified that Mr. James Phillimore had suddenly come in from the rain, opening the front doors to the house. One of the butlers had asked him if he needed anything, and James had replied that he was to fetch his umbrella. The butler had offered to retrieve it for him, but James Phillimore declined, preferring to retrieve it himself. All three of the staff went elsewhere in the large house after their master went into the study, tracking wet footsteps after him.

When asked if anything out of the ordinary happened, one of them, the maid, fancied that she heard a loud crash somewhere in the house, but then felt that it was just the thunder from the storm. The other two said that they didn't hear anything of the kind.

Holmes had asked how many umbrellas were in the house and all three of them said that there was only one umbrella in the whole house, the

We had been on task all through the night and into dawn...

umbrella that was now missing.

Dawn had arrived and Holmes decided to shut the door. After a brief breakfast near the Strand, Holmes did not want to stop. I could say at that time that he had found the problem that he was seeking and that it was the kind of problem that kept him engaged.

His first movement was to find any relatives of the two Egyptians who had assisted the missing Mr. Phillimore and who had committed the murder-suicide in Cairo. This he effected through Scotland Yard, of all places. They had already had two relatives there for questioning and kindly forwarded them to our sitting room at Baker Street.

Our company included the cousin and wife of both the murdered man and the homicidal suicide, respectively.

Youssif and Naira had come separately as they could not bear to be in the same room with each other. Youssif was the cousin of the murdered Ehab who had assisted James Phillimore in the excavation of Sethotep's tomb.

"I am glad to be summoned to here, Mr. Holmes. It is a rare honor to be in the presence of someone like you," said Youssif in perfect English with a slight Egyptian accent as he sat down in the chair before us. He was clothed as one of the better classes of society, with a perfect cravat, grey frock-coat, and Harris tweed pants.

"That tomb that Phillimore had excavated, I tell you, was cursed. Look at what has happened. My cousin, killed by a raving lunatic before he killed himself. And now Mr. Phillimore up and gone without a trace. *Inshallah*, this business will hopefully clear itself up."

"We are very sorry for the loss of your brother," consoled the detective. He sat with his face propped his two arms which were perched upon the armrests. "But pray, what leads you to think that the tomb of Sethotep is cursed?"

"There are other uncanny fates for those who come into contact with the secret of the tomb's existence. Phillimore had ransacked the tomb and milked it for all it was worth, with the result of hundreds of ancient Egyptian artifacts now in the cabinets of the aristocracy of British society. It is a marker of status to own something from ancient Egypt. As you may already know, there are plenty of ancient Egyptian fakes and it is easy for any Egyptologist of worth to tell the difference. Of course, the artifacts from the tomb of Sethotep were authentic. These commanded such high prices and caused so much consternation for the Egyptian government. My homeland desperately wants them back since they were smuggled, yet the British government has possibly turned a blind eye to the whole underground market in the effort of not setting a precedent that would eventually oblige them to return the holy grail of Egyptology back to Egypt: the Rosetta Stone, now in the British Museum. Phillimore was involved in a dastardly business, I tell you."

Youssif looked intently at me and then at Holmes as if we were the ones who would put a stop to the underground market of Egyptian artifacts in London.

"Those who were there at the tomb have succumbed to some terrible fate," added Youssif. "Ehab and his murderer, Morad. Before the discovery of the tomb, I had known Morad to be the gentlest of persons, very devout. It was only after his contact with the tomb of Sethotep that he had become avaricious and greedy."

"Is there any information that you can tell us? Any other behaviour that Ehab and Morad exhibited that seemed suspicious?"

Youssif, slightly agitated, was thinking of the time when he was last in Cairo before the tragic murder-suicide. He remembered Ehab as acting quite nervous and constantly holding a statue of Osiris, the Lord of the Underworld. This statue was made of electrum, a combination of gold and silver that the ancient Egyptians were fond of, and Ehab had explained to me all about the tomb and that he had succeeded in hiding from the inventory books that Phillimore kept this particular statue. This electrum statue of Osiris was never found after Morad killed my cousin, though I had implored the Cairene police and detectives to look for it."

Holmes sat and thought for a while as our guest continued about the tomb being cursed and that those that entered it were fated to madness, violence, or suicide.

After Youssif's visit came Naira, the widowed wife of Morad. She had arrived to Baker Street clothed in all black, showing the respect that most ladies of Victorian society would show for a husband now deceased.

"Dear mademoiselle, thank you for visiting. Please accept all of my condolences as I am sure you know this is a very sensitive time for you. But if you please, tell me all that you know about your late husband for the sake of preventing further violence in the future. As you know, there has been the disappearance of the eminent James Phillimore, discoverer of the tomb of Sethotep in Egypt."

"It is all connected, I tell you, to the Priesthood of Set here in London," she said immediately, her voice raspy. "They needed something for their occult and unknown purposes, and they worship Set, the Deity of Evil. Do not you know that the name Sethotep means 'Set is Pleased'? I would not dare to enter that tomb for any amount, nor would I venture to speak to even one of these new Priests of Set in London."

"How far of an involvement do you think this Priesthood of Set here has in this case?" asked Holmes.

"Oh, every inch of it, I would say. The last I heard there was some idol that they were after, some statue of Anubis or Osiris, I do not know. It was supposed to be of great importance to them. No one is allowed near the tomb of Sethotep as decreed by the Egyptian government, not even Egyptian nationals. The closest that the Priesthood of Set can get to the tomb of Sethotep was through Ehab and Morad, now dead. And I wouldn't be surprised if Mr. Phillimore is found dead as well, eventually. Dark currents have been unleashed since the discovery of the accursed tomb of Sethotep."

"Do you know of any Priests of Set that we can question here?" I had asked, all absorbed in the insinuations of the widow.

"Well, they are not difficult to find. There are not many of them, but they do hold a temple gathering in the Limehouse district of the city. Set is an evil deity, the originator of evil upon this earth. Whether they are harmless or not is for you to find out, Mr. Holmes. I, for one, think they are the ones responsible for most of what has been happening."

Sufficiently content with the questioning of Naira, Holmes accompanied her to the door. She left, going back to her home in the West End.

"Any thoughts as of yet, Watson?" he had asked me.

"I am all sodden with thoughts, Holmes. There is something to this business, no doubt about it. Where is Mr. Phillimore and is he still alive?"

"I have to admit, I am still as much in the dark as you at the moment, but presently I assume that there will be some clarification to the matter."

"There are just so many reasons that Mr. Phillimore could disappear. For one, he could have been kidnapped by the Egyptian government and held in secret custody. Another reason that he would disappear is that he is escaping from some sort of dark secret or dark society. Yet another reason would be that one of his family members had murdered him to benefit from the huge estate he had. And yet another—a curse from visiting the tomb of a pharaoh that worshiped Set, a God of Evil, as we have learned to-day."

Holmes had raised an eyebrow at my last sentence. He had picked up his violin and was deep in concentration on the music and on the case. It was not difficult to read his brow in such moments.

"There is also the French government as well," added Holmes. "Perhaps a jealous French archaeologist such as Dr. Gustave Janvier could not handle a mere apprentice of his taking the fame and glory for the archaeological find of the 19th century. Perhaps this dreadful Priesthood of Set here in London has some answers. I think one of our next courses would be to have Lestrade round up all of these Priests of Set for serious questioning. We must remember what I have said before, no doubt recorded in your chronicles: that when you have eliminated the impossible, whatever remains, however improbable, must be the truth."

"And yet there have been rare cases where the most complex solution was the right one."

He nodded in assent as he amused himself on his violin.

Our next steps would have to wait until we were both fully refreshed. He first planned to visit the half-brother, Mr. Henry Phillimore, for a decipherment of the scrap of papyrus that Holmes had found and a round of interrogation of all of the modern day Priests of Set after the Yard was done with them.

✳✳✳

Taking a hansom cab at evening from Baker Street through the foggy streets of London, we called upon Mr. Henry Phillimore, Egyptologist. His study was sumptuously decorated with plenty of books on ancient Egypt and the ancient Near East, including books on Hittitology, the study of the ancient Hittites of the Anatolian Peninsula. Holmes immediately noted an idol of Osiris that looked as if made from a combination of silver and gold—electrum, as detailed earlier in this account. It was hard for me to contain an interjection of revelation. I did successfully contain my surprise from our host.

Holmes started his inquisitions immediately.

"Mr. Phillimore, we have found a piece of evidence that may relate to the case of your half-brother's disappearance. It was found in the remnants of your brother's ashtray."

He gave the piece of papyrus with its fanciful hieroglyphs to Mr. Henry Phillimore. He had adjusted his glasses closer to his eyes and surveyed the manuscript near a window which had strong daylight to provide him ample illumination.

"Yes, this piece of papyrus holds a spell. It is a spell from the ancient Egyptian Book of the Dead, the text that is used to prepare the deceased for the afterlife. This particular spell is a fragment of a spell from the Protection from Peril section of the Book of the Dead. It is spell number forty-one, which prevents the utterer from being slaughtered by the demonic servants of Osiris."

Holmes and I had looked at each other.

"Are you saying that your brother was in danger of being slaughtered by demonic servants?" I had asked, my voice catching in my throat briefly.

"I am only stating what I translate from this fragment. This spell is recited if someone wants protection from the demonic servants of the Underworld. Anubis was the first Lord of the Underworld while Osiris was the later Lord of the Underworld. It is possible that my brother was suffering from delusions or really was in peril of being killed by demons."

Immediately I had looked at Holmes. His face was impassive, hard to read. He was taking in all that Mr. Henry Phillimore was asserting.

"What reason do you have to believe that your half-brother was in preternatural danger?" Holmes asked the Egyptologist.

"Spells are spells. The Book of the Dead of ancient Egypt contains chants and recitations for finding your way through the underworld and what exactly to say at certain points there in the afterlife before the Egyptian gods. I am not sure why James would burn such a priceless treasure as an original Book of the Dead. But then many Book of the Dead papyruses have been found so there is really no lack of them."

"Do you have any idea where your brother could be at the moment?"

At this, Mr. Henry Phillimore's eyes had started to mist. Overall, his countenance had taken on a look of mourning.

"I have no idea, Mr. Holmes. That is why I am glad my nephew has come to you seeking your assistance in the matter."

"Has your brother had any enemies, any persons that harboured any malice toward him?"

"None that I can think of. Perhaps the Egyptian government. He and his two confidantes in Egypt had really crossed the Egyptian government with their sale of contraband Egyptian pieces."

"Thank you for your time, Mr. Phillimore," said Sherlock Holmes as I had a perplexed look upon my face. Henry Phillimore had led us with good hospitality out into the street with a warning about a curse and that he too was going to recite certain spells from the ancient Egyptian Book of the Dead for his own protection.

Naturally our next proceeding was to question the Priests of Set. There were only three of them, all of them local Londoners unique in their reverence for the evil Set. They were released from detention at the Yard a few days earlier.

The Priests of Set had all proved to be within their temple in the Limehouse district during the time of Phillimore's disappearance at 11:33 a.m., according to the Yard.

After this confirmation of the Priest's whereabouts, I wrote to organize my thoughts.

The letter from a father indicating that he had found a lost tomb, the greatest archaeological find of the century.

A murder-suicide in Cairo from the two known Egyptian confidantes that helped James Phillimore excavate Sethotep's royal sepulcher.

The missing umbrella of Mr. Phillimore.

The missing idol of Osiris or Horus made of electrum, a combination of gold and silver. Could it be the idol in Henry Phillimore's study?

A French archaeologist with possibly nefarious designs upon an inexpert who had taken the spotlight away from him.

The extent to how far the Egyptian government would go to repatriate back all the priceless ancient Egyptian items from Sethotep's tomb.

A curse from an ancient tomb from a pharaoh who worshiped an evil god, Set.

The extent to how far the British government would like to keep everything regarding Britain's own trade and collection of Egyptian antiquities hush and productive.

All of these and more I had written to keep track of what was occurring. Holmes had much wanted to visit Sethotep's royal tomb in Egypt for further investigation, but this was beyond what was possible at the moment given that the Egyptian government had prohibited anyone coming near to the newly discovered tomb.

It was during the very next day after we had visited him that we had the news that Mr. James Phillimore's half-brother, Mr. Henry Phillimore, was found dead due to strangling in his apartments.

Mr. Henry Phillimore lay cold in his chair, a purplish tinge to the surface of his skin. He had been murdered with an elastic cord which bore an ankh pendant, the symbol of life that was held by Egyptian deities on tomb walls. There were also traces of something smouldering on a hastily set up altar in the corner of this gentleman's private study. The altar looked incongruous with the taste and style of Mr. Henry Phillimore,

Egyptologist from the University of Cambridge.

There was a photo of the father that Henry and James had shared, framed and displayed prominently on the desk in front of the strangled man.

As the Yard and local constables were summoned to investigate, Lestrade came on the scene of Henry Phillimore's death about the same time that we did.

Lestrade's conclusion was that none of the Priests of Set could account for their locations on the night of Henry Phillimore's murder. They were all rounded up for extended custody at the Yard again.

Naira and Youssif had their locations accounted for during the murder. Youssif had added to his interrogation to communicate once again to Holmes that this was the work of the tomb's curse and that he had best turn away before the curse started to operate on him.

We observed and noted what we could from the crime scene. Of any outstanding clues that Holmes searched for, there were only three: a hastily set up altar, the missing idol of gold and silver that we had seen earlier, and the elastic cord holding the ankh symbol of ancient Egypt twined deeply into Henry Phillimore's throat.

✳✺✳

It was during this time that I was beginning to have the most tremendous and terrifying nightmares. After we had found Henry Phillimore dead from strangulation, something seemed to have taken hold of me, and I could hear footsteps creeping up behind me at night. I felt a sheer sense of pure terror as I walked the district around Baker Street. I had made the resolve to not walk about alone at night. Even as I was walking up the steps to 221B and Holmes's consulting-room I would fancy that I heard footsteps following me up the stairs, my heart palpitating in terror. I had taken a sudden glance at times to see what was making the unnerving noises, finding that there was no one there.

In these darkly fantastic dreams that I had, I felt that I was back in Egypt in the time of the pharaohs. I had seen an embalming priest cut into the side of the abdomen of a recently dead royal and saw the red blood flow onto the obsidian knife. Incenses and fumigations were being burned in the room and there were strange bonfires that kaleidoscoped into the scenes. I saw Isis standing before the throne of Osiris, the Lord of the Underworld, looking at me with a frown on her face and whispering to her husband, Osiris, Judge of the Dead and the Underworld. One tableau blurred into the next and I witnessed another scene of thousands of Egyptians gathering to build the Great Pyramid of Giza. Next the tableau of my dreams altered to a vision of ancient Egyptian priests of Set who summoned the very being of Set in elaborate rituals to conquer London.

Indeed, I had become so nervous and my blood had run so cold that my state descended precipitously. Holmes seemed to be unaffected but I seemed to be suffering the trauma of the opening of a tomb that never should have been opened.

Holmes, on observing this shocking state of mine, hastily busied himself with other cases. He did not look frightened at all. He implored that I get enough rest and to be calm, but I had told him that the other cases that he was occupied with should be put on hold. It felt as if something imminent and evil was about to descend on all London and that Holmes was the only person standing in between this evil and our fair city.

In such a sorry state, Holmes had roused me up for a journey to the Continent. He felt that a change of scenery would lighten my nerves. We were to visit Paris for a chat with Dr. Gustave Janvier, mentor and archaeologist that oversaw the expeditions to Egypt in which Mr. James Phillimore located and excavated the accursed tomb of Sethotep.

I had packed my valise and we drove to take the 5:15 train from Charing Cross for the Continent.

Holmes had read the whole of The Times during the journey by train and settled to a comfortable sleep. I had drifted off into a slumber as well, fraught with the tiniest bit of horror, yet still more restful than the dreadful dreams I was having at Baker Street.

In Paris, we walked along the Avenue des Champs-Elysees and took in some museums before arriving at our appointment with Dr. Janvier.

When we had knocked on the door, a maid had placed our calling card on a silver tray and carried it upstairs to where Janvier's main study was. On the landing above the first flight of stairs, he had appeared, hobbling. It was evident that he was using crutches to move about. To our surprise, he only had one leg, something that no one had told us about.

"Ah, the eminent Monsieur Holmes, *mon Dieu!* Please, come upstairs into my study. We shall have a tete-a-tete and exchange information for I have heard of the inexplicable chain of events in London and Cairo."

We hastened up the stairs to see the contents of his study. Janvier did not hide his collection of ancient Egyptian artifacts, some of them worthy

In Paris, we walked along the Avenue des Champs-Elysees...

of being displayed in the Louvre, the same museum that held the Mona Lisa. He proudly displayed the finds of all of his expeditions to Egypt, in fact, flaunting them with no reservations.

Taking a chair in Janvier's finely appointed and furnished office of study, Holmes launched at once.

"Monsieur Janvier, thank you for agreeing to such a visit. As you know, your colleague has completely disappeared and his half-brother has recently been killed. James Phillimore's son is searching for him. There have been strange things happening in London lately and we have come to you to shed some light upon all of it."

"You have come here with more motives than one, no doubt," he replied, his eyes cast with a faraway look. "But I will answer your questions to the best of my ability."

"Do you harbour any jealousies towards Mr. James Phillimore, who discovered the archaeological find of the century during one of your expeditions?"

"I do not," he replied firmly.

"Do you have any idea as to where Mr. James Phillimore is if he is still alive?"

"That I do not know. I wish I could be of help in this matter."

"What do you know of the Priests of Set in London?"

"I do know that they are a fanatical group that worship the evil deity of ancient Egypt. I know that there are not many of them. From what I have heard, there are only three of them in all of London. There is no modern day Priesthood of Set here in France."

"What can you tell me about this scrap of papyrus I found at the scene of Mr. James Phillimore's vanishing?"

He retrieved a magnifying glass and read the hieroglyphics out loud to himself. Closer he brought the scrap of papyrus to himself and discerned the ancient writing upon it.

"*Oui,*" he nodded to himself in self-assent. "It is not from the ancient Egyptian Book of the Dead, without doubt, though it looks to be so."

I evinced a look of surprise. We had brought it to James Phillimore's brother before his untimely death and he had translated it to be a spell of protection from the Book of the Dead.

"You have come to the right person. I am an expert in the Book of the Dead, along with the other ancient Egyptian books: the Pyramid Texts, the Coffin Texts, and so forth. This is no spell written here but a set of instructions written in a modern day hand using Egyptian hieroglyphs.

Yes, *oui*, I can tell. The Egyptian hieroglyphs here are used flawlessly but phonetically, where each hieroglyph stands for a syllable. It says 'Umbrella —in cellar—I put it there.'"

I saw my companion's eyes light up. Holmes had never needed to write notes for himself. I had written this on the top margin of the British Medical Journal I had brought along with me.

"Yes, curious," Dr. Janvier continued. "You seem surprised, gentlemen. Though these hieroglyphs are hastily written, they do indeed say exactly that: 'Umbrella—in cellar—I put it there.' What did the other translator say?"

Holmes kept to himself and did not mention that the brother of his former colleague had translated it in a different way, that he had translated it into a spell of protection from the Book of the Dead.

"Well, if you do not believe me, have yourselves confirm it independently by another Egyptologist or person versed in the hieroglyphs of ancient Egypt. Can I be of further use to you gentlemen?"

"Where were you during the day of Mr. James Phillimore's disappearance?" asked Holmes.

"I was giving a paper at the French Society of Egyptology."

Holmes had asked for proof and Janvier seemed unruffled. He looked through the programs of past society meetings and supplied us the program and minutes for the French Society of Egyptology's meeting, proving that he was there during James Phillimore's sudden vanishing.

"And where were you the night that his half-brother Henry was murdered?"

"I was at the Louvre here in Paris curating a new exhibition of Egyptian artifacts. You may visit the Louvre and ask the staff, they will settle that I was there the night in question."

"Have you ventured close at all to Sethotep's tomb?" asked Holmes, bringing out his clay pipe. Holmes had put the strongest tobacco into his pipe while the French archaeologist had brought his out as well, an elegant brier-root pipe that he puffed upon while continuing his answers to Holmes's questions.

"I have not, though I wish I could. You know that the Egyptian government has forbidden anyone, especially foreigners, from going anywhere near the tomb. It is a shame that it is so, for I would, like any Egyptologist, adore studying it to complete the history of the Twentieth Dynasty of Egypt. Apparently, this pharaoh was so evil that subsequent pharaohs have acted as if he had not existed at all. They did what other pharaohs did during ancient Egyptian history—if they did not like a predecessor pha-raoh, they wiped him or her cleanly from the record.

"You see, gentlemen, the ancient Egyptians lived for the afterlife. They were obsessed with life after death. To have a pharaoh's name erased from temple walls, records, and the official king lists caused a removal from existence entirely. In ancient Egypt, when a name is erased from their cartouche or hacked out, then that person no longer exists. In ancient Egypt, it is the worst fate that a pharaoh can have, or anyone dead in ancient Egypt, to experience.

"As for Sethotep, there are rumours that his tomb was in particular cursed. There have been many tombs that had possessed this same warning. The talk of curses is mostly put there to stop any potential thieves from ransacking the tomb.

"Sethotep is translated to 'the God Set is Pleased.' This pharaoh was on the throne for only a short while, most likely because of his unorthodox religion—obviously this pharaoh worshiped Set. Set is the Deity of Chaos and the one who hacked his brother Osiris to pieces, scattering the parts all throughout Egypt and into ancient Byblos. It was Isis, the greatest magician of Egypt, who had gathered what parts she could, restored, and resurrected Osiris."

"Tell us what you can about Mr. James Phillimore," Holmes requested, now more at ease with the French Egyptologist.

"As to his relations? Why, only his half-brother and his son," he replied.

Dr. Janvier continued on his account.

"Once he was exiled from Sethotep's tomb by the Egyptian authorities and exiled from Egypt permanently he had come back to your home country and started a business trafficking underground in the antiquities found in Sethotep's tomb that he had secretly brought with him. There were quite many of them. He had even brought the sarcophagus of Sethotep with him to London. Though where Sethotep's sarcophagus is, who can really say. The last I heard was that the British and the Egyptian governments had come to a rare agreement about it. They had jointly said that the sarcophagus be repatriated and brought back to Egypt from London. Egypt had also wanted an idol made of a combination of silver and gold, of Osiris or Anubis, one of the Gods of the Underworld. The Egyptian Museum in Cairo claims that this electrum statue had a rare spell to 'reawaken the dead,' which claims to be the words of Isis herself."

My eyebrows had quivered at the suggestion of this last piece of information. Holmes had taken notice of my reaction.

"The governments of Egypt and Britain disagreed on the idol and only agreed on the sarcophagus being sent back, the last I heard."

"What else can you tell us about James? He has vanished quite impossibly from a locked room. Are you sure you were not jealous in any way at his discoveries? Of his fame? Of his wealth? What of his personality, can you tell us more?"

"Gentlemen, s'il vous plait, I do not have a jealous bone in all my body. James had the eye and the luck to find the tomb of a pharaoh that the world would marvel at, and he did. Oh, if only everyone should be as lucky as James Phillimore! To find an unspoiled tomb of a previously unknown pharaoh and make your mark on the world stage! Yet he was scorned by the Egyptian press and worshiped as a hero by the Western press. His stature here in France is a bit tarnished since my country feels that I should have received the renown.

"You certainly do have a lot of questions yet I will put every effort into answering them all. As to his personality, well, he seemed to always have his head in the clouds. He was a romantic, oui, that man. Always showing the other workers of the expedition his skill in the arts of stage magic. It seemed that after his discovery of Sethotep's tomb he had changed overnight, that he had become automatically a serious Egyptologist, as if someone had given him an honorary doctorate in the study of ancient Egypt. He was conferred these honorary doctorates by some universities later but in the days after his discovery, he became far more serious than before about ancient Egypt. He kept visiting the temples at Karnak and the temples throughout Egypt. He was obsessed with temples after his discovery of Sethotep's tomb. He kept studying the mummies in the Cairo Museum and was reading all translations he could find about the Egyptian Book of the Dead.

"As for his vanishing, could it not be merely a magician's trick? He was, after all, a stage magician. And why make such a fuss about an umbrella? It was raining, and the man went to get his umbrella—it is quite normal but it sounds fantastic, does it not? As if an umbrella has powers to bring us to other lands, other worlds, to make us fly through the air."

"What do you know of his now recently deceased brother?" Holmes asked in an easy, genial way.

"You know that they were half-brothers though rather close as half-brothers go. They both had the same father. Of their family history that is all I know. Henry never was married. He was married to Egyptology, as I am. After the discovery of Sethotep's tomb, they became closer, with

James, I am sure, sharing all of the details of Sethotep's tomb and what it contained with his half-brother. The two had always held a fascination for Egypt, with Henry obtaining his doctor of philosophy degree in Egyptology around the same time that James found the tomb of Sethotep. During the digs with me, James was writing, usually to his brother in London. I never looked at what he was writing. I was never one to go prying about in the privacy of people who were working for me."

"Was there anyone who harboured any animosity or bitterness toward Henry Phillimore?"

"None that I know."

"Who stands to benefit from the wills of James and Henry Phillimore?"

"How should I know that, Mr. Holmes? I am not of their family. My, you are relentless, dear fellow, in your questioning."

"What do you know about Ehab and Morad, who worked for both you and James Phillimore?"

"Greedy types. Always willing to go where more money was to be found. They had started out as friends on my expeditions and excavations but had turned into avaricious monsters after the discovery of Sethotep's chambers by James Phillimore. It was lucky that James Phillimore was not in Cairo at the time of the murder-suicide. I do feel that James could have been swept up into their world of violence and death. All three of them, Ehab, Morad, and James were selling on the underground markets the artifacts they had found from Sethotep's tomb. They had emptied the tomb of its contents, priceless things. It had made the Egyptian government, of course, very angry, along with Egypt's Supreme Council of Antiquities. All three men had become fabulously wealthy by their underground business, but look at where they are now. Two former friends who killed each other over greed and one hero of archaeology vanished. Yet another instance that illustrates that wealth cannot purchase happiness."

Janvier held a placid calm on his face.

"*Eh bien*, if you will excuse me, gentlemen, the hour is getting quite late and I am due at the Louvre again for more curatorial work," he said as his staff had come into the room to light some of the gas-lamps. "If you wish, you may accompany me to account for my whereabouts during the time Henry Phillimore was so unanticipatedly murdered."

Holmes had accepted his offer and we did account for his being in the museum in Paris the night of Henry's murder.

We then had a fine late dinner in the dining-room of a hotel near the Louvre museum, chatting over glasses of port and pastis. We then returned to our own hotel in the Champs-Elysees to ponder our meeting with Dr. Janvier.

米米米

Returned home in London to our rooms at Baker Street, I had fallen prey yet again to evil nightmares of the most grotesque and the elaborately Egyptian. States of unreality folded upon me during the night, visions of the dead rising, the chanting of priests from rolls of papyrus, floating down the ancient Nile River colored bloody to Luxor, the city of the dead. Here I saw pharaohs wrapped in linen rising from their sarcophagi, at first only one of them, but as my dream continued, there were three of them following me around Waset, the ancient name of Luxor. Temples rose above me, towering above as if they were built not by humankind but by giants, rising beyond as far as eyes can rise, and that strange incense of what I could not tell burning in the night as chants to foreign gods and goddesses droned beautifully and frighteningly, weaving into the echoes of the places of worship. Soon priests had joined the wrapped and walking pharaohs in their pursuit of me, and it was when I had run in terror and stumbled onto the ground that their dusty hands covered my mouth so I could not breathe or utter a scream that I woke up drenched in sweat.

I came down to the room where Holmes was sitting and noticed I was shaking and had a perfect want for fresh air. I realized how long I had slept as the shadows started to form upon the windows and the carpets. It was past four o'clock.

To me, it looked as if Sherlock Holmes had sunk into the deepest of glooms, of those melancholies that he was known to have from time to time. I could see that the facts of this case and all the branches of possibility that led out from it were puzzling to him, not an ordinary feat for the greatest detective the world has ever had the fortune to have. These nervous states of his mirrored my own during this time.

It was with some effort on the part of myself and Mrs. Hudson that we at last roused him from his black mood in his armchair and had him stroll about for some fresh air and nourishment. This was at considerable trepidation for me; though I wanted Holmes to be at his sharpest again, I was still in stark fear of those footsteps behind me that I fancied I heard.

Some days later Holmes had brought the piece of papyrus that both Henry Phillimore and Gustave Janvier had translated. The Egyptologist who translated it for us was unknown to both the Phillimores and

Janvier and had confirmed Janvier's translation, which meant that Henry Phillimore had lied that it was a protection spell from the Book of the Dead.

Holmes was now on the trail to find where the missing electrum idol was, and he had a suspicion that the Priests of Set in London had it. On it was a spell of Isis that was supposed to have the power to raise the dead, according to Gustave Janvier. The government of Egypt had wanted it as much as the Priests of Set probably wanted it. Holmes also desired to come into contact with those who had bought Egyptian antiquities from Mr. James Phillimore. He had certain questions that he wanted to ask of these customers. Till then, Holmes had decided to give himself an easy sleep. I had administered him a sedative. It is a curious thing that he never had a horrid dream while investigating this entire case.

✳✳✳

"What are some of the elements that indicate that someone has vanished?" asked a much improved Holmes as we were at elevenses the next day, a tea and coffee break usually held at 11 a.m. We were at a tea room near Baker Street and I had taken a cafe noir along with some biscuits. My nerves were in a very slight wreck as I had had another bout of disturbing dreams of black magic in Egypt of long ago.

"Well, I would have to say a general search and the family and friends of the missing person claiming a disappearance. There would have to be a lengthy amount of time to have passed to consider someone as 'vanished.'"

"What factor do we have that leads to conclude a vanishing of Mr. James Phillimore?"

"The wet footsteps leading to the room where he went to fetch his umbrella. We saw these dried footsteps clearly leading to the room but not out of it. And a room locked from the inside."

"Who was present at the time of his vanishing?"

"Just his staff, a maid and two butlers. All three of them saw him return back for his umbrella, go to his study, and shut both doors."

"Did they see him shut both doors?"

I had to rethink what I had just said. From what we gathered from our inquiry of the maid and the butlers, none of them had confirmed that they had actually seen Mr. James Phillimore lock the double-door behind him. It was my inference alone, not based on what we gathered.

"You are right, Holmes. None of the three had seen him shut the double-doors of his study."

He continued his considerations while being aware that no one else hear us.

"Why would someone who is in haste for his umbrella to go back outside in the rain shut the door if he is just retrieving his umbrella?"

I had not thought about what Holmes had just mentioned.

"There is something to that, no doubt, Holmes," I had remarked.

"My dear fellow, there lies the problem. Mr. James Phillimore enters his finely appointed house in Grosvenor to retrieve his umbrella. He then disappears. We don't know if he had locked his room or someone else had. It is only with the Yard's help that the doors are opened. Only three people saw him go into the room, possibly only viewing the back side and not the front side. No noise is heard for a while from the room by the house staff of the one maid and two butlers, besides the loud crash the maid fancied she had heard, until one of the butlers had knocked on the locked doors to tell James Phillimore that dinner was to be served. It was then that they had called the local authorities for help in opening the door and finding the master missing. Vanished, as if into some other existence."

I thought about all of this. The dried footsteps now seemed too deliberate.

"When you eliminate the impossible, the truth appears as the remains, probable or improbable," I paraphrased Holmes in front of him.

"Precisely. You know my methods, Watson," he said as he sipped at his coffee.

"I still cannot see how he can vanish, much less escape, from a locked room with no chimney, no windows, and no means of exit besides the locked entrance."

"Let us take for instance the dried footsteps. Obviously deliberate. And also the fact that Phillimore was a stage magician. Stage magicians always performs feats of trickery and illusion."

"Holmes, after this, I think a revisit with the maid and two butlers should be in order. Yet there are so many avenues with this case; we still have to question the three Priests of Set, find customers who bought Egyptian artifacts from Mr. James Phillimore, find the electrum idol that was stolen from Henry Phillimore, and more."

"What is intriguing me is that perhaps if we approach the entire enigma from the start, then we can perhaps lessen some of the avenues of investigation."

It was evident that Holmes was now one step ahead in the case. I can always report when he was at the cusp of breaking the entire dilemma and

"Let us take for instance the dried footsteps..."

only awaiting the confirmation of it through more investigation. It was at these points that he seemed always to be more at ease, as if emerging from the murky clouds that he wallows in perhaps purposefully, maybe taking some deliberate pleasure in wandering his own internal shadows. It could have been that wandering into the dark sometimes allows him to find the answers that he seeks.

"Sometimes to go forward one must go back to the beginning," he said.

And so we went back to the beginning, James Phillimore's house and the locked room that James had taken leave of this world from.

Holmes had, to my utter surprise, not proceeded to inspect the locked room again but asked the maid and two butlers if there was a cellar.

Indeed there was, and he was shown to the door of it.

Opening this door, there preceded a long and steep stairway to the dank recesses of the cellar. Bringing his torch and his magnifying glass to the stairs, he was able to discern slight marks to the wooden stair, and it was bent out of the regular straight descending path into a crooked one, marred with marks and even some evidence of broken wood in places on the stairway down.

Holmes went all the way to the cellar while I elected to stay on the ground floor, too frightened by the dark subterranean area of the house. I felt that I had visions of something unholy climbing the stairs up to grab me and to scare all of London into submission.

In the cellar Holmes had found occult Egyptian symbolism and geometric circles drawn on the ground. He found attempts to mummify cats, dogs, and birds in the cellar. These mummies were created successfully as Holmes had them brought later to Oxford's Egyptology department to validate. They were black things, things I felt that were not of this world when I looked at them. Oxford declared them perfect mummies in the style of the ancient Egyptians and had requested to keep them in their research collections.

Holmes had also tested to see if someone positioned outside of the study could lock the double-doors from the inside. He found this to be possible, and I had tried it and did lock the double-doors from the inside while shutting the doors from the outside after many attempts.

At Scotland Yard, we had finally arrived to talk to the Priests of Set, to glean any information that we could get from them while they were in custody as the prime suspects of the murder of Henry Phillimore.

Upon arriving, Holmes had requested of Inspector Lestrade if their temple in the Limehouse district had been searched for anything of relevance. Lestrade replied in the affirmative, and Holmes had asked about an Egyptian idol of Osiris. Lestrade seemed at sea about Egyptian idols and gods for this and that, so we both had asked him to see what they had recovered from their temple of evil.

We found the idol of electrum sure enough. There it was, the exact idol made of electrum, of luminous silver and gold, of the Lord of the Underworld, Osiris. Sherlock Holmes peered deeper into it to see if there was any writing. He confirmed that there were Egyptian hieroglyphs and that the hieroglyphs were probably Isis's spell of resurrection as detailed by Dr. Janvier. He later had another independent archaeologist of Egypt verify that it was a spell of resurrection by the Goddess of Magic, Isis.

Before we arrived to their cells, Lestrade had informed us that one of them had broken down and confessed to the murder of Henry Phillimore.

"Why did you strangle Henry Phillimore?" Holmes asked the confessor behind bars.

"Because he would not give us the idol," said the Priest of Set, his eyebrows shaved and completely bald of head. The voice was grating, and if I must describe it with utter truth, the voice felt insanely malevolent.

"Who do you intend to resurrect?" asked Holmes.

"Sethotep," he mumbled. "Sethotep."

"Is he here in London?"

"Of course he's here in London," he stared defiantly at the detective.

"Where is the sarcophagus of Sethotep?"

"Henry's brother smuggled it here to London. We don't know where it is now."

"Why do you want to bring back an evil pharaoh? What are your purposes?"

This time, another of the Priests of Set, in another cell, answered.

"We believe that the world has far descended into evil already that it takes a greater evil to clean it up. London is doomed either way."

I had heard of strange cults in London before, but never one where I heard that it took a larger evil to take care of a smaller evil.

"And all three of you entered Henry Phillimore's study where the idol was that had the spell of Isis written on it to resurrect Sethotep. And Henry

Phillimore was not willing to lightly give it to the three of you so you murdered him and took the idol."

"Very good, Holmes," responded the Priest of Set who confessed. "That is exactly it."

"And your next plan was to go after James Phillimore to learn where the mummy of Sethotep is in London."

"Now I see why you are called the greatest detective in London," he replied sardonically, his voice still seemingly otherworldly, still unnerving.

"What role do you have in the disappearance of James Phillimore?" I asked them.

They all three were silent.

"None whatsoever," said the confessor.

"We do have a little hand in it," said one priest.

"I think we have a bit more of a 'little hand' in it, Mr. Holmes," said the formerly silent third Priest of Set.

"All three of you give conflicting answers. It does not bother me," stated Holmes confidently. "I am glad that you will not get your wish of 'resurrecting' Sethotep. Sethotep has slipped from your grasp. Come, let us go, Watson. We are wasting our time with these dedicated to such evil. Know that evil sent out is evil returned. You three are an example of this."

※※※

Holmes was resolute and determined to go to Egypt because he had a strong notion that the sarcophagus of Sethotep was in transit to Cairo and from there, to the Valley of the Kings, the necropolis where pharaohs rested in their tombs.

He had thought that he needed special permission from the British government and the Egyptian government to have access to the tomb of Sethotep and the sarcophagus of Sethotep if it indeed was back in its tomb.

Imagine our surprise when we learned that the sarcophagus of Sethotep was in the British Museum, waiting to be repatriated back to the government of Egypt. The British and Egyptian governments had made a compromise—they would return the sarcophagus of Sethotep with its contents if they would stop their attempt to bring back the artifacts from Sethotep's tomb that were sold on the London underground antiquities market by James Phillimore. The Egyptian government knew that they were mostly irrecoverable anyway, scattered in private collections throughout the United Kingdom but the sarcophagus of the pharaoh is what they felt was essential to the tomb and to their pride. Therefore, the agreement between the two governments was struck.

Holmes had requested a private examination of the sarcophagus of Sethotep in the British Museum. He had wanted no one else in the room besides me. The British government allowed him to do so given he had done so much for the Crown in past cases.

We arrived in the middle of the night when all the workers, curatorial, and museum staff were away. A security man led us to the areas reserved for conservators, academics, and archivists, where the sarcophagus we were looking for was located. When we were alone in the room with it, we found that it was already in a packing crate and ready to ship back to Egypt.

I still felt that footsteps were following close behind during that night visit to the museum, and I dare not turn around. Holmes said that he heard nothing and that they were all delusions possibly from the stress of the case and the overworking of a strong imagination. It sounded like a compliment while at the same time being an admonishment.

Holmes removed the top lid of the crate with a crowbar that he had brought with him in addition to some other tools.

There shone, even in the obscurities of the dark, a resplendent and almost glowing solid gold sarcophagus. The head was elaborately made with onyx eyes, the pharaoh beard in lapis lazuli and carnelian, and the crook and flail made of turquoise and gold.

We stared for some time in mesmerised states before Holmes carefully removed the upper casing of the sarcophagus. I trembled deliriously, knowing that this was the mummy of a baleful pharaoh, one so evil that pharaohs after him had condemned his name and hacked it from memory for all eternity. One so evil that his devotees in London had wanted him to be brought back from the dead.

The casing removed, we saw a bandaged figure. The bandages of linen that wrapped the mummy still looked new, as if made with modern methods.

The arms were crossed as all royal mummy's arms were crossed. There was no trace of dust on the mummy, just the scents of natron, herbs, and spices.

Holmes with the tenderest of care started to lift the bandages from the face. I couldn't bear to see, and recoiled, my back against the wall, shirking in mortal terror.

Holmes did not seem the least bit concerned or terrified.

"So there you are!" he gasped aloud. "We were wondering where you had disappeared to!"

A smile had overtaken Holmes's face.

I inched closer until I could finally see. There, bandaged though visible, was the face of Mr. James Phillimore, his eyes forever closed in death and his being wrapped in the linen of mummies. It was horrific to me and will forever haunt me.

There were evidences that the neck had broken and other markings indicating the suffering of a sudden and deadly fall on the mummy of Mr. James Phillimore, according to Holmes.

✳✳✳

"You see, my dear Watson, it is all so simple."

It was a fine morning and things had seemed fresh and brighter. I, though, had thought the matter far from simple. I was relieved that the Priests of Set had not unleashed a revivified Sethotep on the whole of London.

"Mr. James Phillimore had died on the morning he had retrieved his umbrella."

It was only the two of us again at elevenses at the same tea room we had patronized earlier. There was no one in ear's distance from us, Holmes had made sure of this.

"That morning was very rainy, and Mr. James Phillimore had, of course, reason to get his umbrella. We learned that there was only one umbrella in the whole house, according to our examination of the maid and the two butlers. He entered his study, the wet shoes creating tracks that would later dry. There were no other tracks besides these. It seems as if Mr. James Phillimore had vanished. The maid and two butlers go to other parts of the large, sprawling house of Mr. Phillimore. A crash is heard by the maid, but this could have been attributed to the thunder and noise of a storm. The other two, the two butlers, do not hear anything because of the outside thunder and rainstorm.

"Mr. Phillimore does not find his umbrella in the study as he had anticipated. He found a note in hieroglyphs, the one that Mr. Henry Phillimore had lied about. The note said: 'Umbrella—in cellar—I put it there.' Now, it stands to reason that two Egyptologists, the brothers James and Henry Phillimore, would communicate in hieroglyphs often to keep their skills in Egyptian hieroglyphs sharp. Therefore, after Henry

Phillimore's use of the umbrella, the only umbrella in the whole house, he writes a note in Egyptian hieroglyphs to his fellow Egyptologist, his brother James, as to where the umbrella would be. Of course, he'd put this on James's desk.

"James goes to the cellar in search of the umbrella. His shoes by now had dried because of the large carpet in the study. He goes to the cellar door and down those steep, torturous steps. However, he slips and falls to his death, an accident. We saw the marks on the steps leading down into the cellar. This was the crash that the maid had heard: the fall of James Phillimore down the cellar steps. We must remember that people have different levels of hearing ability. In this occurrence, the maid had the keenest sense of hearing.

"Who should be outside the house and waiting but his own brother, Henry. Seeing that James had not emerged from his house quickly after fetching the umbrella, he goes inside to see what is delaying James. The maid and the two butlers are elsewhere in the house, assuming that Mr. James Phillimore had retrieved his umbrella easily and gone into the rain, so they do not see Henry Phillimore enter.

"He goes right to the cellar, knowing that the cellar is where the umbrella would be since he had left the umbrella there.

"He finds his brother dead from the fall at the bottom of the stairs.

"Here, he has to think quickly. It is true that Mr. James Phillimore was drifting away from the Anglican Church according to his son, Hartley. We saw in the cellar all the Egyptian occult markings and paraphernalia of Egyptian religion. We also saw that Mr. Henry Phillimore was strangled by the Priests of Set with an elastic cord holding the Egyptian symbol of the ankh. While it seemed that the Priests of Set had strangled Henry with their own elastic cord, it was actually Henry's own elastic cord with his own ankh on it. Yes, Henry was a follower and worshiper of the ancient Egyptian religion. That hastily set up altar was not what the Priests of Set had put up on the murder scene of Mr. Henry Phillimore. It was Henry Phillimore's own altar, dedicated to worshiping the good Egyptian gods, not the evil one, Set.

"We also know from the account of Mr. James Phillimore's son that 'strange incenses' were being burnt in his house after James Phillimore's break from traditional religion. We can also deduce here that Mr. James Phillimore became, like his brother, a worshiper of the virtuous ancient Egyptian gods."

Suddenly it became clearer, as if a picture had suddenly come gradually into focus.

"Both of them being devotees of ancient Egyptian religion, what is the most important rite?"

I sat staring at Holmes, marveling at his skills of deductive reasoning yet again.

"Preparation for death. Preparation for the afterlife. The ancient Egyptians were obsessed with preparing for death. This is done through being made a mummy in the proper way and buried properly on the west bank of the Nile River in Egypt.

"We saw in that cellar the experiments on cats, dogs, and other animals in mummifying them. Successful experiments, as we had confirmed.

"Now why would Henry want to mummify his own brother?"

Again, I sat silent, hardly touching my tea and held rapt in his explanations.

"Because in mummifying his brother James, that would allow him to get past the lifelong Egyptian ban of James visiting Egypt. Henry performed a mummy switch!"

My sense of amazement was thrilled at this conclusion. Now it was starting to make much more logical sense.

"The sarcophagus of Sethotep was still in London and was soon to be repatriated back to Egypt in a rare agreement by the governments of Egypt and Britain. Egypt would have the golden coffin of Sethotep and the British Museum would get to keep the James Phillimore Collection of relics from the tomb of Sethotep. That was the compromise between the two governments.

"So Henry Phillimore, in haste, took up the thin body of James Phillimore, his brother, outside somewhere and hid it successfully. He then burned the note in the study but did it too hastily. Why did he burn the note? Because he did not want to be accused of murdering his own brother. This was why he lied about the deciphering of the hieroglyphics when we questioned him.

"He then locked the double-doors from the outside to make it seem as if James Phillimore had vanished into the very air, away from this world.

"Having left the house of James Phillimore with the maid and two butlers never seeing him, Henry hastened to his apartments, probably in the dark, with the body of his brother. Skilled in their mummification experiments, Henry, in his chambers, made his brother into a mummy in the exact ancient style of long ago Egypt. This he switched with the mummy of Sethotep in the sarcophagus.

"All that remains now is to discover what happened to the mummy of

Sethotep and if we should inform the authorities of what we know.

"The beliefs of the afterlife of Henry and James, I feel, should be respected. It is not for us to judge their beliefs. It is obvious that the whole family has a love of ancient Egypt. That love for Egypt and its history and religion ran deep and will probably do so for future generations. I have been studying ancient Egyptian religion and the goodness of the vast majority of their beliefs. If we were to suddenly tell everyone what we know, then James Phillimore's body will not reach Egypt and he will no longer be existent in the next life, according to his religion. It was his wish, probably the most profound and serious wish, of James Phillimore, to return to Egypt, even if it was after his own death. His brother had found a way. I can find of no more loyal a brother than Henry Phillimore. It is a shame that the Priests of Set had to murder Henry, a kind and loyal brother, in a bout of evil-driven zeal."

I had tacitly agreed as Holmes had resumed sipping his cup of coffee. All my fears and nightmares about the supernatural, of all the instances of footsteps following me, were all due to my imagination about ancient curses from cryptic Egyptian graves.

"I agree, Holmes, that the disappearance of Mr. James Phillimore should remain a mystery," I assented. "Good heavens, what a clever way to get around a lifelong ban from Egypt!"

"Perhaps there is some mechanism that Henry Phillimore has put in place to make future researchers of the mummy of Sethotep believe it is the mummy of Sethotep in the sarcophagus and not the mummy of his brother. It is indeed curious. Perhaps the mummy of Sethotep is already in Egypt and will be switched again by confidantes in Egypt loyal to the Phillimore brothers. They will, therefore, switch back the mummy of Sethotep into the coffin and bury the mummy of James Phillimore in the sands of Egypt, as he so desired."

✳✳✳

Later, we did find that Holmes's hypothesis of another mummy switch in Egypt was correct. This was years later, though, when the clamor and Egyptian pride around the return of the mummy of Sethotep being returned to Egypt had calmed.

The mummy switch in Egypt was performed by other worshipers of the ancient Egyptian religion in Cairo. They took the new mummy of James Phillimore and replaced it with Sethotep's mummy in secret.

It is with relief now that I am able to tell this before untold case because neither Holmes nor I know where the mummy of James Phillimore is buried in the Valley of the Kings in Egypt. James Phillimore's confidantes had hidden him well, too well. Perhaps one day it too will become an "ancient Egyptian" grave of incredible significance thousands of years from now.

THE END

STORY SPARK

The incipient spark for this Sherlock Holmes mystery about Mr. James Phillimore was inside the well-known vaults in the mind of every Holmes fan. These vaults are described by Watson in "The Problem of Thor Bridge." I, as much as you, want to enter these vaults to read these locked away cases, so carefully hidden by Watson from the view of the public. In the vaults that Watson writes about are untold cases, tantalizing cases that for some reason or other privy to Holmes's well-being, had to be kept secret from the public, sealed as mysteries indefinitely.

Among these unwritten tales by Watson is this enticing morsel, here in verbatim:

"Among these unfinished tales is that of Mr. James Phillimore, who, stepping back into his own house to get his umbrella, was never more seen in this world."

Just this one sentence from Arthur Conan Doyle has sparked the imaginations of his legions, most probably because of the mention of an umbrella. An umbrella conjures up for us thoughts of fantasy, of flying away, of entering other worlds and other places not bound to the earthly realm if we just hold onto its handle. We all know the tradition that an umbrella should never be opened indoors, yet, eagerly, I yearned to open the umbrella out of the doors of Watson's vaults to unfold the tale that fills this gap in the Holmes canon.

Not only is this tale a fulfillment of where James Phillimore and his umbrella are, it is also a locked-room mystery, one I've wanted to write for seeming eons. It is also a missing persons case, though it wouldn't be a mystery tale from me if there wasn't at least one or more murders in it. Preferably more than one.

The reader will see that this story is a metaphoric tree from which sprout complex branches going here and there, pathways traveling from the main stalk that are either planted in the supernatural or in the probable. As in all Holmes's cases, the solution is firmly within the rules of the probable, the real, though the play on the fantastic is much alluded to.

Ancient Egypt is prominent in this work since I endeavored to heap even more intrigue into the account. Egypt is, to all intents, mystery at its core. Having returned from my first visit to that country, I saw the ancient temples, archaeological sites, and hieroglyphs, including Tutankhamun's treasures. I saw countless artifacts from the 3000 year history of pharaonic Egypt that were breathtaking, and the visit expectedly deepened my natural love of this field of study. People seem to be automatically drawn to Egypt as if by magnet with its tales of mummies, curses, and pyramids, with its hovering feeling of mysteries unsolved. I drew on my own Egyptological knowledge from avid reading in the field and from my affiliation with the American Research Center in Egypt (ARCE), the resources of the University of Chicago's Department of Near Eastern Languages and Civilizations (one of the most sizable in scope in the country), and through my contacts in the department, building a solid foundation on Egyptological lore and scholarship. Weaving in Egyptology was the most amusing process about writing this Holmes adventure and it was also an adventure for me.

There is a MacGuffin in this plot, which the astute reader will discern. This MacGuffin is portable and fits nicely into the adventure by bringing about possible peril to London society.

Spell 41 as seen in this story (on the MacGuffin!) is a real spell from the ancient Egyptian Book of the Dead found in the Protection from Danger section. It's a spell that "prevents the deceased from being slaughtered by demonic servants of Osiris." The exact words to the spell can be found in John H. Taylor's *Ancient Egyptian Book of the Dead: Journey Through the Afterlife*, a valuable source.

A favorite character I invented in this piece is Dr. Janvier, the Egyptologist in France. His French surname, "Janvier," means "January" in English, therefore his name could be read as Dr. January. Names evoke volumes about character, and Dr. January has future possibilities just by his name. I do feel that Dr. January, or, Dr. Janvier, as he'd like to be known, could appear in my future Holmes stories since he's also an authority on other areas that Holmes could utilize for his science of deduction.

We had a whole gallery of suspects here, so many of them. There were two that were practically invisible during the whole narrative, though some of those reading this Holmes adventure could have wondered about them. Never mentioned are the mothers of the half-brothers, James Phillimore and Henry Phillimore. These unknown two could have factored into the chronicle of Mr. Phillimore's disappearance and could have been unseen suspects in the narrative. I could have angled it that way but chose to have them inserted between the lines of thought.

If ever you find that corner of unlabeled Egyptian artifacts in the British Museum that Holmes and Watson encounter in the opening of this adventure, you now know why they are there.

✳✳✳

DEXTER FABI -Dexter Fabi is a visual artist and writer from the Chicago area. The many hats he has worn include teaching English as a second language in Japan, being a college teacher in California, maintaining an online store of rare and vintage books, and being an information technology administrator for a company in downtown Chicago. After receiving his Master of Science from DePaul University in computer technology, he worked in the industry for years until becoming an educator. Working in the mediums of digital and handmade art, he has exhibited his artwork in the Midwest and in Europe for the World Science Fiction Conventions in Kansas City and Helsinki. He has garnered awards for his art, including an award of First Place in The Waukegan Public Library's Ray Bradbury Creative Contest for Visual Art in June of 2015, held by the very same library that Bradbury himself visited and loved as a child growing up in Waukegan, Illinois. He continues creating for art shows every year. In the course of his writing, he is also the recipient of the literary award of Best Short Story for *The Royal Wedding of Oz* at the annual Winkie Convention presented by the International Wizard of Oz Club. Among his many hobbies are Egyptology, cinema, genealogy, languages, folklore, baseball cards, pulp fiction, listening to music, and reading, his eternal obsession. He lives in the suburbs of Chicago and is a full-time tutor.

Sherlock Holmes

in

"The Adventure of the Irregular Heartbeat"

By
Jonathan Casey

Throughout the years that I have been associated with my intimate friend Mr. Sherlock Holmes and chronicled those adventures that have ignited so much public interest in the inner-workings of the vast underworld of our great city, I have tried, to the best of my modest abilities, to showcase those extraordinary qualities of his that have so impressed and, at times, baffled me. I have remarked elsewhere about Holmes seemingly having an inhuman will-power when engrossed in the middle of case, and it is indeed true that we have been involved in an almost uncountable number of situations which would have tested and probably broken the resolve of even the most battled-tested Englishman. It is for this reason that I continue to see it as my duty to the public at large to bring to light those instances in which the light of Providence has shone in even the darkest of times. But, as he has been wont to do when I bring up the subject of what he has labeled my "fanciful exaggerations", Holmes very recently chided me for such a stance, requesting instead that I present a more well-rounded portrait for inspection in the gallery of public opinion and reminding me that he has in fact been mistaken a time or two. In line with his wishes, I present the following narrative of a situation that pushed Holmes to the very edge of his reason and which had me at the same time finding myself in a struggle to keep up with it all.

It all began one night in the middle of as harsh of a winter as I had seen for some time. My rounds had kept me until late in the evening, as an elderly patient of mine had taken a fit of horrific seizures, which took me several hours to stabilize. I admit to being quite troubled by the whole of the evening, and as a precaution, I alerted a colleague at St. Bartholomew's who agreed to check in with and transport my patient for further observation if necessary. As I trudged my way toward Baker Street, I could not help but notice that I was the sole traveller attempting to brave the storm—no small feat in the middle of our metropolis; I had not even so much as passed a hansom for at least half an hour. The brim of my hat had been gathering a considerable amount of snow from my trek, and as I stopped and shook my head to clear it, I considered that the faint glow of the gas lamps backlit the snow in such a way as to make it seem that the specters of those long gone from this world had come back for their own stroll in the night.

I was still mulling over such bizarre and curious thoughts when I reached the front door of 221B. The downstairs windows were as black

as the night of the New Moon, and it took me a moment to remember
that Mrs. Hudson had left two days prior to visit a friend whose ever
more frequent letters had managed to be persuasive enough to get her to
leave her post as gatekeeper of two of the most unruly and unpredictable
tenants that she could have ever imagined having stay in her home. The
patience of that dear, dear woman still amazes me to this day. It appeared
that the light of our rooms upstairs was still blazing bright like the beacon
of the lighthouses in the sea-faring stories in which I had gotten wrapped
up as of late. I could feel the pain in my leg and the burning of tired eyes
beginning to set in, and I hoped that instead of facing some pressing
matter of national importance, I would be able to find the comfort of my
warm bed and a glass or two of brandy before I drifted off into the arms
of Morpheus.

As I slowly ascended the staircase to our dwelling, I questioned whether
or not I had taken a wrong turn somewhere and ended up at the opera
house instead of Baker Street. My senses were flooded with the incredibly
sorrowful rising and falling of passages coming from what could only
be Holmes's violin. Despite my reluctance to stay awake any longer than
necessary, I found that I could not move from that spot on the landing,
lest Holmes cease what sounded like a very intricate and brilliant exercise
in virtuosity. I have remarked previously that he was not always the most
considerate flat-mate when it came to the hour in which he chose to work
on his hobbies, but I would never intrude on those activities which gave
him respite from the constant working of his marvelous mind. I could not
have been standing there longer than five minutes when the movement fell
apart and I could hear some muttered curse escape from inside our rooms.

"You may come in now if you wish, Watson," said Holmes. "This blasted
thing has bested me this round, but I will get it yet. Besides, your leg seems
to be bothering you far more than it has in some time. You really must
learn to take care of yourself as well as you do your patients."

I was not sure if I should take the latter statement with the amount of
sarcasm I suspected was attached to it, but I was in no mood for arguments.
Opening the door, I observed my friend gathering up a jumbled stack of
composition paper and shoving it into a drawer. After having hung up my
coat and hat, I made my way to the sideboard and began to pour myself a
brandy.

"Wait just a minute, Holmes," I said, my mind finally catching up to
reality. "How in the deuce could you possibly have known, well, any of it,
without even opening the door?"

Normally, such a question would at least elicit a chuckle of frustration from my friend, but on this occasion, I found that he was in even more bitter spirits than he had been when I had left him that morning. He was still attired in the same grey tweed suit he'd had on earlier—though he had swapped out the grey jacket for his black smoking jacket—and his face looked considerably haggard and worn down. I stole a glance at the mantle to see if the morocco case containing his hypodermic syringe was still in its usual place, but I was quickly rebuked for such a caring consideration.

"Really, Watson," he snapped. "Your obsession with my occasional dabbling with a perfectly-crafted, reality-dulling solution knows no limits."

He walked over to the mantle, picked up his pipe, and shook his head as he made his way to the window. The pipe finally lit, and my friend was engulfed in a cloud of smoke, making me wonder if he had taken to parlour tricks as a new hobby.

When the smoke cleared, he continued, "But, perhaps I am over-reacting. Besides, I have not yet answered your question, the answers to which are obvious to anyone with at least a modicum of logic and reason."

I sat down in my chair and listened to the crackling of the fire, knowing that he would continue on now, explaining my movements from the time I had left the premises to the time I had found myself with unexpected orchestra tickets.

"It is now two o'clock and in this weather, you will not find many cabs willing to brave the elements for what may only amount to a single overnight fare. Therefore, it is reasonable to assume that you have been active for an extended period, most probably since after lunchtime, the time you were to see that older fellow whose visits you save for last because they do not typically take you more than fifteen minutes. Undoubtedly, you were delayed by an unexpected turn in his health, a turn which occupied and tried your mental and physical faculties until at least a couple of hours ago. From there, you found yourself without a means of transportation other than your own fatigued body, so you set off on a snow-filled journey to Baker Street. During your journey, I would wager very confidently that you failed to see the man following you…"

"Following me!" I exclaimed. "Whatever do you mean following me? I was the only one out there for miles."

"As I was saying, you failed to see the man following you and made your way to 221B. With your leg now aching from your travels, you found the staircase up to our rooms to be a daunting task and, as it turns out, one that you undertook approximately ten seconds slower than normal. In fact, on the sixth step, you slipped—no doubt because of your wet boots— causing the board to squeal."

As was usually the case, I was astonished at the accuracy with which he described the details of my day, but I was even more flustered over the fact that there had been a mystery man tailing me without me having even the slightest hint of him being there.

"That is all very well and good, Holmes…" I began before he interrupted my tired attempt at anger.

"He is long gone now, my dear fellow," Holmes said. "And even with my considerable abilities there is not much hope that I would be able to track him in weather that leaves footsteps filled in with fresh snow within mere seconds."

Sensing my frustration, he continued, "However, I must admit to being glad at this turn of events. I feel that I have become increasingly frustrated at the lack of interesting cases as of late, and I find that my mind has been marinating in a deep pool of stagnation, the likes of which is quite new to me. Sure, it is true that the case of the Bewlay Brothers was of some interest, but that resolved itself quickly in the end."

He stopped and stared out the window for what seemed like hours before going on. "No, this will just not do. And it is in such times that I find myself pondering the idea that life, as dangerous as it was in those days, was much more interesting with Professor Moriarty lurking in the shadows and waiting to strike. London has become a predictable place, one which seems to run on gears and offers no hope of anything other than an endless loop of the mundane."

I had heard him make remarks such as these several times since his still unbelievable return to the land of the living, but I could not help but get the sense that he had fallen into a darker chasm of despair than at any time previous.

He extinguished his pipe and waved his hand in the air dismissively.

"Enough of this," he said. "You best be off to bed instead of listening to my prattling about deceased criminal masterminds. Besides, I am sure tomorrow will bring something of interest."

"If you say so, Holmes," I said with a yawn.

I retreated to my room, and for a moment, I could have sworn that I heard the clasps of Holmes's violin case being opened for another go at that passage which had frustrated him earlier. I waited for the screech of the bow, but it never came, and before long, my eyes succumbed to the darkness.

Awaking in the most abrupt and jarring of ways is something to which I had grown quite accustomed in the time that I had spent serving with my fellow countrymen in Afghanistan, but it seemed to be a particular habit of Holmes to find new ways to rouse me from my slumbers. Such was the case the following morning when at a quarter past eleven a torrent of metal disks came crashing down upon me like a meteor shower from the heavens.

"Quick, Watson," said Holmes in a hurried tone. "We must be off at once!"

With that statement, he exited the room in a flash, and I was left to pick up the pieces, which in this case were made of gold and silver. Shaking my head of the cobwebs and the possible concussion I had suffered, I began collecting the sovereigns and shillings that lay scattered about my beaten and worn down frame. Dressing did not take me more than a moment, and after slipping my Webley into my jacket pocket, I bolted to the door to try to catch Holmes who himself was already halfway down the staircase. My leg was not in full agreement with the course this morning was taking, but such was the life of a doctor turned biographer.

Stepping into the garishly bright light of the sun which reflected sharply off of the newly minted coat of snow, I covered my brow with my hand and found myself face to face with a carriage from Scotland Yard. I mounted the step and entered the carriage and waited for Holmes to explain what in the world was happening.

"Where to first, Mr. Holmes?" asked the constable in complete deference to my friend's wishes. This demeanor in and of itself was the first signal to me that matters were rather grave. While his years of service to the Yard had ingratiated Holmes inasmuch as such an institution can truly accept a private citizen, it was rare that he was given such command of a situation from the emergence of even the most bone-chilling calamity.

Upon his inaudible reply, Holmes entered the carriage, and we were off at a brisk pace to a destination unknown to me. At first, I suspected that my friend would remain silent and lose himself in the mental processes that so efficiently put together the most disparate clues into a functioning whole. But just as that thought passed through my mind, he began his brief dissertation.

"It is incredible, Watson!" said Holmes excitedly. "Six banks in one morning's time. This is really one for the annals of crime."

His enthusiasm aside, I noted a hint of reservation in his voice, something that I could not understand given the present circumstances.

Here was a case tailor-made for the great detective, and yet, I could not shake the sense that he was troubled by some fact which he had already ascertained well ahead of everyone else involved. I hoped Holmes would soon take me into his full confidence right then and there, but that was not to occur until later.

Thrusting three documents, one newspaper, and one telegram in my direction, he continued, saying, "I have been to three of them already and intend to see the other three within the afternoon. It is really most peculiar, Watson. Each of the vaults remains perfectly intact, and other than the doors being left wide open, there is no other discernible sign of foul play."

"Surely the lack of funds in the aforementioned vaults is indicative, is it not?" I asked somewhat smugly.

A slight smile played on his face, and he spread his hands out like a pastor ready to discourse on the Gospel.

"There is the rub, my dear fellow," Holmes said, pausing for a moment before continuing. "An inventory of each vault has shown there to be nothing missing—nothing at all. Everything down to the last half-penny is in its proper place."

As it did the previous evening, astonishment set in, and I did not envy Holmes the anxiety or, if he did not feel anxiety, hyper-focus that engulfed his very being in these instances. Indeed, surgery required prolonged periods of maximum intensity at times, but there was always an end in sight within hours, not the weeks that were sometimes consumed by the most daunting of his cases.

"You cannot be serious," I said, shaking my head back and forth in disbelief. "What could possibly be the motive for such a thing?"

"Therein lays the crux of the matter," he remarked casually.

Holmes reclined and steepled his fingers in front of his face, and it was in this position that he remained for the remainder of our journey. I busied myself with reviewing the materials that he had presented me. Other than the scrawled message of confounded alarm from our old comrade Lestrade, which I found amusing on its own merits, I found nothing of significance in the accounts presented.

We had been traveling at a good clip, and when the carriage rounded the next corner of the following intersection, a familiar sight came into focus. The front of Cox and Co. stared me directly in the face, reminding me that I had not made any monetary deposits in much longer than I cared to admit. The constable slowed up the horses, and, all things considered, he seemed rather jovial. To be in such spirits, he must have been blessed with an awareness that did not see as far into the murky depths of the future as my friend's own mind did.

Prepared to battle through the gathered throng of disaster chasers who lived vicariously through the peril of others, Holmes and I alighted from the carriage and made haste to the office of the bank manager. He did not seem familiar to me, and it occurred to me that he must have begun his employ in my hiatus from the practice of financial competency. The man did not appear to be older than thirty, but his hair had begun to grey on the side, and I observed a cane leaning up against his side of the desk. The nameplate on the tidy desk indicated that the man's name was J.C. Adams.

Mr. Adams removed from his jacket pocket a worn cigarette case and extracted a cigarette that appeared to be monogrammed in the area under his fingers. "Welcome, gentlemen," he began. "It is an honor to meet you at last, Mr. Holmes, and you as well, Doctor. Chicanery and robbery is certainly a nasty business, and it is unfortunate we have been fated to meet under such circumstances. If you would care to share a smoke with me before we delve into the matter at hand, I can have my secretary run to get you whatever you would like."

Dispensing with pleasantries, Holmes brusquely turned his attention to the problem that had commanded his attention all morning long. "Will you lead us to the vault at once?" he asked.

Mr. Adams set down his cigarette and struggled to get to his feet. Taking hold of his cane, he got himself into motion and led us to the vault. Not being his physician, I was unsure of his exact condition, but I surmised that it was muscular in nature.

Reaching the vault, Mr. Adams clicked his cane down on the floor twice in apparent frustration and said, "I truly hope that you can get to the root of the matter, Mr. Holmes."

"That is certainly my intention, sir," Holmes replied. "And if you will excuse me, there is work to be done."

Mr. Adams turned immediately in acquiescence before Holmes said, "Has a proper inventory been completed yet?"

Shaking his head, Mr. Adams replied, "No. As you and the doctor have no doubt noted, I am limited in my efforts, I'm afraid, and I did not feel it prudent to allow anyone else in the vault until the Yard sent for you."

"A wise choice, sir," was the only comment that Holmes could muster before he lost himself for the better part of an hour in the minutiae of his examinations. Every corner of the room found itself under the magnified gaze of my friend, and he spent a considerable amount of time investigating the vault door itself. The few statements that escaped him under his breath led me to believe that there was not much to be found.

Exiting the bank, Holmes said, "It is like the others, Watson. Wholly unremarkable—and yet!—exceedingly remarkable just the same."

"The vault looked perfectly full to me," I said, wishing I had just a stack of the currency I saw inside that room which could have paid the debts of some small nations.

Holmes nodded in agreement, "It was indeed. Though, it is a several pieces lighter now than it was when we entered."

He patted his jacket pocket, and I was hoping beyond hope that he had not done what he was intimating.

"Do not let your heart be troubled," he said with a curt laugh. "I have not resorted to such means lightly. The storm you weathered upon waking at that late hour was the fruits of my labor this morning. I feel that an examination of the contents of each vault is necessary, but not under the gaze of those buttoned-up number crunchers whose only care is the lining of their own coffers. Thus, the transportation of a sampling of each vault's contents to Baker Street is of the utmost importance. And before you chastise me, please check your own pockets."

I did so and could not help but laugh. "Unbelievable." Departing from Cox and Co., the carriage began its circuitous journey to what was to be its penultimate destination. Perhaps I had been mistaken about Holmes's uneasiness after all, I thought. I looked out the window of the carriage and saw the sun beginning to fall behind a new accumulation of dark grey clouds, and I feared that we were all to be buried alive again by nightfall.

✳✳✳

The remainder of the afternoon provided no more useful information and was for all intents and purposes rather dull. The final two banks were not dissimilar to the situation that we had encountered at Cox and Co., though it does not do me credit to inform my readers that I became involved in a heated exchange with one most particularly offensive banker.

By the time that we reached Baker Street, the wind began to howl wildly in its course around the snow, which had begun to fall heavily. The light of the gas lamps once more showed the way for anyone who cared to find their way through the tempest, and I was extremely delighted to find myself in my armchair near the fire.

Holmes took to his studies immediately, and I knew better than to ask any questions during such an intense scrutiny. But it was he who broke the silence after a couple of hours had passed.

"If I am not mistaken, we have a visitor." Holmes said. "Enter!"

The door to our rooms opened slowly, and in walked a young boy who could only be one of those street urchins that Holmes was always so ready to employ in his efforts. The boy was a wee bit on the shorter side and could not have been more than seven or eight years of age. His face was covered in uneven layers of dirt and soot, and an unruly collection of blonde hair escaped from underneath a ratty cloth cap which looked like it had been through all of the wars in human history. The boy saluted Holmes and awaited his marching orders.

"Ah, Little One," Holmes said endearingly. "Prompt as always. You know, Watson, she really has been a great asset to me since my return to the art of detection. And, as it happens, she is particularly adept at trailing oblivious doctors by foot."

Feeling like a Neanderthal, I began to process the information in my mind so as to be up to speed with the others in the room. The dirt on the child's face was intentionally applied to hide that fact that she was of the fairer sex. After all, it was dangerous enough for the boys who made up that motley band of ragamuffins Holmes so titled the Baker Street Irregulars to be out on errands for the great detective, let alone a little girl.

"Holmes!" I shouted. "You mean to say that this is who was following me?"

"Bravo, Watson," he said jestingly. "Your deductive skills are certainly improving. Please pardon my white lie last evening. Little One is skilled at remaining unseen and unheard, and she will certainly need to put those talents to use this evening since Wiggins is away keeping watch over our dear landlady."

Before I could interject, the girl began speaking with Holmes. "Wha'ever ya need, Mr. 'Olmes," she said proudly. "You can count on me."

"I must warn you," Holmes said, with a dire look on his face. "Though it will appear that you are in the safest of environs, you must remember to be ever-vigilant."

"I's always the careful sort, Mr. 'Olmes."

Extracting a guinea and a scrap of paper from his pocket, Holmes walked over to the girl and knelt down in front of her.

"You must return here immediately after your complete your mission, is that clear?"

Saluting him, she grabbed the items from his hands and was off before

"Ah, Little One. Prompt as always."

I could register what had happened.

"I am not sure where to begin, Holmes." I started. "Why does Mrs. Hudson need watching? Surely, she is in no present danger."

After acquiring his favorite pipe and filling it with a considerable amount of shag tobacco, he sat down in his chair and smoked it silently for the next few minutes. Setting his pipe down, he disappeared into his bedroom and returned with a small stack of clippings from the *Times*. He dropped the papers on my lap and made his way back to his chair. Reading through them quickly, I found numerous horrible stories, the most remarkable of which were of a suicidal broker who had severed his own jugular, an apparent prostitute who had died of strangulation and was left on a train platform, and a revered army commander who had died of a heart attack.

"He has returned, Watson," Holmes said mysteriously as he stared into the fire.

"Who has returned, Holmes?"

"The proof is all there, don't you see it? It is all there, hidden in plain sight in the printed text of the periodicals!"

"Forgive me, Holmes, but I don't see what any of this has to do with banks or really what these situations have to do with one another at all."

"How obtuse you can be sometimes, Watson. Must I really have to digress into such tedious explanations of the facts when it should be obvious to anyone what is happening here?"

"If you would like me to converse with you on the subject, it would be beneficial to me to have a rudimentary understanding of what it is we are actually speaking about."

"Professor Moriarty!" Holmes exclaimed. "He has returned, and I cannot for the life of me grasp how that can be so."

I admit that my heart skipped several beats before I could find the gumption to reply. "That is impossible, Holmes. You yourself told me that you saw him collide violently with solid rock before his final descent into the abyss of the Reichenbach Falls. And I must say that it is really unlike you to be more absorbed by the ghosts of the past than the problems of the present."

With his hands steepled once more before him, he willed his stare further into the fire, almost as though he were a seer trying to conjure a vision from the flickering flames. "But there is no mistaking him, is there? The hallmarks are clear."

I tried unsuccessfully to question him further on the matter for the next half hour, but he would say no more, other than that more light would be shed on the subject once Little One returned from her travels. Seeing no use in trying to pry open the palace of his mind, I poured myself a brandy and nestled into the comfort of my chair and began to flip through the pages of a new novel I had been neglecting. In this state of suspension we sat, hearing nothing from the outside world but the screaming of the wind. I confess that I was uneasy about that poor girl being out there in such conditions, but we are each given our respective lot in life, and that was hers.

After more than two hours had passed, Holmes began pacing in front of the fireplace in a most impatient manner. Like the pendulum of a clock, he moved back and forth and back again until I began to feel dizzy trying to keep up with the constant motion. The twentieth pass completed, he stopped cold, nodding to himself in obvious approval of a conclusion he had just reached.

"We have no choice," he said resolutely. "We must move quickly if we are to ensure Little One's safety."

Within seconds, we found ourselves lost in the blustering wind of night. Try as we might, we could not make out anything more than a meter ahead of us, as the snow continued to fall heavily and drift in the gusts. I followed Holmes as closely as I could, but after a time, I began to lag slightly behind. Not wanting to get lost in the snow globe that our city had become, I attempted to double my efforts and closed the gap considerably.

When I was finally a couple of paces from Holmes, the unmistakable report of rifle fire devoured our senses and echoed like an explosion off of the nearby buildings. To this day, I am still not sure what streets we were traversing when it happened, but I am certain that Holmes could provide a detailed accounting of our steps if such a request were to be made. At that moment, the only thing of which I was aware was the gouge that had been created in the bricks that had been decimated by our unknown assailant's large-caliber round. I can only assume that the bullet had passed through the space between Holmes and me. Sensing the need for expediency, my friend grabbed my arm and began to lead me on at breakneck speed down the twists and turns of back alleys and streets that I could not possibly find again on the clearest of days if I tried to do so.

Before long, we slipped into the side door of what looked to be an old and decrepit red brick building, and I followed Holmes up three flights of stairs to the front of a heavy oak door. Stopping dead in his tracks, Holmes waved me back down to the previous landing. His eyes darted in every direction as he made his way cautiously toward the door. Nailed to the middle of the door was what looked to be a folded letter closed by an ornate black wax seal. Holmes plucked the paper from the nail tore it open immediately. The missive read as follows:

> Mr. Holmes,
>
> It is not safe for you here, but then it is not safe for you anywhere in London. There is really nowhere that you can go now. I have been observing you of late, and it has been incredibly disheartening for me to find your mind to have become so frail and your manner so complacent. I myself am feeling quite well. Perhaps my recovery will be exactly what you need to recover from your morose state. You will be seeing me soon.
>
> - J.M.

In the time that it took us to read one short message, we had found ourselves transported back in time to my home all those years ago, and I stood motionless waiting for Holmes to tell me that he had to close some imaginary set of shutters on the non-existent windows for fear of air guns. But Holmes did not survive dangerous situations with such spectacular wanderings of the imagination, and as would be expected, he was in this case quick to action.

"There is a hidden exit to this building, and we must get there in seconds if we are to have a chance at escape."

To our surprise, we did not encounter any resistance in the street below, and I once again found myself lost in a maze of twists and turns, racing along more roads and throughways than I knew existed. The second building we entered seemed to be abandoned, and I was confident that we had finally reached some form of sanctuary in which we could take a moment to catch our breath. Alas, my thoughts were little more than optimistic musings in the middle of a firefight, as we found yet another missive nailed to the door to which Holmes had taken me. The contents read much the same as the first, and it was clear that battle lines had been drawn.

Never one to be upstaged, Holmes turned to me and said confidently, "He is not as clever as he thinks. For there is one place that should be open to us yet!"

Within three quarters of an hour, we found ourselves approaching a foreboding manor on the outskirts of town. It was almost unnoticeable in the thick of the storm, as the black bricks seemed to blend in with the darkness behind it. The spires stood a menacing watch over the gothic showcase in which we were now fully engrossed. As we reached the steps of the manor, we slowed our speed, and Holmes produced a large key that I had never seen before. There was no missive nailed to this door, a positive sign if our previous experiences were any indication. Holmes inserted the key into the keyhole, and sure enough, the door clicked open, and we were inside the foyer in the blink of an eye. Clearly, Holmes had been here before, and he led me into the sitting room and prepared a fire.

"Rest here, Watson," Holmes said. "I will be back downstairs directly."

With that, Holmes disappeared from the room, and I was left with far more questions than I had any answers. Deciding to heed Holmes's advice, I sat down in a comfortable leather armchair, absorbed the warmth of the fire, and began to take in my surroundings. The room was subtly but impressively adorned, and there was a piano in the corner opposite me. The walls had built-in bookshelves, and the collection appeared to be arranged more meticulously than one would find any library's corresponding stacks to be. Eventually, my eyes settled on the mantle of the fireplace in front of me, specifically a framed picture of what appeared to be a husband, wife, and child. They appeared perfectly at peace with the world, and that was a feeling that comforted me in that moment of anxious fear. I stood up and walked over to the mantle to examine the photograph further.

The photograph was faded, and I struggled at first to make a more detailed examination of it. I could not shake the feeling that I had met the gentleman in the photograph previously; he very well could have been a previous patient of mine. He was tall, thin, and he wore round black spectacles. To the man's left stood a woman whose beauty could not be hidden, no matter the condition of the photograph. She had all of the features that a man desires in the fairer sex, and her hair was pulled up in a lovely, haphazard way around her face. In the middle of the two stood a little girl. I smiled at the photograph and wished that Mary and I had had the opportunity to have children. As happy as I had been for Holmes to have come back from the dead, I had been just as sorrowful to realize that Mary would have no such return to this world. Sitting down, I rested my head back against the chair and then jumped up suddenly.

While it may be fair for Holmes to say that I do not possess an incredible deductive prowess, I had more moments than he would like to give me credit for. In looking at the photograph again, it was all so obvious now, and to say that I was shocked would be the understatement of our time. The man underneath the disguise was Holmes himself, and the woman next to him none other than Irene Adler. As to who the child was, I could not yet say, but I had my suspicions that we were searching for her this very night. I had no idea how the photograph could have been taken, but I had no doubt that Holmes had devised some clever way of manufacturing it from multiple images.

I have said time and time again that Holmes had no room in his makeup for romantic entanglements due to the effect that he felt that such concerns had on one's rationality and reason, and I hold to that general assertion. Whether it was a notion of my own brought on by the ghost of Mary or just my own exhausted hope for my solitary friend, I cannot say, but in that moment, I wondered if there was a small part of Holmes that wished that he could have had a family such as the one depicted in the daguerreotype that lay before me rather than the isolationistic lifestyle that he had chosen for himself.

Hearing his footfalls on the steps, I sat back down in the chair. When he entered the room, I could see that he had transformed himself into the man in the photograph.

"I hope to return within a few hours, Watson," he said. "You will be safe here. And thankfully, no one will be looking for one Jonathan Stone on the streets of London."

"Godspeed, Holmes," I said, not knowing what else to say. "And I demand an explanation of all of this upon your return."

To my surprise, he was able to force a smile. "Good old, Watson." Then he was gone into the darkness, and I was left to wonder. Before long, the exhaustion overtook me, and, try as I might, I soon lost the war and sleep overtook me.

✳✳✳

The next day, I awoke to the familiar sight of my friend, sans disguise, sitting in the armchair opposite me, his cold, grey eyes fixed in a perpetual state of intense concentration. The dim glow of the light of early morning silhouetted his angular features in such a way that I could not help but be reminded of the vigil that we had held in the empty house across from the sanctum sanctorum that was Holmes's beloved Baker Street. But now was not then, and in the present, I wondered about Little One, where Holmes had gone, what time he had returned, and whether or not his travels had been fruitful. Upon sensing my waking, he blinked and turned to me, and it is not an understatement to say that his look was grave indeed. I tried to formulate the first of my numerous questions, but, as was his custom, he took center stage and delivered a brief monologue, the first of two that morning, that shook me to my very core.

"She is in a safe place now, Watson," Holmes began solemnly. "But due to my actions, she lies in a state in which no child should ever find themselves. It took me several hours to trace her movements, and in the end I found her on the doorstep of Baker Street with only her little broken face peering out from the pile of snow that had accumulated in the night. She was still breathing, though just barely, and at once I set off to bring her to refuge. Even with the storm, I quickly made my way to Diogenes, and there she remains, under careful watch of a team of Mycroft's best physicians."

He removed from his pocket a crumpled message and held it up, saying "On the way to Diogenes, she spoke little, but even in her condition, that poor girl's singular goal was to relay to me the location of the information she had collected. She did not fail me."

There and then he became silent and walked around the room with his hands clasped behind his back. I wanted to say something, but I found that words had completely escaped me in that moment. I continued to watch him, wondering about the machinations that were occurring inside of his head. Before long, he sat back down in his armchair.

"I have tried, I truly have," Holmes began again, his hands once more steepled before him. "However, it troubles me to think that the reality of this situation may be beyond the scope of my reason. The pieces have been placed before me, and regardless of their arrangement, they do not correspond with what I know to be the truth. Moriarty cannot be, and yet, he is. From the outer darkness of those blackest of memories that we shared those years ago, my dear fellow, Moriarty lingers like an incurable plague dismantling those in his path from the inside out."

He stopped for a moment, a grim grin forming on his face. "But to be sure, we must venture into the lion's den, Watson. It is there and only there that we can find the clue that is tugging at the edge of my consciousness. I hope that I am not speaking out of turn in assuming that you will accompany me, my dear fellow. You are more than within your rights to remain here, and I would not think any less of you if you were to do so."

Standing up, I shrugged on my jacket, patted my jacket pocket proudly, and asked, "Where does one find a lion's den in London, Holmes?"

Within the half hour, we found ourselves hidden in an alley across from a nondescript white building. The city had returned to life following the night's barrage, and we could see the streams of passersby making their way along both sides of the street while cab drivers tried in vain to dodge the snow mounds and the citizens who were navigating in and out of the thoroughfare without regard for anyone else but themselves. Just as he had in the stairwell the evening before, Holmes constantly looked this way and that, trying to get the lay of the land in the way that only he could. Even with such an endless flood of information before him, I had no doubt that he had already determined the secrets of everyone that passed. If we had been in different circumstances, I am confident that he would have revealed that the woman in the wrinkled purple dress had just come from some sordid affair, that the one-toothed cab driver with the severely chapped face had fallen asleep outdoors last evening after consuming four bottles of whiskey, and that the young man who wore a suit that cost more than the down-payment for my former home was embezzling funds from the firm for which he consulted.

Instead, he said, "In my estimation, Watson, we are not being watched, which leads me to believe that we were successful in our efforts at going underground last night. Even so, it would still behoove us to be as cautious as possible now. In thirty seconds, that brougham down there will be directly in front of us. Before it gets here, I will cross into the courtyard over there. You will need to get into the brougham, close the door, and slip out the other side when you are at least two streets down from here. By then, I will have unlocked that side door for you—that is, if I encounter no resistance inside."

I was unable to process this information, and I found myself entering the brougham just as Holmes had instructed. Not knowing what other destination to give, I told the driver that I would like to go to the address for my billiards club. Perhaps my gambling had gotten out of hand after all, I laughed to myself. At the time Holmes had suggested, I left a sovereign on the seat, departed through the other door, and tried to look inconspicuous as I made my way to the side door of the building into which Holmes had entered. Upon my reaching the door, I was pulled by an invisible hand and dragged inside by my coat collar.

"I apologize for startling you, my dear fellow, but that vendor on the corner struck me as odd, and I had only a moment to get you in here without anyone noticing the door opening."

"Where are we, Holmes?"

"This, Watson, is the home of Professor Moriarty."

"For heaven's sake, Holmes! What in blazes are we doing here?"

"I have told you before that I have been in these rooms three times, so I know my way around. The building appears to be empty at the moment, but it is still immaculately maintained, which is telling. The air has an almost medicinal smell to it, does it not?"

"Is it not possible that you could have opened the door and been face to face with the man himself?"

"Possible, yes, but not probable. I highly doubt that he has been back here since he trailed us to Switzerland. The message from Porlock that Little One obtained did confirm that the professor's belongings have remained here. More than that, however, Porlock would not say. Now we are here, and there is one thing in particular that I wish to examine."

He led me to a study which was not dissimilar to the room in which I had found rest overnight. A large desk stood in the middle of the room, and all of the items on it were arranged most meticulously, with not a piece of foolscap out of place. The only imperfections I could see in the whole room were sets of two notches in certain parts of the floor. Surrounding us were rows of beautifully carved bookshelves that depicted scenes of the great battles of bygone ages, and on the wall behind the desk hung the infamous painting that Holmes had mentioned to me once. Unfortunately, I had no more time to capture the image of the room in my mind, as Holmes interrupted me.

"It would stand to reason that a man would write in his own hand those thoughts which are most important to him, would it not?"

"Yes, I suppose it would."

"Now, you will recall that I have seen different documentation and cheques that the professor had endorsed. What was peculiar about those cheques is that no two signatures matched one another. Therefore, even if Scotland Yard were to have the capability to ensnare him, he would still be able to maintain a plausible level of deniability. There is a cunning brilliance about disguising your hand even in the most mundane of your affairs."

"I fail to see what this has to do with anything, Holmes."

After he finished speaking, he clearly turned his attention elsewhere and began scouring the spines of the books on the shelves. Most of the selections were titles that would only be of interest to the most invested of scholars, and I imagined that many of those had only been read by a handful of people in the world—whether or not the rest of us were missing

"For heaven's sake, Holmes! What in blazes are we doing here?"

out on some gnostic secret, us laymen would never know, and considering whose rooms I was in at that time, I was fine with that notion. Finally, Holmes extracted a volume and held the book by the spine and extended it out towards me like a drunken preacher on the street corner.

"Behold, Watson, the first printed edition of *The Dynamics of An Asteroid*, that seminal work which propelled Moriarty into the stratosphere of academia."

I realized that we had not come all this way to simply marvel at a copy of a mathematical treatise, so I waited for him to continue as he flipped through the pages of the text.

"I learned long ago that inventors and the intellectual elite, no matter their accomplishments, are never satisfied with the final result of their greatest work. Thus, they spend their lives trying to tinker with brilliance. What they fail to understand is that their talents could be better served creating again rather than trying to constantly perfect that which has already been created and perfected. Such is the case with Professor Moriarty. Look here."

Holmes turned the book in my direction, and I could see numbers, symbols, and words scrawled in the margins of every page in the book. Reaching into the inside pocket of his jacket, he withdrew the missive that we had found on the door of his first safe house. He set the missive down next to the book and began an intensive study with his magnifying glass.

The silence of that room was deafening, and I prayed that we would soon be on our way out of that dreadful place. Suddenly, he slammed his magnifying glass down on the desk, and his face assumed a nasty scowl.

"What a fool I have been, Watson!" he growled. "How many times have I said that it is a fundamental flaw for an investigator to reach conclusions without the proper data to support those very same conclusions? Supposition and conjecture are futile. Facts are what matter, and facts we shall have. I know that I have asked you this when I have erred in the past, but please remember this occasion and remind me of it if ever I become veiled in the cloak of arrogance."

To my surprise, he took a seat behind the professor's desk and pulled out his cigarette case. He motioned for me to do the same, and so I reclined uncomfortably in the seat opposite his.

"You recall my monograph on handwriting?"

"Yes."

"Good. Then you have no doubt in my abilities to make a proper comparison of documents to determine their provenance and legitimacy."

"No, certainly not."

"Then I tell you with confidence three things. First, the handwriting in the margins of this book and the missive that we found matches that of Professor Moriarty, of that there is no doubt. Second, he did *not* pen the aforementioned missive. Finally, you and I can both rejoice over the fact that Professor Moriarty *is and has been* quite dead at the bottom of the Reichenbach Falls for some time now."

So stupefied was I then, I was convinced that he had finally lost his mind. "Holmes," I exclaimed with disbelief, "that does not make any sense. How could the handwriting match that of Moriarty's so exactly and it not be his?"

Holmes nonchalantly took a drag of his cigarette and knocked the ash onto the top of the desk. He must have sensed that I had grown incredibly impatient at this point in our adventure and finally brought me up to speed with him—or, so he thought.

"The answer to that, Watson, is that there is a great mind at work here, one who would have me chasing ghosts instead of he who is clearly of the most diabolical kind."

"That is not an answer, Holmes."

"Tut-tut, Watson, frustration does not become you," he said. "Nevertheless, I hope that we shall know all before we are through. Every stage of this investigation must be reexamined from the beginning, and every clue must be viewed through an entirely different lens than the fool's lens that I had used previously."

He extinguished his cigarette in the middle of the table and said, "Although the professor is dead, we are still in very real danger. The bullet that passed between us and the current condition of Little One are indicative of that fact."

He said no more, and after ensuring that we were not under surveillance, he hailed a cab, and we found ourselves on the way to Baker Street. Breathing a sigh of relief that Holmes had at last had a moment of clarity, I could not be happier to be heading back to the familiar confines of 221B.

※ ※ ※

Upon our return to Baker Street, I found my mind at odds with itself, the events of the last few days and, in particular, the last few hours weighing quite heavily on me. The paradox of Moriarty was a conundrum that I could not begin to understand in that moment, and Holmes was not of the mind to dispel such feelings, as he typically did not allow himself to be consumed by the fleeting emotions of a situation. However, I could not help but recognize that when he had been sure of Moriarty's return at the start of our journey, that thought had shaken him to his core. But as only he could, Holmes had in one instant grasped the reality of the situation and immediately shifted his focus from the impossible to that which remained. This ultimately left his great mind and his reason unburdened, and to say that he was now on the offensive would be to put it lightly.

While I knew full well that I could still be of use in this matter before the end, I also knew that my friend's talents and processes were what were of immense importance at that moment. Thus, I was left to my own devices, doing little other than relaxing in front of the newly roaring fire. Eventually, I decided to begin a thorough accounting of the events as they had unfolded so far—the life of a scribe, indeed. In full disclosure, I would be remiss if I did not acknowledge that my true hope was that I might glean some hidden fact from the words that I scrawled wearily along the page.

Meanwhile, Holmes immersed himself in far more important matters, namely a systematic examination of the currency with which he had so coolly absconded. After a quick rearranging of his various ongoing experiments, he spread out across his chemical table the numerous coins and proceeded to actively inspect each piece with such an intense scrutiny that I doubted he would be finished until the wee hours of the following morning. Just as he had in the vault, he would let slip occasional mumblings, but that was all I heard from him for some time. Every now and then, I would glance over and hope that the turning point would come, but as the old wives' tales suggest, a watched detective does not deduce. Not surprisingly then, it was not until my head had begun to loll back against my armchair that Holmes's revelation was made.

"The genius of it, Watson!" Holmes exclaimed, the sharp clap of his hands echoing off of the walls. "Whoever has devised this scheme is a worthy adversary indeed. Our friend Lestrade must count himself fortunate that I have not yet retired to beekeeping on the Sussex Downs."

"Out with it, man! What have you found, Holmes?"

He motioned me over to the table and directed my attention to the guinea that lay beneath the gaze of his microscope. After I viewed the first coin, he replaced it with a second, and it looked virtually identical to me. We completed similar exercises with the sovereigns and shillings, and I was still at a loss as to what he was driving at.

"Would it surprise you to know that certain pieces that you have just examined are counterfeit?"

"Not particularly, Holmes. I assumed that you wanted to examine the currency for inconsistencies. Therefore, it was only logical to assume that you thought that the currency was not legitimate."

"Good, Watson. We will make a detective out of you yet," he said. "But in stating the obvious, you failed to comprehend the crucial piece of information that I just relayed to you a moment ago. A thorough inspection has shown that it is only *certain* pieces that are counterfeit, not all. Now, one may make the argument that counterfeit currency could have made its way into the pockets of our unsuspecting citizens before settling into the hands of our banking institutions undetected. However, this appears to be something else entirely, as the characteristics of these pieces lead me to suspect that they were all produced by the same hand and deliberately inserted into each of the banks. Notice the almost hidden mark in the edge of this guinea here. That mark is the signature of the forger that created it, and no one looking at that coin would ever be the wiser, probably mistaking it for a ding in the course of everyday transactions. However, for us, that mark is everything. That I am not familiar with this particular mark does surprise me, as I thought that I was acquainted with the majority of the forgers and counterfeiters in London."

"That is truly amazing, Holmes," I said. "Though, I don't understand what purpose this would serve. If the counterfeit coins are this good, why not just manufacture them and spend them?"

"Surely you are not that obtuse, my dear fellow," he said. "If someone could replace legitimate currency with the fake variety, would they not be able to siphon out as much of the real stuff as they wanted? To be sure, it takes some work, but as I said, it is all undetectable. And then where does all of the power lay?"

"I still don't understand. Someone had to break into bank vaults—six of them, in fact—in order to pull off this ruse, did they not? Is that not far riskier than spending a counterfeit sovereign?"

"You are not seeing the bigger picture here, Watson. There is something far more nefarious than counterfeiting and theft at work here. I am sure of it."

"So what is our next course of action, Holmes?"

He made his way over to the mantle, withdrew his jack knife from the correspondence pile, and strolled over to the window overlooking the street below.

"The darkness has settled in nicely, and I think that the remainder of our evening would be best spent in the vault of the first bank that was disrupted."

"Really, Holmes. You must be out of your mind. Scotland Yard will be out in full force, and I highly doubt that even they will be receptive to your wanting to snoop around bank vaults at this hour."

"We do not have a choice, and what Scotland Yard doesn't know will not hurt them. The banks did not trade yesterday or today due to the fear and uncertainty they felt about their respective fortunes, but they will certainly do so tomorrow and by then, our evidence will be all but lost. It is vital that we determine the total amount of counterfeit currency in that vault. Time permitting, we must attempt to do so at the other banks as well, but beggars cannot be choosers. Quick, there's not a moment to lose."

He slammed the jack knife into the stack of correspondence on the mantle, and then we were off once again, racing into the black of night toward the ever-treacherous future that lay before us.

※※※

Despite my apprehension, Holmes and I slipped unseen into the bank. I could not help but notice that the constables on patrol were rather lax and predictable in their beat, so much so that even their increased presence would not have stopped a crying infant from making its way unnoticed into the institution they were tasked with protecting. Little wonder then, that six banks had been so infiltrated, I thought. And so it was that my friend and I found ourselves at what was to be the beginning of the end of our adventure.

Once we were sure that the coast was clear inside, I opened the shutter of the dark lantern, and Holmes made quick work of the locking mechanism on the vault door. The door swung open silently, and we entered the monetary mausoleum. The swiftness with which Holmes undertook his examination was a sight to behold, and as the candlelight of the dark lantern flickered, I marveled at the drama of the shadow play that was being acted out by my friend on the wall behind him. I stood transfixed, watching the shapes on the wall, and I was troubled that others could only imagine such greatness from the black and white text of my printed tales. I knew that it was rare that I could take a moment in the midst of the action to reflect on the surrealism of it all, and I hoped that there was not some greater darkness that would overtake us in the end. Such pessimism would seem unwarranted as long as my friend was on the case, but even if the professor was gone, his shadow remained—though, perhaps the silence of my surroundings had led to an unquiet mind.

The hours passed in this way, and scribbling the final tally in a tattered ledger, Holmes turned silently, left the vault, and began a search of the building for the accounting records. In recounting this tale, I would ask that my readers forgive our entering into the land of the lawless, as it was our sifting through numerous registers and financial transactions that finally put us on the right track.

Of course, the revelation came from Holmes in his typically dramatic fashion. Throwing the record book in the air so that it could crash onto the desk before him, he closed his eyes and listened to the sound echo off of the walls until it faded into the silence of the night. Whether it was the interplay of the shadow and the light I could not say, but I would testify in a court of law that I never saw his face more determined than it was at that moment.

"Chasing ghosts indeed, Watson!" Holmes said. "Look at the final accounting at the bottom of the column there."

As I reviewed the records, Holmes proceeded to withdraw from his jacket pocket the ledger book containing his calculations of the counterfeit currency within the vault. A comparison of the two showed that the figure reflected on the page of his ledger book was an exact match to that of the number showing in the column of the bank records.

"Amazing, Holmes," was the only reply that I could muster.

"If you have been paying attention, you now understand that this account was one of Moriarty's bank accounts, a fact that really should have been obvious to me much earlier. He is rebuilding Moriarty's empire, Watson, brick by brick! And in doing so, he is assuming for himself the mantel of that which should never be again. Therefore, we must not allow this sinister line of succession to continue."

"It is almost four o'clock, Holmes. We must go now if we wish to reach any of the other banks."

"No, Watson, that will not be necessary. I know now exactly what we will find there. I have something else in mind. You must return to Baker Street. Be sure to take all necessary precautions, and I will join you by midday."

My travels back to Baker Street proved uneventful, and I found myself anxious to take action. I spent my time cleaning and reloading my Webley to ensure that it was ready if called upon. It did not seem like more than an hour had passed, but before I knew it, it was noon. While no one may know the day or hour of the Lord's return, Holmes himself was nothing if not prompt. So it was that the great detective threw open the door of our rooms before the bells had finished tolling the twelve o'clock hour, and it was a good sign that he appeared to be quite satisfied with the results of his mysterious errands.

"It is all coming together now, Watson," he said, sitting down in his chair. "But right now, we can do nothing but wait. What do you say to a lunch at Simpson's, my dear fellow?"

The growling of my stomach was answer enough, and we spent the remainder of the afternoon eating an excellent roast beef, imbibing of a brandy of a particularly fine vintage, and discussing matters unrelated to the events of the last few days. It was an enjoyable enough scene, and even though I wanted answers, I was not about to ask for them. I had no doubt that Holmes read my occasionally unsettled thoughts as they passed through my mind, but he did not remark on them.

Several hours later, dusk began to set in, and we returned to our rooms once more. When we reached the front door, a particularly overzealous deliveryman accosted us. After a quick exchange in which the man handed several telegrams to Holmes, he was just as quickly lost in the crowd.

"From Mycroft," Holmes remarked as he read the first telegram. "Little One seems to be holding her own and should soon be on the road to recovery."

"That is excellent news, Holmes," I said.

He nodded his head in agreement and said, "Yes, we were bound for some good news, were we not?"

He continued to review the other messages as we ascended the stairs to our rooms. When I opened the door, I was shocked to find a man sitting in Holmes's chair with his back to us.

"Who are you, sir?" I yelled, drawing my revolver. "And what are you doing in our rooms?"

Holmes stepped forward and placed his arm in front of me in a sign of warning. He motioned for me to hold my ground while he slowly advanced on our uninvited guest. After navigating around the perimeter of the room so as to have a clear view of the man, Holmes laughed and then shook his head. To my astonishment, the intruder had no response to the presence of the great detective—in fact, he did not move or make a sound of any kind.

"I believe it is safe for you to lower your weapon, Watson," Holmes said.

"Unless London has been overrun by a swarm of the undead, this man can do you no harm now."

We both crossed the room to the chair in which the man sat, and we found his throat slit from ear to ear, the entirety of his torso covered in his lifeblood. If that was not macabre enough, we found a telegram card nailed forcefully into the frontal bone of the man's skull. It read:

> Mr. Holmes. Here is your forger. I am done playing games with you. You and Dr. Watson are invited to my residence tomorrow evening for our denouement. I expect you at 7 o'clock.

"How morbid, Holmes," I said. "I have not seen a sight like this since that Devil's Foot affair."

Somehow, Holmes smiled and said, "My efforts this morning have clearly affected our adversary most remarkably. It seems that he has become impatient and grows weary of his own schemes."

"He sounds crazed if you ask me."

"I assure he is very much sane."

"How do you know, Holmes? You speak now as if you know who is behind all of this."

"The who should be clear, Watson, but there are still particulars of the why that require clarification. You should know that I have a trick up my sleeve yet. Rest assured that all will be revealed tomorrow evening."

But I did not rest that night, and as I stared into the darkness above my bed, I hoped that this waking nightmare would soon be over.

※※※

The next morning and afternoon passed by in so painfully slow a manner that I was convinced that I would be dead of sheer anticipation before the events of the coming evening set in. Holmes himself seemed rather content and after a brief absence from our rooms, he returned and busied himself with a new chemical experiment and a rearrangement of some of the old papers that comprised the records of those cases in which he had been involved before our partnership had begun. I hoped that was not some last act of getting his affairs in order, but for his part, Holmes did not seem the least bit concerned. Troubled as I was, I tried to take solace in that fact. Besides, however willing my friend may have been to give his own life to rid the world of Moriarty, I doubted very strongly that he would be so willing to do so to exorcise the professor's ghost from the soul of our city.

At a quarter past six, Holmes hailed a brougham, and we began our trip to the end of the line. During the ride, Holmes said nothing, and I was left to watch the city pass by before my eyes. Half an hour passed, and I felt my heart palpitate uncomfortably at the sight of Professor Moriarty's home. After several minutes, we stepped out of the cab, and Holmes paid the cabbie most generously, telling him to wait at a nearby pub for the next several hours until his services would be needed again. This physician's mind wondered at the future functionality of this particular cabbie after his detective-sanctioned binge.

We could not see any light emanating from the inside of the building, but there could be no doubt that someone was awaiting our arrival. The front gate was open, and Holmes pointed to the front door, which had been left slightly ajar. Checking his pocket watch, Holmes lit a cigarette and casually smoked it, seeming as though he were on an evening stroll.

"Holmes, can we get this business underway?" I asked.

He continued to smoke until the clock reached seven, and, returning his watch to his pocket, he said, "Watson, it is rather presumptuous to think that our host would want us to barge into his home before our appointed time. But the hour has come. Follow me."

Once inside, we could see flickering light coming from a room not far down the hallway, and I recalled from our previous excursion that the room was the professor's study. Following Holmes, I patted nervously at my jacket pocket, ready to draw my revolver at a moment's notice. Reaching the door of the study, Holmes pushed the door open, and we entered into that sinister sanctuary. My breath caught in my throat when I saw the man sitting at the professor's desk.

"Ah, Mr. Holmes, Dr. Watson," Mr. Adams said coldly, taking a drag of his cigarette. "Welcome to my home. Please, have a seat."

We did not move, and he continued, "Oh, from the look on your friend's face, Mr. Holmes, I can see that you have not yet brought him into your full confidence regarding this matter."

"If he did not have my full confidence," Holmes said matter-of-factly, "then he would not be here."

This comment set loose a fit of cold, blood curdling laughter that played demonically off of the walls. I watched as Holmes took a seat across from the man, and with much reluctance, I did the same. I wondered whether this would be the moment that Holmes took charge of the matter, but he

Holmes paid the cabbie most generously...

seemed perfectly fine with letting the conversation proceed casually.

"Watson, I introduce you to our host, Aleister Whills," Holmes said. "I must give you credit Mr. Whills, you certainly do your former mentor proud."

"I appreciate you saying that, Mr. Holmes, I really do," Whills said. "Surely a man of your intellect can see the brilliance of what I have been able to accomplish."

"Truth be told, Mr. Adams or Mr. Whills, whatever you like to be called. I don't see that you have accomplished much of anything," I remarked sarcastically.

"The truth is actually quite to the contrary, doctor, and I doubt if even Mr. Holmes has yet grasped exactly what I have been able to achieve. My work far surpasses anything that even Professor Moriarty could have dreamed of."

Shockingly, Holmes came to the professor's defense, launching into a diatribe whose aim I confess I did not see at the time. "I would disagree strongly, Mr. Whills. Despite the fact that the professor and I were very much of different minds as to the human condition, his intellectual abilities were superior to those of anyone else of this generation, including my own."

He reclined back in his chair, steepled his fingers, and continued, "But you, you appear to be nothing more than a feeble, confused young man, desperate to be counted amongst the upper echelon of cerebral achievement. However, nothing you have done to this point has shown you to be so."

At that comment, Whills's face expressed a look of such immense outrage that any onlookers would have thought that even in his limited physical state he would find the energy to dive across the desk at Holmes's throat. However, that was not to be, and in seconds, he was once more reserved and collected, and he silently smoked his cigarette, seemingly allowing Holmes to continue.

"You see, Watson, Aleister was a student of Professor Moriarty's before he lost his chair at the university. The professor, being of a particularly esoteric nature, must have seen a bit of himself in Aleister and quickly sought to foster the young man's interest in complex and highly theoretical mathematics. This is not to say that the professor had any human connection to the boy—he simply wanted to extract from his mind any ideas that he himself had not yet contemplated. So it was that Aleister worked closely with Moriarty for two years, trying to do just the same. At the end of Aleister's second year in university, Moriarty's dealings in the criminal underworld lost him his chair. While this did not affect the professor very much at all, him having his syndicate to occupy his time, it had a considerable effect on Aleister. With the professor gone, the heads of the university saw Aleister's work as dangerous, representing a nasty reminder of the past that they would much rather forget. Thus, his work was left unfinished, and he was left with the choice to either finish his schooling in the field of economics and finance, an offer the university extended unhappily, or be disbarred from the institution altogether. Aleister chose the latter and was not heard of again after completing his studies. Instead, he assumed the name of J.C. Adams and became entrenched in the banking sector."

Whills clapped his hands in mock applause and gestured to Holmes, "Please, continue, this is quite thrilling stuff."

And so Holmes continued, "In that investigation you so-titled *A Study in Scarlet*, Watson, you remarked that I lack a certain knowledge of astronomy. That description was accurate, and it actually has hindered me in this investigation. Please remind me to complete a thorough study of such areas in which I need education so this does not happen again. You see, the name J.C. Adams in long form is John Couch Adams, the famed mathematician and astronomer who was involved in the discovery of the planet Neptune. A more proper moniker for Aleister I could not imagine, nor could he, obviously. I am not certain, but I suspect that over the course of the years, he tried to correspond with Moriarty to no avail. Here was a man abandoned by the only person who understood the workings of his mind, and I came along and robbed him of any possible chance of ever collaborating with the professor again by sending him tumbling over the Reichenbach Falls. Recently, Mr. Adams took over the management of Cox and Co., a position which gave him access to some of the most intriguing documents he could have ever hoped to hold in his hands, the private papers of Sherlock Holmes which are housed in the dispatch box of John H. Watson."

"You mean to say, Holmes, that—" I started to interject.

"Yes, Watson, he intruded on your privacy and in doing so found something he did not expect to find: relics of Moriarty—those six cheques that I obtained and discussed with Mr. Mac around the time of that Birlstone affair. I regret that I did not make that connection much sooner, so sure was I that Moriarty had risen from the depths. But even so, Aleister was left with only one course of action, to manufacture events to bring me into the fold. For revenge or amusement, I still cannot say. And with that history lesson, the floor is yours, Aleister."

Whills extinguished his cigarette and stood up slowly, grasping his cane. "A seemingly perfect reconstruction, Mr. Holmes. Quite typical really of the flowery monologues that Dr. Watson includes at the end of your adventure stories. However, as I knew you would, you miss the point entirely."

He picked up a stack of papers from a table and held them up to Holmes. "These papers contain the calculations of your exact movements from the moment you first read of my actions in the newspaper. Professor Moriarty was able to trace the movements of an asteroid from an armchair, and in so doing he made me realize that I could do the same with human beings. What is it you like to say, Mr. Holmes? Data, data, data. Well, using Dr. Watson's writings as a base, I created a data set that allowed me to calculate the dynamics of the so-called 'Great Detective'. Using methods far beyond you or the doctor's comprehension, I was able to expand upon the data I was presented with and reach the true Holmes Constant and its related variables. After all, with enough data, the actions of any human being are quite predictable, are they not? As long as I could start the equation properly, the end result was all but guaranteed. That is why everywhere you went and everything you did was under my control."

"Splendid, Aleister, truly splendid," Holmes said with a grin. "See Watson, how we have been reduced to nothing more than a calculation."

"Is that not what you do, Mr. Holmes, in your supposedly brilliant deductions?" asked Whills.

"Human beings are not pieces of rock floating in space and are nothing if not unpredictable, and while my deductions are formed on the solid foundation of my observations, there have been many times where even I have been surprised."

"No, Mr. Holmes. You will not take this from me. All of this was a showcase for you to see what I am capable of. And, in truth, you must realize that you have no legal means to stop me, no evidence tying me to any of the things that you have been investigating. I have been careful. Despite my condition, I was able to pull it all off without the help of accomplices other than that forger who most likely still remains in your rooms at Baker Street. If I am not to be able to use my mathematics in the way that I intended in my youth, then I will be left with no choice but to use my talents in the furtherance of the professor's vision. With my calculations proving to be as accurate as they are, I do not see how you will be able to stop me. And our future interactions will allow me to further refine my work. And one day, people will say that, 'All is as Alesiter wills'."

"Despite your intelligence, you do not even have the capacity see how your calculations are flawed, do you? The fact that you fired a bullet at us on a certain street, and Watson and I retreated to the closest of my safe houses is not the mark of predictive genius on your part. Clearly, you considered that you might err, as you posted notices in at least five of my safe houses, and you did not even locate the place where Watson and I actually sought refuge that evening. All you proved is that you have much time to spend reviewing public records and corresponding with Colonel Moran. That your mathematical theory is sound is far from proven."

Whills slammed his cane down into the floor and growled, "This conversation is over, Mr. Holmes. I bid you and Dr. Watson good evening. Though this interaction proved more unpleasant than I had hoped, I look forward to our next meeting."

"A rather poor host you are, Aleister," Holmes said removing a cigarette from his case as he stood up from his chair. "I would have thought you would at least allow us to share a smoke before departing into the harsh cold of this winter night."

Whills forced a laugh and said, "As you wish, Mr. Holmes."

Holmes lit his cigarette and sat back down in his chair. Whills reached into his cigarette case and found it empty. He sat down at the desk, organized his stack of calculations, and removed a fresh cigarette from the drawer.

"It seems that I am lucky to have restocked my supply this morning, Mr. Holmes," Whills said. "A really fine blend you know, I will have to give you the name of my private tobacconist sometime."

Whills lit the cigarette and inhaled deeply, "Doctor, you may find it interesting that my physician has devised a method for incorporating my medicine into this commonplace habit of mine."

"How ingenious of him," I said sarcastically.

Holmes finished his cigarette and said, "Until our next meeting, Aleister."

Whills stood up and walked around the desk so that he could be face to face with Holmes. Suddenly, a look of surprise consumed his face, and he fell stiffly to the floor. From the sounds I heard, I surmised that he had broken at least five bones in the fall. To my surprise, he did not say a word or make any movements whatsoever.

"You know my methods, Mr. Whills," Holmes said with a casual arrogance as he stared at the man lying helpless on the floor. "Apply them."

With that comment, Holmes walked over to the bookcase and removed from it the professor's own copy of *The Dynamics of An Asteroid*. Seeing the rage on Whills's helpless face, Holmes tossed the book into the fire and just watched as the pages burned to ash. Walking over to the desk, Holmes picked up the stack of Whill's calculations and made a move toward the fireplace once again. Just then, he stopped and looked an almost empathetic look at the pitiable wretch on the floor. Shaking his head, he put the calculations inside of his jacket.

"Someone will be by to collect you directly, Aleister." Holmes said. "My brother has assured me that you will have a place where you will have all the time you need for your mathematical musings."

With that comment, Holmes and I departed the room and exited the building through the front door. Surprisingly, our cabbie was alert and waiting at the ready for us.

"All went as planned, Mr. Holmes?" the cabbie said.

Holmes considered and said, "Yes, I believe it did. Please ensure that Mycroft's men are sure not to break him any further. You have your instructions for his transport, yes?"

"I do, indeed, Mr. Holmes," the cabbie said.

"Excellent. I think Watson and I will take in the air of the night and make our way back to Baker Street on foot."

"As you wish, Mr. Holmes," the cabbie said.

As we passed along the streets that led us to our home, I continually cycled through the events of the night in my mind. Holmes had once again prevailed, and I felt guilty that I had ever doubted our safety.

"Now, now, Watson, don't trouble yourself," he said out of the blue. "It is only logical that the shadow of Moriarty would have made you feel that way, my dear fellow. But let us rejoice in the fact that the professor's ghost has now been put to rest."

✳ ✳ ✳

Over the course of the next week and a half, Holmes and I had no discussions about the incidents that had taken place while we were on the trail of Aleister Whills. The weather had finally started to let up, and I was once again free to resume my usual routine of tending to my patients. I was very glad to learn that my elderly patient had made it through his bout with seizures. Though he would grapple with them for the remainder of his life, I was grateful that he still had life remaining after that horrible day those weeks ago.

One afternoon, I returned to Baker Street and found that Mrs. Hudson had returned from her travels. She looked positively refreshed, no doubt because she was not sleeping with one eye open wondering what portion of the criminal underworld would be mounting a full assault on her humble abode the next day.

"Dr. Watson, it is so very good to see you again," she said with a short embrace. "How have you been these last few weeks?"

Not wanting to trouble the poor woman, I said, "I have been doing about what you would expect."

She shook her head in obvious disapproval. "No doubt that he had you out at all hours of the night without as much as a proper meal for days. Before you go upstairs, come inside and I will fix you something."

Mrs. Hudson prepared me a mix of cold cuts, scones, and tea, and within minutes I was sure that I would not eat again for weeks. As the meal concluded, Holmes began to play his violin, the sound echoing loudly even downstairs.

"Amazing that you still allow us to live here, Mrs. Hudson," I remarked with a laugh.

She smiled and said, "Who else would look after you both, my dear?"

"Who indeed?" I said. "Thank you for the meal. It was much needed after my rounds today. Do you mind if I remain here until he is finished?"

"Not at all, doctor, not at all," she said.

Suddenly, the music ceased abruptly, and Holmes yelled, "The violin is back in its case, Watson. You may return to your rooms now without the worry of further musical misadventures today."

Thankfully, my leg was feeling much better, and the stairs did not prove as difficult as they had on the night that had begun our adventure. Entering our rooms, I saw Holmes scrawling away on what looked to be his composition paper. I took a seat in my armchair and took a breath of relief that my tasks for the day had been completed. Within a few minutes, Holmes neatly folded up the stack of composition paper and placed it within an ornate envelope. He addressed the envelope and set it on the mantle.

Turning to me, he said, "That business with Aleister Whills was certainly nasty, eh, Watson?"

"He was a madman if you ask me, Holmes," I said.

"Perhaps, but I would argue that there is a small bit of psychosis in even the greatest of minds."

"Not yours, though, Holmes."

"I am not so sure of that, Watson. We have both discussed the idea that were the course of my life to have been altered, I could easily have been a master criminal. I am only glad that my talents are spent on this side of the law instead."

"Count me appreciative of that as well, Holmes. Since you are open to the topic, there is still something that is unclear to me. What exactly happened to Whills that led him to be so immobile?"

"Watson, I truly thought you were finally on the right path to thoroughly understanding the art of detection. Once I ascertained Aleister Whills's true identity, I set out at once to determine the nature of his condition and the remedy he received for it. You may recall that when he was in the guise of the bank manager, he did not offer us any of his own cigarettes. Additionally, I noted that Moriarty's study had a medicinal smell to it. Upon learning that Whills had specialty cigarettes manufactured, I realized that inhalation was the primary means by which his treatment was administered. Thus, I found a means of opportunity for disabling him should that become necessary. I snuck into his physician's rooms that morning and replaced the medicine with a paralytic agent of my own creation. From his physician's records, it did not take me long to determine Aleister's smoking habits, and I knew that he would need to smoke more heavily if he became overburdened, otherwise, his muscular pain would become most intolerable. You may have noticed how I pressed him and critiqued him from the start of our conversation so that he was not in control of himself. That he was quick to frustration was evident by the marks in the floor of the study, as he has a habit of roughly tapping his cane into the ground. If I may say so myself, I knew that I was more than capable of prolonging the conversation until he had to replenish his supply of cigarettes. And, with the victory seemingly in hand, he would not deny my request to share a smoke with him. The rest is as you know it to be."

"That is brilliant, Holmes!" I exclaimed.

He made the mocking gesture of bowing before me, and I was sure that the play had finally drawn to a close. Just then, there were two successive knocks at the door, and Holmes bade the guest to enter. I was unsure if this was to be the start of another case, but when the door opened, I was overjoyed to see Little One standing at the threshold. It appeared that she was still in rough shape, but she seemed to be on the mend and the smile that graced her face was enough to dismiss any concerns about her well-being.

"Whatcha need, Mr. 'Olmes?" Little One asked.

"Little One, yes, it is good to see you back in better spirits," he replied. "I have an important task for you."

Holmes walked over to the mantle and picked up the envelope he had set there earlier. As he walked over to hand her the envelope, I was able to see the person to whom it was addressed.

"Please make sure that this is posted at once. It has been delayed for far too long already."

Taking the envelope from him, Little One saluted him and said, "You gots it, Mr. 'Olmes."

"Little One," he began, "I realize that I never did ask you for your name. I seem to have just created a name for you based on you being the youngest of my Irregulars and that is what stuck."

"They always said that me mum called me Lily," the girl said.

"Lily it is, then," Holmes said to her endearingly.

With a final salute, she was off on her mission, and I knew that the woman on the receiving end of that letter would be happy indeed.

THE END

"The Mists of Reichenbach"

To my recollection, the first Sherlock Holmes story that I ever encountered was *The Adventure of the Red-Headed League*. I believe that I was either in elementary or junior high school, and that story was part of a short story workbook that my fellow classmates and I had to complete. While I found it to be a very interesting and clever story, I don't think that I fully understood at the time the significance and creativity of what I had read. After I graduated high school and moved on to college, I picked up a leather-bound book containing the entire Holmes canon. I proceeded to read *A Study in Scarlet*, and, though it may be heresy in Holmes circles, I freely admit that I was not a huge fan of that novel.

Several years passed, and I saw the trailer for an upcoming movie titled *Mr. Holmes*. The trailer reignited my interest in the Sherlock Holmes character, and I began reading the canonical short stories and was soon through them in no time at all. I then read *The Sign of the Four* and couldn't put it down because it was such an exciting story from beginning to end and includes all of the characteristics that make up the most classic of Holmes tales. *The Hound of the Baskervilles* was next in line, and then I finished off *The Valley of Fear* in one afternoon.

Upon my completion of the canonical adventures, I began to seek out any Holmes pastiches I could find and read them one after another (40 or 50 in a year's time according to one count). As I write this, I have countless Holmes novels and short story collections piled up in stacks not unlike those of an attorney's office. The Basil Rathbone and Nigel Bruce movies and radio tales are, of course, classics as well, and modern television interpretations like CBS's *Elementary* (which is my favorite TV interpretation of the characters—though the series starring Ronald Howard and BBC's *Sherlock* are great as well) provide great new twists and turns on the characters and plots.

I have always been told that I have an old soul, and I think that may be part of the reason that I enjoy these stories so much—they transport the reader to a different time and place and challenge him to match wits with Holmes to solve the latest mystery plaguing the foggy streets of London. Additionally, I have always tried to help people in any way that I can, so I can relate to Holmes's determination and hyper-focus when trying to resolve a situation for those clients who have sought his assistance.

In my search for pastiches, I stumbled upon a series called *Sherlock*

Holmes: Consulting Detective and really enjoyed the way that all of the different contributors interpreted the characters. Writing short stories and novels is something that I have always done as a hobby. My method of writing stories usually follows the method employed in the *Esquire* period of my favorite author, F. Scott Fitzgerald—small stories that tell a complete tale and pack an emotional punch in the span of 1000-2000 words. Before this, I had never tried to have anything published, but it had long been a dream of mine. So it goes that in early 2019 I messaged Mr. Fortier with a plot description/outline for a story called *The Adventure of the Irregular Heartbeat*, and, after adjusting a few plot points at Mr. Fortier's suggestion, I began writing the tale that you just read. It was an incredibly fun and rewarding process, and it was fun to have my parents reading pages along the way and providing feedback on the characters and the way that the plot was progressing. I am very grateful to Mr. Fortier and Airship 27 Productions to have the opportunity to have my story published as part of this collection.

I knew from the beginning that my story would have to utilize Moriarty, as the Moriarty character has been a favorite of mine since my first reading of *The Final Problem*. And, like *The Sign of the Four*, I wanted to include all of those pieces that make up my favorite Holmes stories— the introductory deduction sequence, the interwoven mysteries, the Baker Street Irregulars, a cunning foe, The Woman, etc.—and try to do them justice. I hope that I have done so and that you enjoyed the story. I look forward to further Baker Street Adventures.

✳✳✳

JONATHAN CASEY—is a Child Welfare Caseworker from Pennsylvania who majored in the field of Criminology at Wilkes University. He enjoys playing guitar and spending time with his two West Highland White Terriers, and he is still searching for The Woman. He does not use social media much these days but can be reached at Taylor67914@yahoo. com if anyone has questions or feedback.

Sherlock Holmes

in

"The Woman on the Ledge"

By
I.A. Watson

"Mrs Whitten," Holmes pleaded, "please don't jump."

The young widow tottered on the balustrade, a half-step away from plummeting five floors to her death across the pavement of Threadneedle Street. Afraid that closing on the distraught woman might prompt her to destroy herself, Holmes and I halted in place, six paces too far off to be able to grapple a suicide and save her life.

"Mrs Whitten," I called out. "There is no need for such action. There have been mistakes, yes, but..."

The lady on the ledge choked back scornful laughter and a sob. "Mistakes? You know hardly anything!"

"I know that you are young, with your life still ahead of you..."

Holmes laid a hand on my shoulder to caution me to silence. I was saying the wrong things. My friend took a deliberate pace backwards, right to the roof door through which the distressed widow had gained access to the summit of the Lavenheim Merchant Bank.

"You are aware of who I am?" he asked Mrs Whitten.

"You are the detective that Mr Petherward engaged."

"I am the detective whom that detective consulted, but otherwise, yes. I am he who discerned that you had been extracting information from your employer's study desk, private financial data which might be used to great advantage in the trading of stocks."

"Then you know I am a guilty woman. You have exposed my crimes. It is the cell or the fall. I... I cannot face the cell."

"Your crimes are not so great," I encouraged her. "Yes, you copied paperwork that old Petherward brought home. Advance notice of the loans and investments that Lavenheim might approve is of commercial value to an unscrupulous trader. But though you conspired to fraud, you might receive only a light sentence, perhaps not even a custodial one if you tell us who set you on."

"We know that you did not act alone," Holmes noted. "But I perceive now that we have not uncovered the whole of the story. Not anything like it."

Mrs Whitten wavered on the ledge. On the street below, a passer-by saw her slim form balancing on the railing and called for her to be careful. Others looked up and discovered the drama. A crowd formed.

"Please apologise to Mrs and Mrs Petherward for me," the lady on the ledge requested us. "They were considerate employers. Mrs Petherward deserved a better companion."

Holmes seized upon a chance to further his enquiries. "You answered an advertisement for a place in the Petherward household two years ago. Was it always your intention to infiltrate their home in search of confidential documents?"

The widow scowled indignantly. "Of course not! I just… It happened."

"Your family lost its fortune in l'Union Générale crash of 1882," Holmes recounted, referring to the infamous Paris Bourse stockmarket crash eight years earlier that brought a quarter of the pre-eminent brokers of Lyon and Paris to the brink of bankruptcy. When shares in the Union Générale had risen in price sixfold in but a few months many unwise investors were tempted to commit their fortunes to the bank, only to lose all when it collapsed with a loss of four billion francs. Mrs Whitten's father, Mr Oliver Standard, was amongst those men who found themselves ruined in the disaster. The loss had perhaps provoked the stroke that had left him a bedridden invalid.

"I supported them!" Mrs Whitten retorted sharply. "I tried. When Davy's pension proved insufficient I sought reputable work."

Our enquiries had already uncovered the sad death of Leading Hand[1] David Whitten aboard *HMS Agincourt* in March '85, a tragic accident that had left his wife of eight months a widow at twenty.

"You had a good upbringing and a refined education," Holmes knew. "You were well qualified to be a lady's attendant, a bright companion for the ailing and aging Mrs Petherward." We knew from Mrs Whitten's bank account that she regularly transferred more than half her stipend to support her parents. There was no indication that she had ever received payment for or made profit from the information she had stolen. "When did you first begin to abstract data from your employer?"

The widow looked to the pavement of Threadneedle Street and the growing collection of gawkers lining the road. "Am I to make confession then, before the end?" she asked us. "I suppose I might as well. Todd is away and safe. You cannot now find him. His enemy can harm him no more."

I glanced at Holmes to see if the name meant anything to him. "Todd Thornton," the detective supplied. "Formerly of Penge Street, Ealing, but now absent from his lodgings. He and Mrs Whitten have been walking out together for some seven months now. Mrs Petherward was rather bracing herself for her companion's eventual resignation when the pair announced their nuptials."

---

1 The Royal Navy equivalent of a corporal.

"Thornton and I were informally engaged," Mrs Whitten admitted. "We had planned... well, that is irrelevant now."

"Please allow us to adjudge relevancy," Holmes urged his precarious subject. "I urge you not to kill yourself, but if you must, then do not do so without explaining matters. Tell me when and why you began to copy such confidential documents as Mr Petherward brought home from this bank. Sometimes around last Christmas, I suspect. December 27th, perhaps?"

The widow's intake of breath betrayed that Holmes had hit the mark. "How did you know?"

"An examination of the stock market," my friend answered. "Lavenheim's finally realised there must be some flaw in their client confidentiality and referred the matter to a specialist who forwarded the problem to me. I was swiftly able to discern the pattern of opportunistic investment that your secret partner utilised. His methodology was rather uninspired, I must say. A less crude exploitation of the information would likely have never been spotted. He was greedy."

"Yes, it was when you say," Mrs Whitten confirmed. "I knew where the study key was kept. I managed to procure a wax mould of it and have a copy cut. When the family were settled for the night, I slipped to Mr Petherward's desk and made hand-copies of the files he kept there."

"That must have been a lengthy process," I considered.

"I had all night. Just after Christmas, that was the first time."

"And on many occasions thereafter," Holmes declared. "Now tell us why. Tell us about Mr Todd—and his enemy."

Mrs Whitten shivered. I feared she might fall. "It was three years since Davy... since I was left alone. I met Todd last summer by chance as I was shopping for Mrs Petherward. He struck up a conversation and we met again. I sometimes saw him on my half-days off. We began courting at the end of November. It was Christmas Eve when he asked me to be his wife."

"Did he ask you to copy those files?" I asked, trying to keep disapproval from my voice. I do not care for the exploitation of ladies.

"Of course not! Todd would never... You have to understand, I was the happiest woman in the world on Christmas Day! To find true love, not once but twice in a lifetime, is... was..." Mrs Whitten wiped her eyes. "We were engaged on Christmas Eve, but the very next night Todd told me we must break it off. He asked me to release him from his promise."

"Had Thornton made his offer in front of witnesses?" I wanted to know. After all, a breach of promise of marriage is legally actionable.[2]

---

2 As mentioned in the footnotes for "The Impossible Coin", Breach of Promise was common-law tort in England up to 1970, until when a woman could sue a man who had reneged upon a promise to marry her, and receive damages known as "Heart's Ease".

"It wasn't like that. Todd was trying to protect me. At last he broke down and told me all."

"Pray explain," Holmes urged the widow.

She took a deep, rasping breath. "You cannot find Todd now. He is escaped from Britain, with another name and a new life. Only that comforts me."

I was puzzled. "You said he was not your partner in crime in the stock-trading fraud."

"He was not. That was another—his blackmailer. His enemy. You see, Todd tried to break our engagement because he was being leached dry by one who had a hold on him. He did not want me to be sucked in, to be tied to a man who might at any time be arrested."

"Arrested for what?" Holmes asked.

"For murder."

Holmes leaned back on the door-lintel, his eyes gleaming. "Whose murder?"

Mrs Whitten glanced again at the street below, but determined to continue unburdening her conscience. "Todd—before he called himself that—he had a mother. A mother who raised him alone, who meant everything to him. She fell ill, with tumours in breast and lungs, and she was in a good deal of pain."

I winced in sympathy. Such illnesses are far too common, and unless excised early with dangerous surgery are quite incurable.

"She begged Todd to help her," Mrs Whitten continued, "to put an end to her misery."

"He assisted her suicide," I understood. Such things are not unheard of, though they are technically murder.

"He bribed a physician for some medicine that would do it. The doctor agreed, but only if Todd wrote a note of hand explaining that it was he, not the supplier of the drug, who was responsible for administering it."

"Hold," I objected. "That would not insulate a medical practitioner. He would still be accessory. He would lose his license at the least, if he was not convicted."

"Todd was told that the warrant was only a precaution. But after he had eased his mother's passing, that letter was a confession that might have hanged him."

"The doctor blackmailed him?" I was outraged that a man of my profession might stoop to such a breach.

"No. The letter was stolen. Todd never found out how, or by whom.

When a demand for payment for silence came, he went to the doctor to accuse him, but the man was dead, his household dispersed. The note must have been among the physician's effects."

Holmes nodded slowly, as if absorbing these new developments into that massive brain of his. "The man who would be Todd fled," he surmised, to speed the account along. "He changed his name and ended in Ealing. That is why I can find no record of Todd Thornton before April 1889. He has only been Todd Thornton for fourteen months."

"But his blackmailer traced him," I guessed. "At Christmas he caught up with him."

"Exactly," Mrs Whitten agreed. "Well, at the beginning of December. Todd was forced to pay over almost £400, the whole of his inheritance, in three sums, and was instructed to liquidate the last before New Year or be exposed. He did not want me tangled in that mess."

"Quite right, Mrs Whitten," I approved.

"But you were," Holmes intervened. "Between the time you heard of Thornton's blackmail and your abstraction of information on the 27th. How?"

"I received a letter, made on one of those typewriting machines.[3] The writer knew all about me, and about my engagement with Todd. He threatened to destroy our happiness, to see Todd on the gallows if I did not procure certain information for him from Mr Petherward's study."

"He asked for specific materials?"

"No. Only that I make copies of whatever was there, with special reference to any files pertaining to future investment recommendations. Which firms would receive loans, which would declare dividends, that kind of thing."

"And you did it," I knew.

"What else could I do? He held Todd's life in his hands."

"Did you tell Mr Thornton of your actions on his behalf?" Holmes asked.

The lady shook her head. "He had enough to fear, without knowing I was dragged in as he had dreaded. Besides, the note warned me not to."

"How did you deliver your information?"

"At first I was required to post it, to a post office box in Cheltenham. I sent material an average of once a week, and received new instructions afterwards. Often the letters responded to information I had sent on, requiring me to search for particular points or find clarifications or confirmations."

3 The first commercial typewriters were introduced in 1874 but were not common office equipment until the late 1880s.

"I daresay I could tell you what many of the queries were," Holmes admitted. He had been thorough in unpicking the murky insider trading that had so breached the Chinese walls of the Empire's commerce. "You said you posted it 'at first'?"

Now the lady's look to the spectator-filled pavement was almost yearning. "Three months ago, on March 30th, I was required to deliver the papers in person. I was directed to a seedy hotel in Romford, where a man awaited me. He was of undistinguished height and build and he wore a mask that covered his entire face. He spoke in a raspy whisper."

I didn't like the way the widow's story was unfolding. "Why the face-to-face meeting?"

"I could be interrogated on what I had read, including those parts I had not had time to copy."

Holmes's long face was sober. "And what else?"

Mrs Whitten glared at him. "He had the power to destroy the man I love," she snarled. "I am a young, attractive widow. What else do you think the blackmailer required of me? And I paid him."

My jaw set. "He blackmailed you to that?"

"Each time he summoned me from then on, yes." The lady clenched her fists as if she could strike the blaggard. "Todd... Todd never knew."

Holmes is ruthless in his investigations. I need not recount his detailed cross-examination about the sordid details of the blackmailer's demands of Mrs Whitten. Suffice that I was disgusted and appalled. "Holmes, we have to find this monster and end him!" I declared.

"Indeed." One might have mistaken my friend's response for indifference, but I recognised it as being the distraction that comes from immense deep calculation. "Mrs Whitten, why did you come to Mr Petherward's office here at the bank yesterday?"

"Why do you ask when you already know?" the widow asked miserably. "Of course you know! I came to steal the account book."

"Account book?" I glanced to Holmes for clarification.

"A bank like Lavenheim's is not like our domestic institutions," Holmes lectured me. "It is headquartered in Flanders, with branches across the world. The minimum deposit to open an account is twenty thousand pounds.[4] Of particular use to investors who wish to avoid domestic taxes[5]

---

4 Equivalent to £560,000 in modern sterling value.

5 The first modern income tax was levied in Britain from 1799 to 1802 to subsidise the cost of weapons and equipment for the French Revolutionary War. It returned in 1803 until 1816, again to cover costs of opposing the French (Napoleon). Prime Minister Sir Robert Peel, who gave his name to the 'peelers' of the world's first modern police force that he

"Each time he summoned me from then on, yes."

are some foreign accounts in nations with different financial regulations. The 'account book' to which Mrs Whitten alludes is the ledger that lists such entries, along with the identifying numbers and pass-codes that would allow deposits to be withdrawn. Correct, Mrs Whitten?"

"Yes," the widow admitted. "Mrs Petherward sometimes sends me here with messages or small tokens for her husband. I am known to his secretary and am admitted to his office to leave things on his desk. I could find the account ledger and leave with it in my bag."

"A dangerous and risky gambit," Holmes judged. "Your masked blackmailer learned that I was investigating and decided to close up shop with one final coup."

"It was my choice. He agreed that if I did that, got him the book, then he would set Todd free. He had made a fortune from the materials I copied. He would give Todd a ticket, passage to another country and a new identity where he could never be found or prosecuted. If only I got the account book."

"A book with which the villain might extract the contents of any numbered account at Lavenheim's Continental branch!" I exclaimed.

"Or by which he might blackmail those account-holders who might prefer Her Majesty's Exchequer not to know about income for which taxes have not been paid," Holmes suggested.

I looked at the lady on the ledge. "Your story is a tragic one, madam," I told her. "No judge or jury hearing it could fail to be sympathetic. Come down from there. Let us help you. I offer my word…"

"You haven't heard all," Mrs Whitten spat. "You don't understand! I came here yesterday—you are clever detectives, you have uncovered it all by now—I took the book, knowing I would be discovered. It didn't matter. I could elope with Todd and we would be gone, gone before anybody could catch us. But our enemy had one last filthy trick to play."

Holmes had already anticipated it. "He revealed to Mr Thornton that you too had been the subject of his blackmail. He told of your espionage in the Petherward house. He also recounted to your fiancée the other payments he had abstracted from you in your personal meetings with him."

I bit back an oath. I have rarely despised a felon as much as I did this vile specimen who had brought the young widow to the parapet above the street.

"That is what he did," Mrs Whitten said. "Todd was disgusted. Why

initiated, reintroduced the tax as a temporary measure to help balance a deficit national budget in 1842. This temporary measure continues to the present day.

should he not be? I am disgusting. What I have done…"

"You were corned and abused by an unscrupulous villain," I assured her.

"Todd has gone to his new life, his escape. I am glad of it. But his letter to me was clear; there is no place for me with him in that new life."

"You did not see him before he departed?" Holmes checked. "His rejection came by letter?"

"Yes. Enclosed in the same envelope as another instruction from my tormenter in the mask. He writes that since I will not be departing with my betrothed he has other uses for me. He has ample evidence of my crimes to ensure my compliance. He proposes to introduce me to… gentleman whom I shall entertain and from whom I am to extract useful information. Since I have prostituted myself to him, as he says, why should he not then prostitute me to others?" Mrs Whitten choked on a sob. "I prefer the ledge."

Holmes frowned. "May I see the letters?"

Mrs Whitten shied back. I thought for a moment that she might go over the ledge right then. "I am not so foolish as to let you come within range to seize me," she warned.

"You may feel that self-destruction is your only recourse, but are you not also interested in accomplishing the downfall of him who has done you such wrong? The study of the typed letter is a very new art, but one to which I have devoted some effort. Each typewriter has its quirks and distinctions, as different from all others as each man's hand or the imprint of his favourite boots. Given a chance, I can discern the brand and age of machine upon which your message was typed. The quality and origin of the paper may tell me more. There are a dozen different techniques to examine a hundred signs, any of which might lead me to your tormentor."

"He is hidden. I told you. He cannot be found."

"No, *he* told you. What reason have we to trust to his word? Surely we have every evidence to the contrary."

"Give Holmes a chance," I begged the widow. "Why give your blackmailer the final satisfaction of accomplishing your death to complete his getaway?"

The lady on the ledge slipped a crumpled envelope from her jacket and hurled it towards us. I stamped down hastily to prevent the paper from being blown off the roof.

Holmes took the letter, first examining the commonplace envelope and then removing the contents for inspection. There was a typewritten note as Mrs Whitten had described, and a handwritten message on cheap waiting room stationary.

"This is… indeed telling," Holmes murmured, staring intently at the evidence. "Much that was previously obscure now becomes depressingly clear."

I saw the colour mottle Holmes's face. I had seldom seemed him so angry. "Holmes?" I probed.

"Here is what I deduce from your letter, Mrs Whitton," he told the widow. "Todd Thornton is a man in his late thirties, sturdy but of average height, with sallow skin and grey eyes…"

"What?" the young woman gasped. "How can you know that?"

"Because I have encountered him—and owe him some strokes of the crop across his back before I'm done with the miscreant! You know him too, Watson. And the blackmailer—we have met him before."

"Indeed?" I racked my brain, considering the many unpleasant characters that Holmes has bested over the years. "You recognised Thornton's handwriting?"

"I recognised his typewriting,"

"No. It was the blackmailer who sent those notes. Todd Thornton's letter was penned by hand."

"I recognised both. We have encountered this same typewriter previously. It was the property of Westhouse & Marbank of Fenchurch Street, though I do not doubt that it has since been removed from that company, probably without their consent."

"Westhouse & Marbank? But they were employers of…" I caught up. "Your description of Thornton! It is *he!*"

Mrs Whitton, discerning that we had discovered something but not comprehending what, made a despairing gasp. "What are you talking about? What do you know? How can you known Todd?"

Holmes soberly folded the documents and stored them in his cigarette case. "I have difficult news for you, Mrs Whitten, things that I am loath to reveal to a distraught lady who stands on the precipice of self-destruction."

"Tell me now or never," she demanded, "for my next step will be my last."

"It need not be," I urged her. "There are better choices to make."

"Tell me the truth!"

Holmes assented. "Your story was suspicious from the start. No, I am not impugning your veracity, but that of the circumstances which you endured. Your chance meeting with Todd Thornton was very convenient, for your affection for him left you vulnerable to coercion—you, the very person whom a blackmailer seeking forbidden financial information might wish to suborn. Everything you were told about Thornton's situation, about his past act of clemency and the difficulty in which it placed him, are entirely at your ex-fiancée's word."

"I met the monster who ruined him," Mrs Whitten insisted. "He ruined me too!"

"Your masked tormentor, who knew so much about you and Thornton—was he not of the same build and stature as the suitor whose life you sought to save? In short, *might then not be the same man?*"

The widow shuddered at the idea. I feared she might faint.

Holmes was not done. "And at the last, his aims accomplished, was not this final message the ideal way for both Thornton and his 'enemy' to both disappear, leaving you deserted to take the blame for what has been done?" Holmes suggested. "But as I say, as soon as I saw these notes the sordid plot was evident."

"Holmes has seen this handwriting and the typewriting before," I knew.

"Where?" the widow dared to venture.

My friend told her. "The writer was then called James Windibank, but wrote under another name with a typewriter from the financiers' office where he was employed. The slurred letter 'e' and the defective 'r' are quite distinctive, then and on the document here. He used typed communications in anonymously courting his own step-daughter, since she would have recognised his distinctive handwriting, with the characteristic 't'-whorl and eccentric 'f' that your Mr Thornton also evinces."

"He courted his own step-daughter?" Mrs Whitten puzzled.

"She would come into control of her inheritance if she married," I explained. "Windibank's idea was to use another identity to court her, jilt her, and break her heart so that she might never wed and he would remain in guardianship of a fortune he had already significantly plundered. When Holmes exposed him he fled—ahead of a good horsewhipping."[6]

"He vanished almost three years ago, some time before Mr Thornton came into existence," Holmes mentioned. "He managed to straddle the edge of the law but was too cowardly to face his wife and step-daughter. I predicted then that no good would come of him."

Mrs Whitton shook her head violently. "You expect me to believe that my Todd is… is a married man, his own blackmailer, and… and that he abused me even as he turned me into a thief and a… a… No, I cannot accept it!"

"If your fiancée was indeed James Windibank, there is no depth to

---

6 The unpleasant Mr Windibank was exposed in 'A Case of Identity' in *The Adventures of Sherlock Holmes* (1891).

which the bounder will not stoop," I assured her.

"There may be a way to resolve the question," Holmes noted. "I will need to approach the ledge, but I will not venture close to you."

Holmes edged past the suspicious lady and peered at the gathered crowd below. "We have been here for some time," he pointed out. "An idle throng of well-wishers, thrill-seekers, and ghouls have assembled below to witness what comes next. Word has spread rapidly. You have an audience in the hundreds, Mrs Whitton. And, I'll warrant, one special spectator."

"You mean that Windibank may be down there?" I asked.

"Todd is gone—far away!" Mrs Whitton insisted.

"Then you will not object to staying here and keeping all eyes on you while I slip downstairs and hunt the crowd? Watson, come to where I am standing, where you can be seen from below. Appear to be entreating the lady to reconsider her choice."

I shifted as he asked. "You really think that Windibank might be watching?"

"His cruel final missive is designed to achieve one of two ends. Either he ensnares Mrs Whitton in a life of indentured prostitution or she elects to escape that fate by ending her life. Both ends suit his needs in different ways. Naturally he will be watching to see which option the lady takes."

I saw the first splash of doubt break through Mrs Whitton's misery, a new kind of hurt.

"Go," I told Holmes. "I will keep this lady company."

The detective hurried off, his whole intellect now dedicated to finding and capturing his quarry. Mrs Whitton shuddered again, standing on the top of the ornamental balustrade, gripping the building's flagpole with whitened fingers.

"Tomorrow may be worse," I confessed to her. "But it might be better. If you let go and fall, you will never know."

"I thought I had been a noble fool, to throw myself away for love," she told me. "Now it seems a may just have been a fool."

"Your choices were made honourably, whatever the circumstances behind them. You have been much ill-used. But the Petherwards seem like decent folk. All is not lost."

We talked. I tried to keep the conversation going, knowing how much depended on keeping her attention on me and away from the fall.

She jerked and pointed. "Look!"

In the throng below, Sherlock Holmes had approached a spectator in darkened glasses and a thick overcoat. As we watched, the fellow lashed out at the detective with a briar walking cane. Holmes twisted it from him and used it to deliver a sharp cut behind his quarry's kneecaps to prevent escape, then three blows across his back.

Holmes ignored the disturbed crowd, apprehended his grovelling adversary in a full-nelson, and frog-marched him into the bank.

"Do you know him?" I asked Mrs Whitton.

She nodded yes. Tears covered her face. "It is Todd! What Mr Holmes said… it must be true."

"With the capture of Windibank, the Lavenheim ledger will be recovered. His confession will release you from the charges against you. This time he will not slip away or escape the arm of the law."

The widow looked at the ground five storeys below, at the gawking crowd, at the darkening sky, at the place where James Windibank had stood.

"Please come in," I asked her. "I should hate to see a scoundrel win. I should hate to see a kind lady destroyed for her loyalty and care." I doffed my hat and held out a hand to her.

She reached out slowly, stretching, then grasped my palm urgently as if I could pull her back from the abyss. I drew her in, folded my arms about her, and walked her from the ledge.

THE END

A Man in Need of a Thrashing

I.A. Watson discusses Mr James Windibank

Even Homer nods. No Canon story has come in for as much criticism as 'A Case of Identity', the third short story about the Great Detective, first published in *The Strand Magazine* of November 1891 and included the following year in *The Adventures of Sherlock Holmes*, the first collected anthology volume. It is one of those stories whose sentiments have not aged well, concatenated by a dubious authorial interpretation of the law and by the villain escaping unscathed.

Margaret Brown's oft-quoted review of the story for *Proceedings of the Pacific Northwest Literary Society*, Summer 1987, in her article 'A Hundred Years of Sherlock Holmes - Looking Back on the Centenary of *A Study in Scarlet*' summarises many modern objections:

"Much as I admire Sherlock Holmes, I am always seized with impotent fury at reading the end of 'A Case of Identity'. What a patronizing arrogance, to decide for [Miss Mary Sutherland] whether or not she could stand hearing the truth! Anyway, he was manifestly unethical to his client. She engaged him to find Hosmer Angel. He found Hosmer Angel. He should have given his client the information she wanted and let her decide what to do with it... Anyway, what is this nonsense about the villain being beyond reach of the law? In British law of that time, a man could be sued for breach of promise. Even a bachelor who proposed to a woman with complete sincerity and then changed his mind could be sued. All the more so a married man who went through an elaborate charade and fallaciously courted his own daughter in law! Any half-decent lawyer could have broken him in court. Of course, the young woman might have chosen not to sue him—but Holmes should have left the choice to her. For me, this story is a dark blot on the otherwise admirable career of Sherlock Holmes."

Doyle himself, finding his way in the still-new Holmes series, perhaps anticipates his audience's dissatisfaction when he reports Holmes's prediction: "That fellow will rise from crime to crime until he does something very bad, and ends on a gallows."—but that is the last the Canon has to say on Mr James Windibank.

Equally unpalatable is Holmes's closing remark to Watson, justifying his decision not to reveal the truth to his female client by quoting 'Hafiz', the 14th century Persian poet and mystic:[7] "'There is danger for him who taketh the tiger cub, and danger also for whoso snatches a delusion from a woman.'" Modern sensibilities are perhaps more outraged at Windibank's cruel deception, less inclined to laugh it off as Holmes does and move on to a new case, and less comfortable at a choice to leave a young woman mourning for her lost fictional fiancée (and presumably never marrying, thereby granting Windibank the very victory for which he plotted).

I am generally cautious in relying upon all but the most common elements of Canon lore in my Holmes stories. I ration myself. The original tales use recurring cast sparingly and, with the exception of Moriarty, never feature a returning adversary. Even Holmes's great arch-enemy only plays a substantial role in two stories.

Therefore I didn't set out to grant Windibank his long-overdue comeuppance. I wanted Holmes and Watson talking a woman off a ledge, and from that came the backstory as to how and why she might be there. It was clear that she had been cruelly deceived and abused by a man she had thought her fiancée, and that his deception included disguise and lies for financial gain. It was also necessary for the central conceit of the story to restrict all events in one scene, including the uncovering and capture of the villain. I needed a Windibank-like cad who would be brought to justice by the close of a single act.

So if I needed a Windibank-esque fellow… why not use Windibank?

The mystery suddenly solved itself. The methodology became clear; we had seen much of it before. And had not Holmes predicted that this rotter would graduate on to other and nastier things? Here the impostor was, guilty as sin. Let there be catharsis.

According to Holmes there were three men and one woman who ever bested him.[8] The Woman we have heard much about. The three men are not specified; but it is certain that none of them was James Windibank.

IW
Deceiving no heiresses or widows
October 2018

---

7 That is, Khwajeh Shams al-Din Muhammad Hafez-e Shirazi, usually known as Hafez in modern discussion.

8 The occasions were mentioned but not specified in 'The Five Orange Pips' (*The Adventures of Sherlock Holmes*, 1891), which is generally held to have taken place in September of 1887.

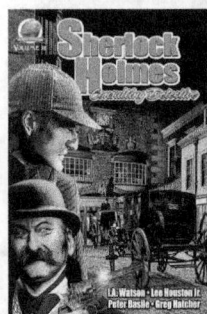

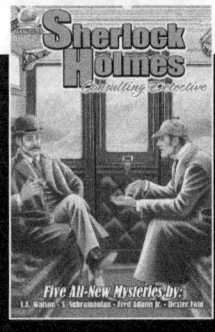

www.ingramcontent.com/pod-product-compliance
Lightning Source LLC
Chambersburg PA
CBHW051124260626
47170CB00005B/1654